ROOT OF EVIL

ROOT OF EVIL

William Harry Hughes

Book Guild Publishing
Sussex, England

First published in Great Britain in 2010 by
The Book Guild Ltd
Pavilion View
19 New Road
Brighton, BN1 1UF

Typesetting in Baskerville by
Nat-Type, Cheshire

Printed in Great Britain by
CPI Antony Rowe

A catalogue record for this book is available from
The British Library.

ISBN 978 1 84624 431 5

In memory of my father ...
My hero, my mentor, my best friend.
Our loss is heaven's gain.

Prologue

'What a stupid day to die!'

Barry Bourne lay on his back, his hands clasped under his head as he stared at the cold grey cracked ceiling. Tears welled up in his eyes as he became enmeshed once more in self-pity. *He would never see Mary again … He would never fulfil his dreams or hopes … He had nothing to look forward to but non-existence.*

'Shit! Shit! Shit!' He swore gently to himself as he looked around his prison cell, feeling the weight of silence press down on his body. He had promised himself he would not get into this state, and he used his forearms to roughly wipe away his tears and lack of control.

The ice-cold tiny cell reeked of urine entwined with the musk of human hopelessness, and the wire-mesh-covered dim light above his head softly illuminated the bare walls once covered in whitewash which had long ago flaked away under the nervous fingernails of previous occupants. By now he was familiar with every brick, every crack, and had read every piece of graffiti that adorned his room, but try as he might to keep his thoughts at bay, his eyes kept going back to *that* door. Not the one through which the guards delivered his food and through which his last visitors had walked, but the other door, the room beyond which would be the last he would ever see. The hairs on his arms stood on end as a chill passed through him when he recalled for the umpteenth time the words detailed in the spine-chilling statement read out so callously to him: 'To hang by the neck until you are dead!'

He had visualised *that* room a thousand times since in his nightmares, the steps, the rope, the trapdoor; everything else became a blur as those nine words screamed inside his head over and over again.

He was interrupted from his stupor by the grating of metal and a small circle of light appearing briefly in the eye-level peephole in *that* door which was quickly darkened by the shadow beyond. Barry knew he was being watched and studied, by a man he would never see, but who was shortly going to end his life in a lawful and professional manner. He recalled reading somewhere how Albert Pierrepoint, the Crown Executioner, had famously got it all wrong the first week he started in 1932. When the condemned man's body reached the limit of the rope, the knot, which should have caused the neck to snap, thereby providing a quick death, instead popped the man's head straight off the top of his body like a cork from a bottle, leaving the surrounding area stained with blood that remained a permanent reminder to this day.

Fear once more starting to overcome him, Barry tried to steady his mind and let his eyes wander around the cell, past the small fold-up table that held his two books, as well as the game board and the open Bible, and through the open bars comprising one side of his final dwelling place, until they rested on the prison officer, quietly dozing in a chair with the front legs off the floor and his back jammed into the corner for support, there to ensure the condemned man did not try to cheat the system by carrying out the sentence himself before the allotted time.

Barry hoped the warder would not wake up soon; he did not want to make small talk or play yet another endless nonsensical game of draughts that every screw appeared to be taught as part of their basic training. He moved his arm slowly and glanced at his watch, one of the few items he had been allowed to keep, along with some photographs of his wife. The luminous dials glowing faintly in the dim light showed four o'clock. Four more hours left and then what? *Shit!* He was scared. *Please! Please! Let it be quick. Stop it! Stop it!* He didn't want to die. He knew everyone had to die sometime, but this surely wasn't his time. It was so unfair, so wrong. Who had given that bastard judge the right to say that on the 28th of January 1953 he was to meet his maker? Only God had that right! Barry knew that he would have to explain it all to Him and hoped He would understand, but what if He didn't? What if God hated him as well?

Four o'clock in the morning, how ironic. A sour smile crossed his face as he remembered that fateful morning less than a year ago when this had all started. He lay there remembering ...

Part One

Chapter 1

Barry to his family and Bob to his colleagues because of his initials, Police Constable Barry Oliver Bourne A165 felt a lot older than his 26 years as he sat on the upturned oil drum, shoulders wedged into the corner where the wall of the garage met the border of the haberdasher's yard, and enjoyed the last half of a crafty smoke in the early-morning chill. He glanced at his watch. In the light from one of the only remaining unbroken streetlamps in the road, it showed four o'clock. *Only two more hours to go.*

He drew on the cigarette before exhaling and watching the smoke as it merged and spiralled into the pre-dawn sky. Smoking in public while in uniform was a flagrant abuse of the Police Code of Conduct; however, he was not concerned about being seen, knowing how unlikely that would be. He had been on this beat for the past eighteen months and knew every shadow and every noise. This part consisted of nothing more than shuttered or boarded shop fronts and newly built offices, with a maze of alleyways through which the wind blew recklessly even on the warmest of days. This constant chill deterred even the homeless low-lifes who frequented the city streets, rummaging in dustbins for food and discarded cigarette butts, from sleeping here – they preferred the more scenic and sheltered surroundings of the park five miles away.

He smiled to himself as he remembered his first solo beat, when the squeak of a dilapidated shop sign had nearly

3

caused him to shit himself. It was almost ten minutes since he had gone to the junction of Lansing Court and Carp Street where he was supposed to have been met by Sergeant Hill, who as usual had not turned up. It would be a bloody good thing when they got radios to keep in touch, instead of relying on the police box or some over-the-hill, overweight shift sergeant condescending to turn up to see if you needed assistance. Still, if push came to shove, he knew that a single loud blast on his whistle would bring one of the bobbies in an adjoining patch rushing over to help.

On a night like this, when all was quiet, he didn't care about missing the scheduled rendezvous as he didn't particularly like 'Podgy' Hill and had no doubt the feeling was mutual. The sergeant was an eighteen-year veteran who preferred the company of the older lads and would often join them on their beats, reminiscing about the old days and wishing away the few remaining years until his retirement. Barry admitted to himself that he probably hadn't helped their relationship; he reckoned Podgy had simply got narked with him for the number of times he had crept up on him and blurted out those stupid words, 'All correct, Sarge!' The sergeant had given up joining him on his beat, and their subsequent mandatory once-a-night meetings suited them both.

Barry blew on the end of the cigarette and watched the ash glow crimson. He nodded to himself – he definitely preferred the night shift. For a start, he patrolled a very quiet beat, which was slowly starting to be rebuilt after the destruction inflicted on the area by the Luftwaffe. But more importantly, it meant he was out of the house and therefore avoided the hassle from Mary in the form of relentless grousing about kids or cash; the absence of either was her constant moan. Mind you, he was glad about the kids, or rather, lack of them, considering she spent all that he earned and then some before the end of each month. The trouble

4

was, Mary had champagne taste and Barry only earned beer money. He had thought about getting another job during his off-duty hours, but if he was caught, or more likely shopped by some jealous colleague who couldn't keep his mouth shut in front of the Super, he would lose not only his job but the company house that went with it, and even his wife's moaning wasn't worth that.

'Sod it!' he said to no one in particular. It was strange how each time his thoughts wandered to Mary and money he always got depressed. He drew on the last of the cigarette before glancing again at his watch: two minutes past four. *Oh well!* Time for one more trip round his patch, to check everything was as secure as it was thirty minutes ago by rattling doorknobs and pulling down on padlocks. He held the unsmoked end of his Park Drive between his forefinger and thumb before flicking it as hard as he could into the black night sky, watching as the sparks danced like fireflies until it hit the top of the wall and fell to earth in a cascade of fireworks before being extinguished in a pool of dog urine.

Barry stood up, pulled down his jacket, and had a guilty check around him. He knew instinctively there would be nobody about, but still he always looked. Satisfied that his unofficial break had passed unnoticed, he moved towards the alley at the end of the lane, between the empty office blocks at the far end of his beat. He knew from experience that if he turned down the next road on his right, he would end up at the point nearest to the police station from his patrol, with just enough time –without needing to check his watch again – to meander slowly towards the station and conceal himself in the shadows of the newsagents until the morning shift arrived. He could then gratefully hand in his beat card and exchange the usual banter with the rest of his shift as they changed to go home.

Still annoyed with himself that he couldn't shake off his despondency over Mary, he moved towards an alleyway that

5

led to Reynolds Street, which was the start of PC Paul 'Dickie' Bird's patrol. No, she would never be happy. No matter how much he got paid, she could always spend it faster than he could earn it. As he passed the end of the alley, in the faint light from the streetlamp at the far end he saw an empty quart-sized oil can lying on its side only six feet away. Without a moment's hesitation, and full of pent-up frustration, he covered the two yards and kicked the can as hard as he could, attempting to send it cleanly onto his colleague's patch. He knew that there was no one in this resident-free area of shops, offices and lock-ups to object – unless Dickie was having a crafty smoke in the street, there wouldn't be another living soul within a mile and a half to disturb. The can lifted gracefully into the air, spinning before it clattered and crashed as it rebounded off both walls and came to rest in a clamorous crescendo on several half-empty dustbins. The heightened noise created by the echoing acoustics of the alleyway made even Barry flinch. He laughed to himself at his own jumpiness, and then suddenly became alert: was that footsteps he'd heard running away? He silently cursed himself for his own stupidity in kicking the can and alerting whoever it was of his presence. He hurried along to the end of the alley, and as he turned the corner, Barry almost tripped over a large canvas bag lying on the pavement.

He stood motionless and surveyed his surroundings, listening to the quiet stillness of the early morning that surrounded him. He was certain he had heard someone running. He removed his torch and, holding it almost at arm's length above his shoulder, shone it down and around to illuminate as much of the area as possible, while the fingers of his right hand snaked through the strap of his truncheon to curl round the handle. Barry was over six feet tall and remained fairly fit; even though it had been six years since he had left the Army after his stint of National Service, he still felt able to hold his own with anyone on a one-to-one basis. He started to relax, and the blond hairs on the back of his neck settled back down as his adrenalin level slowly lowered and his instincts informed him that no immediate danger was present. He quickly scanned the shadowed recesses of the rear entrances of the adjoining shops and office blocks; they gave out no light, for although the war had been over for nearly seven years, still the occupants of these buildings extinguished every light at the end of the day as if the blackout remained in force. He saw nothing out of place.

'Curiouser and curiouser!' he murmured to himself as he made his way back to the corner where the bag lay. Bracing himself, he opened it slowly, ready to leap back if the contents required: many a horrifying tale had been told by colleagues who had discovered *things* in discarded bags. Barry steadily shone his torch onto the contents as he eased open the bag. 'What the ...' The sentence remained unfinished as he dropped to his haunches and gazed incredulously at the hundreds of bundles of one-, five- and ten-pound notes that mockingly stared back at him.

He snapped the torch off and crouched there in the darkness. Was he dreaming? Had he imagined it? He tried to steady his hand and couldn't understand why it was shaking as he switched the torch back on. No! It was there all right. He gingerly pushed his hand right down into the bag, closing his eyes as he did so, feeling under the wads of paper for weapons or something identifying the owner. Why was his hand wet? It hadn't rained for three days. He drew it out and in the torchlight saw that it was covered in blood.

He stood up and under the murky light of the streetlamp used his handkerchief to clean the blood from his fingers, checking his uniform jacket and shirt sleeve with the torch to make sure they weren't stained. Thankfully, neither seemed to be marked and he automatically balled the handkerchief and stuffed it into the canvas bag, carefully avoiding any mess. With a second brief scan of the area he picked up the bag by the handles and made his way back to the entrance of the alleyway. When he got there he looked at his watch to remind himself what the time was, for when it came to making up his pocket book: ten past four. *Was that all?* He put his watch to his ear and listened. The steady tick assured him that it was working correctly and that indeed only eight minutes had passed since he had sat on the oil drum and finished his cigarette.

Chapter 2

'Right,' he said aloud to steady himself as his brain began to comprehend the situation and quickly process the procedures he should follow; even though it was technically PC Bird's patch, it would be his investigation. The area would need to be thoroughly searched, but that was a job for the day shift. First he would have to report it, and it would be quicker to return to the station than to use the police box at the end of Carp Street. Christ, the Super would be pleased, but the night-watch inspector and 'Podgy' Hill would be brassed off. He could see them now; Inspector McFarlane, the Irish idiot, would be having a crafty kip in his office under the guise of checking reports and crime figures, while Sergeant Hill would be gorging on a full English breakfast washed down with a cup of very sweet tea down at the greasy spoon on Buchannan Street. Of the other lads on the shift, some would be working, some would be shirking, but all would be willing the hands of the clock to turn to six o'clock so that they could go home. Well, he would just take the bag into the station and put it directly onto the inspector's desk. Let him make all the decisions – after all, that's what the lazy sod was paid for.

As he walked back down the alley towards his beat area, Barry pondered where the hell all that cash had come from. There were no bookies on that street and none of the owners of garages or premises on his patch would make anywhere near that amount of money in a year, let alone walk about with it in a bag at four in the morning. He wondered how much there was and how long it would take the officers assigned to the investigation to count it – if they kept their hands off it; he had no doubt one or two would try to inadvertently 'lose' a few notes into their own pockets before the official total was recorded in the record. *Typical!* thought Barry. The way he saw it, he had found the cash but the light-fingered day shift would profit from it. Why should they, though? If anyone should gain a bit of extra cash through the find of the century, it really should be him. And why only a bit extra? Why not the lot?

'Finders, keepers!' he exclaimed, before realising he was talking aloud and then furtively looking around to see if the coast was clear as he exited the alleyway. He knew that if he handed it in in his official capacity as a policeman and no one claimed it then it would go to the government. He also knew of at least three colleagues who would give it to their wives to hand in so they could receive any reward if it remained unclaimed in the police property store for six months, but that was out of the question for him, for what excuse would Mary have for having been there at four in the morning?

That was when the idea developed. Out of guilt he stepped back into the shadow of a doorway as he collected his thoughts. *What if I don't hand it in? What if I kept it?*

'Who would know?' he muttered to himself. Suppose he did take it in, it would mean involving everyone in the station, including the Super, and he would have to fill in a report in triplicate, Podgy and the rest of the lads would be required to search the area, and all this would take longer than the time left on shift. With little overtime available at the moment, he was just making extra unpaid work for everyone and they would all be extremely pissed off. However, if he hid it somewhere until he knew where it came from or someone reported it missing, if it turned out to be

10

vitally important then he could always 'find' it again, this time on his patch, and he would get big pats on the back. But pats on the back didn't pay bills; especially the exorbitant ones Mary had run up, and after all, any pats on the back from his workmates, some of whom he knew would keep the money, really meant 'stupid bastard'.

Keep it! Keep it! The words burned into his brain. Why not? Why the bloody hell shouldn't he keep it? If it was legal money then it was bound to have been insured and would be reported lost or stolen; if it was illegal money, then no one was going to come forward and claim it. But what could he do with it until he knew where it had come from?

Again his brain screamed, *Hide it! Hide it now, you prat!*

He answered himself out loud: 'I've already worked that out ... but where?' Where on earth *could* he hide it? The chill that crept up his spine was as much from the winter wind whipping down the cold empty street as from the realisation of what he was considering doing. He took several deep breaths as he tried to come up with an answer: what were his options for hiding the money? Here on his patch? Out of the question. Although it was quiet during the early hours, this area was a hive of backstreet garages and shops used by the local office workers from Reynolds Street, and so many people meant that someone was bound to find it. He couldn't stash it at the station – besides not even having a locker to keep it in, he would undoubtedly arouse the suspicions of the desk sergeant if he walked in from his shift with a canvas bag and no explanation. Home? That was even worse than the police station, as Mary's regular cleaning routine ensured that the whole house was under her scrutiny twenty-four hours a day, and it was in any case undeniably more likely that she had hiding places he didn't know about. No, he definitely didn't want to involve anyone else. *I know I can trust me, but only me,* he thought to himself. Anyway, Mary could never keep a secret and would've spent half of it on

11

fabrics from Marks & Spencer before the week was out. When you lived in a road of police houses, you only had to upgrade your brand of toilet paper for the woman ten doors away to question how you could afford it. How would it appear if the wife of a constable was seen hanging curtains made from fancy, expensive fabrics? Another thing: his best friend Martyn lived only three doors away. Martyn Crowe and his wife Rita were the reason that he had joined the force and moved to this city in the first place. However, he might be able to use his friendship with Martyn, who was in the Criminal Investigation Department – the CID – to find out more about the true owner of the money.

Suddenly, while thinking of Mary, his thoughts strayed to her mother and then to the garden shed that was now practically his since Mary's father had walked out on his marriage. Barry had always been fairly good at carpentry, and after leaving the Army had even fancied setting up in business for himself as a local handyman. The shed had a lock of which he held the only key, and as no one else ever went in there, he knew the money would be safe there, and as it was normal practice for him to go to his mother-in-law's every afternoon when he was on nights, frequent visits to the shed wouldn't raise suspicion. If he could just get the bag into the boot of his car, it might work. But should he leave the bag where it was now and fetch his car back after the shift to retrieve it? He decided not to, for what if he was seen? He wouldn't have any reasonable excuse to go back to his patch once his shift was over, and anyway, what if meanwhile one of the early office commuters discovered the bag? He would have to take it to his car now, he reasoned; after all, if he was seen by one of his colleagues or by the next shift, then he could say he was simply taking the bag to the station to report his discovery. However, if he did manage to get it into the boot of his car unseen and then get back to complete his patrol, the hardest part of the problem would have been solved.

For once, Lady Luck was on Barry's side. The previous day his exhaust pipe had developed a hole which now made his car sound like a diesel train. If he had parked it in the compound as normal, somebody would have shopped him to the bosses – there were those in the force who would happily grass up their own mother if they thought it would mean promotion. So instead he had left it within walking distance of the police station, rather than in the car park at the rear. Barry looked at his watch again: half past four, plenty of time. He could get to his car and back without anyone at the station seeing him, and with just enough time to spare for a last cigarette and an abridged final patrol before clocking off. Even if he turned out not to have time to complete his patrol, there had been nothing to report before he found the money, and if the worst came to the worst, he would just have to swear blind that he had indeed made a final set of rounds and found nothing amiss.

With a deep breath, and wishing his heart would stop pounding in his chest so loudly it could probably be heard a mile away, Barry picked up the canvas bag and moved into the shadows en route to Maiswood Avenue and his car. Forty-five minutes later he was back on his patch, sweating profusely and shaking like a leaf even though the blustery winter weather careered around every corner and chilled the morning air. The sky was starting to lighten and he only had thirty minutes before he needed to be back at the station for shift changeover. But finishing his rounds could wait. More importantly, he needed a smoke and he needed one now. He moved into the doorway of the Co-op as, hands trembling, he dropped the cigarette. Managing to retrieve and light it in one desperate motion, he gratefully drew the nicotine deep into his lungs, hoping that somehow the smoke would pass down to his feet and stop his legs shaking. Apart from being startled by a passing road sweeper while on the way to his car and nearly jumping into the hedge, the whole operation had been so ridiculously easy: he had met no one, particularly none of the bobbies who patrolled the areas nearest the station, and although he was sure he had made enough noise opening and closing the boot to wake the dead, if not the nearby residents, no one had questioned him.

He leaned on the wall in the shop doorway and studied his reflection in the glass. Was he the same person as before? Did he look furtive, as if he had something to hide? Inhaling another batch of calming nicotine, he let the thought pass. He had a lot of planning to do and he had to start thinking ahead to ensure that every possible scenario was covered. If for some strange reason his car were searched now, the cash would be found and he would be up the proverbial creek without a paddle, but that was an illogical worry as there was no worldly reason why anyone should wish to search his car. However, he would feel much safer when he could get the bag and its contents to his mother-in-law's. This shift seemed to be never-ending!

Discarding the cigarette, Barry resumed his beat and tried to conscientiously check all the property and business premises on his now much-shortened patrol route back to the station. He knew he had to appear as normal as possible when he entered, but he could not help feeling that everyone was watching him suspiciously when he did so, and the usual 'Nothing to report, Sarge!' seemed to stick in his throat. Did the desk sergeant suspect anything? Was he to be arrested as soon as he entered the changing rooms? No. From the predictable petty comments and banter exchanged between his colleagues and the next shift, Barry was relieved to see that all was normal, before he finally walked out into the early morning air, which promised a cold but pleasantly dry day, and proceeded to his car.

Making no attempt to go anywhere near the boot when he reached his car – although he had approached from the rear so that he could make sure no one had jemmied the lock in his absence – Barry opened the door and climbed in with a sigh of relief. After starting the car, which indeed sounded like a diesel locomotive, especially in the stillness of the early morning, he pulled out from the kerb, turned left and merged into the light traffic of early morning commuters. Throughout the short journey home, he found himself continually checking his mirror, looking for vehicles that remained at a constant speed and distance; the way a car tailing him would, but saw none.

'Pack it in, it's too late now,' he muttered as he forced himself to concentrate on driving, just as the number 36 bus pulled out in front of him from its scheduled stop without indicating, forcing him to break a little too hard. He had to settle down; he was too jumpy, and if he didn't concentrate on his driving he wouldn't make it home and what would the accident investigation team make of one of their own with a car full of cash? He knew he wouldn't be able to think straight until he had the contents of his boot safely hidden, but then he could calmly plan his next move. First, though, he had to get home safely.

After what seemed like an eternity, with every pedestrian or vehicle intent on making him crash his car so his booty was discovered, he finally turned into his street and gratefully parked in his usual spot outside his three-bedroom, semi-detached police-owned residence. *This may be my house, but it certainly isn't home,* he thought as he locked the car, his hands still trembling slightly. He couldn't help glancing at the boot for one final check before giving the bodywork an assured tap as he turned and noticed the downstairs lights coming on in Martyn's house. *Probably Rita preparing breakfast before getting the kids ready for school,* he thought as he walked up the garden path to let himself into his own house.

Closing the front door behind him quietly before turning to stare straight ahead up the stairs and into the bathroom at the top, he undid the silver buttons of his tunic jacket before unclipping the whistle chain and slipping out of his tunic jacket. He hung it over his civilian topcoat, on the crude hooks that were nailed into the wall recess laughingly called the cloakroom. He paused and toyed with the idea of making a cuppa and having another cigarette, finally deciding against both. First he would only end up having to get out of bed in the middle of the morning to go to the toilet, and second, the smell that Mary detested, the smell of cigarettes, would only give rise to further early-morning bitchy comments and he had too much on his mind for another row.

His boots off now, allowing him the delicious feeling that his toes once again belonged at the end of his feet; he padded his way up the stairs and into the bathroom. At least cleaning his teeth would dilute the smell of smoke and give her less to complain about, he thought as he undressed completely. Silently opening the bedroom door, he carefully folded his uniform trousers over the chair back and quickly put on his pyjamas before moving back the bedclothes as gently as he could, so as not to waken her. He had a lot of thinking to do, but first he had to get some sleep. In her slumber Mary moaned something about cold feet and moved away from his side of the bed as far as she could. He was glad of this and gratefully closed his eyes. Sleep, however, was hard to come by this morning.

Chapter 3

Three doors away in a house the mirror image of Barry's, Detective Sergeant Martyn Crowe pushed back the covers and sat on the edge of the bed, having a wonderful scratch of his nether regions to welcome in the day. He glanced around at the empty space that his darling wife had occupied, still smelling her fragrance as if she remained snuggled next to him, and marvelled at her amazing ability to leave her presence in a room. It was one of the many things about his wife that still fascinated him, even after eight years of marriage and the arrival of two terrors to whom, judging by the noise emanating from the kitchen, Rita was already going full blast trying to attend.

He stood up and stretched his arms as far as they would go, relaxing as he enjoyed another scratch while he moved to the window to pull the curtains a little way back to look into the street. He followed the same routine every morning and loved the start of the day because it was full of unknowns. Seeing Barry Bourne's car parked outside his house, he knew his pal would just be getting into his bed after the night shift and then his usual morning question popped into his head: *I wonder what today will bring?* Martyn pulled on his dressing gown and walked onto the landing before receiving the shock of his life. He could not believe his eyes: the bathroom was empty! This was not an opportunity regularly granted in the Crowe household, but hearing Rita moving about in the kitchen talking to their sons, he paused at the top of the

17

stairs for a brief moment. Rita always managed to talk to the boys; no shouting, no bullying, no threats. He could hear his sons laughing and giggling, and as he moved silently into the bathroom he thought, *Yes, I am very lucky and today is going to be a good day.*

About the same time that Martyn Crowe bent down and turned the taps on for his bath, a few miles away to the north of the city, Charlie Morgan sat in a seedy, dirty bedsit, glaring at himself in the mirror.

'Where the hell is it?' he demanded out loud, 'where the bloody hell is my money?'

The reflection gawking back at him obviously didn't have any answers to the questions barked at it and neither face appeared proud of what it saw: forty-five years of age, thinning dark hair and a stubble-covered pock-marked face with yellow nicotine-stained teeth. The badge of honour, in the form of a puckered pink scar running from above his left eyebrow in a steady curve across his left cheek to the corner of his mouth, gleamed in the glare of the unshaded bulb hanging from the ceiling.

He turned his head slightly to the right to get a fuller view of his one and only souvenir for crossing Alexander 'Big Al' Law, a mistake he would not make again unless he wanted the surgery to be repeated below his waist line, as had been threatened. All over a stupid van load of cigarettes, but that was back in the days when Big Al was only known as Al, the main enforcer for Mack Mackenzie, the racketeer who ran the black market in the city. Charlie and his pal Bobby, both young hoodlums, had heard about the delivery of stolen cigarettes and taken the opportunity to steal the van as the driver opened the gates to Mackenzie's warehouse. Charlie and Bobby hadn't got any further than storing the cigarettes in a run-down lockup and ditching the van before Al and his lads turned up. Bobby hadn't been seen again since being led off by a couple of Al's cronies, but Charlie became the latest advertisement, through the surgical skills of Al and a broken beer bottle, for not messing with any of the four major crime bosses of the city, known collectively as 'The Institute'.

Twenty years later, Al was now known as Big Al; a select member of the inner sanctum of the Institute, having succeeded Mackenzie, he had grown not only in criminal stature but also in brutality, and permanently carried a stiletto commando knife, with a sheath conveniently sewn into the left sleeve of all his suits for the purpose of carrying out swift justice. Charlie, however, had simply grown old and become a walking billboard with the nickname 'Pirate'.

As Charlie looked intently at the lowlife reflection in front of him he caught a whiff of his body odour, a sickly-sweet smell which didn't endear him to anyone who met him, and caused partly by his minor disregard for hygiene but mostly by a glandular problem which was the only thing he supposed he'd inherited from his unknown father. He moved his hand to his face, tracing the scar with the fingertips of his left hand, a subconscious movement he did whenever he was trying to solve a problem and hold back his rage. As he did so his eyes flicked up and he noticed that the upper portion of the mirror was missing, since the collision with an ashtray thrown by his long-departed girlfriend, Gloria. Well, *girlfriend* was a bit of an exaggeration; they both frequented the Crown and Anchor down the road, and when Charlie was a bit flush, he would ply Gloria with enough drink so that she wouldn't be averse to supplying sexual favours in return. The damage to the mirror was caused when Gloria awoke after one particular drunken stupor, to discover Charlie had found her winnings she'd collected earlier from the bookies and that she thought were safely hidden at the bottom of her handbag.

The broken mirror gave Charlie a distorted image as

though one of his bloodshot eyes was twice the size of the other. He leaned forward, clenched knuckles resting on the cracked and unpolished wood of what was once a dressing table, and tried in vain to get the red mist to disappear from his eyes.

'Where the fuck is it?' he growled.

He had put a lot of time and effort into planning this job, working hard to secure the friendship of one of Big Al's lackeys. 'Smithy' was a guard at the offices in Reynolds Street, and since overhearing him boast to his mate in the pub that he was to receive a large package for immediate personal delivery to Big Al, Charlie had cultivated his acquaintance. If it was a package for Big Al and was important enough to require personal delivery by a subordinate security guard, it could only contain one of two things, both of which Big Al now controlled in this city: drugs or protection money. Big Al wouldn't risk having drugs discovered at his home or office, so it had to be money, and if it involved Big Al there had to be lots of it. Charlie knew that he wouldn't have another chance to get his hands on a retirement fund so easily, and it would be all the sweeter if it had belonged to the man who had marked his face all those years ago. He had carefully calculated his plan to the last detail, because he knew that if he got caught he would be a dead man – Big Al would see to that. Once he had his hands on the cash he would immediately leave the country by ferry from Harwich, and so by the time Smithy could tell Big Al what had happened and who was responsible he would have disappeared off the face of the earth. Boy, how he would like to have seen the face of that vicious bastard when he found out that it was Pirate who had screwed him over.

However, it hadn't quite gone to plan, he thought as he relived the past few hours …

Charlie regretted that he'd battered Smithy so badly as soon as he'd done it, but the stupid bastard wouldn't give him the bag. He had expected Smithy to defend it because of who his boss was, but he had assumed that he had only to hit Smithy a couple of times to break his nose and, like all second-rate caretakers who called themselves security guards, that would make him give it up. But as usual, Charlie had lost his temper and gone too far when Smithy wouldn't let go of the bag, and as some of the notes fell onto the ground through the opening, he'd kept on hitting him, even when he fell to the ground too and didn't get up. Anyway, it was Smithy's fault for following him out onto the street after he had threatened him and taken the bag; it was Smithy's fault for not letting him go without a struggle, and it was definitely Smithy's fault for making Charlie lose his temper and beat the crap out of him. Still, it didn't matter, he thought, as he started back through the early winter morning to his now temporary lodgings. It would have been funny for Big Al to know it was him, but that wasn't the important part; he had got the bag, and by the weight of it there was enough inside it to keep him in the sexual luxuries for which he had a lavish taste, for a long time. Charlie was just wondering exactly how much there was and how long it would take him to count it before travelling to the ferry, when he was deafened by a loud clattering sound coming from the alley straight towards him. *Shit, it's Big Al!* He panicked and leapt over a four-foot-high wall that ran down the side of one of the garages, dropping the bag in the process, and hiding until he knew it was safe. When he had climbed back over the wall and returned to the alley, the bag had gone.

'Shit! Shit! Shit!' he had cursed, stamping his feet and waving his arms. *Where's the bloody bag? Who has it? And what made that sodding noise?*

His hands clenched on the dressing table, Charlie sensed rage filling his body again, and retraced the line of his scar as he tried to stay calm. 'Mustn't lose my rag,' he muttered.

21

'Gotta think!' He flexed his back and heard his muscles creak as he tried to force himself to relax and analyse the situation. He would still be OK as long as Smithy was dead and couldn't tell Big Al anything. The word would go out on the street by morning that Big Al had been ripped off and was looking for blood as well as his cash, but Charlie had been very careful and had never met his contact near any of his usual haunts. Big Al wouldn't be a problem … unless Smithy wasn't dead.

'Bastard!' he exclaimed as he started to wonder about Smithy. *What if he wasn't dead? What if he had survived and told Big Al what had happened before he could get out of the country?* Fear of the brutal villain caused him to start sweating with dread, making his usual onerous odour twice as bad. He slapped his hands on the dressing table before turning away towards the sagging broken sofa, one of the few luxuries contained in his unpaid weekly rental.

His fear turned once again to anger. This was to have been his last job, the biggie, the one he had dreamed of and constantly bragged to his associates that he was due. It should have been the easiest and given him the necessary nest egg to enjoy his old age in luxury. As he flopped on the sofa, Charlie saw the half-empty bottle of cheap scotch on the box substituting for a coffee table. He ignored the chipped glass, stolen from the local for just such occasions, and, unscrewing the lid of the bottle, emptied the raw liquid into his throat, feeling the rush of agony as the cheap alcohol tried to work its way through his abused body. *It should have been my cash*, he thought as the pain in his gut made him close his eyes and bend over slightly to wait for the hurt to subside. Another one of the same and he might begin to feel better. He too had got a lot of thinking to do this morning.

Chapter 4

Martyn Crowe knew, as soon as he walked into the police station that morning, that it was going to be one of those days. Over breakfast, as the boys had rummaged in the newly opened cereal box for the 'must-have' promised toy, he had decided to go in early and complete the reports for the two cases he had recently cleared from the backlog of crimes. Although not major incidents – one was purse-snatching and the other drunk and disorderly – it helped the monthly 'solved' statistics so loved by the Commissioner, and cleared a couple of files from his in-tray. But the excitement of the new day that he had experienced on finding the bathroom empty had quickly dissipated with the cries of 'Sarge, Sarge – hey, Sarge' as soon as walked across the car park at the rear of the building towards the side door.

'Give me five minutes and I'll come and see you,' he responded to all the shouts for attention.

As he climbed the stairs, Martyn thought again of the promise the day had held just an hour ago. Then he walked into the CID office and shut the door behind him. Normally, he would take advantage of the early start and shift changeover and have his first and probably only cup of tea of the morning while quietly sorting out what incidents had occurred during the night and seeing which the priority cases were. This morning was not going to be like that, however. It was not going to go as planned.

Standing with his back to the door, Martyn looked at the

scene in front of him. Six desks covered in paperwork sat facing each other in clumps of two, metal trays forging a boundary between each desk to store the case files and notes while in theory providing personal space for each occupier; however, each desk's personal space was in fact taken up with telephones, pictures of families and pen pots. Hundreds of scraps of paper lay in small piles, each scrap containing reminders of messages, phone numbers and names, important only to the officer concerned. As he walked to his own desk at the far end of the office, with the chair back to the wall so that he could supervise the others in the department, Martyn was sure where the term 'organised chaos' had first been coined – here.

At twenty-nine, he knew he had done well to become a detective sergeant in such a short time. He was considered by those older and less senior than himself to be a flier, and by those younger and junior as a sort of hero to aspire to, though they all in reality wanted to knock him off his perch. He winced as he looked at his desk, knowing that the mounds of paperwork had grown overnight. He knew the desk sergeant would place any new cases on his desk for prioritising, reviewing and allocating when he arrived in the morning. However, this morning the pile seemed to be greater than usual – they must be breeding, he thought. It certainly was a lot of 'breeding' paperwork, he sniggered to himself as he hung his overcoat on the hook. He must remember to tell Rita that one. *Bugger!* What was it she had asked him to bring home tonight? He would phone her later to find out – after all, he always tried to phone her at least once a day.

Martyn took another look around the office and, noticing that the area with the kettle and teapot looked like a bomb had hit it, shrugged off the idea of a cuppa and headed downstairs to the commotion below, hoping that he might be able to nip into the canteen and get a fresh mug of rosy afterwards. He fully understood that once he asked the officers who had tried to attract his attention earlier to explain what was bothering them, then all the responsibility of their problem would be his. All they had to say, it seemed, to get themselves off the hook for any future reprimand was: 'Well, I told DS Crowe.'

He entered the uniform charge room. 'Well – let's have it, what's been happening?'

'Got a very bad wounding, Sarge!' said an anonymous voice from the back.

'Anyone we know?' asked Martyn, raising his voice slightly to be heard over the drunk sitting in the corner arguing and swearing with a phantom companion.

The previous, unidentified voice answered, 'Not by name, Sarge, but we think he's one of Big Al's men.'

Martyn closed his eyes. He knew for definite now that today was not going to be the good day he had previously hoped. Anything to do with Alexander Law, aka 'Big Al', was bound to be a bag of rats. It would be trouble from start to finish.

He sighed and said to no one in particular, 'Tell me what happened.' The constable in charge of the office picked up a sheaf of papers and, ignoring the mumbling drunk, crossed over to Martyn.

'Well, Sarge, you know that block of offices in Reynolds Street, the one owned by Law?' Martyn nodded as the constable handed him several sheets of paper contained in a buff folder. 'Well, the officer on beat in that area, PC Bird, found the back door to Law's offices wide open and one of Law's security guards outside in a bloody state. Law has been informed and is on his way down there, but he has already said on the phone that nothing is missing from his premises.'

What a load of cobblers, thought Martyn. *How would Law know if anything was missing if he hadn't even arrived there yet? There has to be more to it than just a wounding – anything to do with that animal Law must involve something highly dodgy.*

25

'Where's the security guard been taken to?' Martyn asked the constable.

'St Joseph's, Sarge.'

'Send someone down to the hospital to make sure the security guard sits tight until I get there. Also make sure to send an extra body down to Reynolds Street to cordon off the area and I'll get the next DC that comes in to take over.'

The constable in charge of the office smiled at Martyn as he replied, 'Already done, Sarge!' Then he turned to instruct one of the officers loitering to remove the drunk to a cell so that he could sleep off his night's revelry and provide welcome relief to the ears of the charge room officer.

'Thanks,' said Martyn as he left the room, knowing that each of the officers' faces held a look of relief that someone had taken charge and they were no longer responsible.

Back in the CID office, Martyn sat at his desk and closed his eyes. 'If only – if only I could nab that bastard Law,' he muttered to himself. Each time a case like this happened, adrenalin surged in every CID officer's veins with the possibility of being the one to arrest one of the biggest villains in the area. Martyn let out a deep sigh. Hundreds had tried and all had failed. The problem of course would be witnesses. No one would talk to him. 'No one's about to snitch, because that would be going against the Law,' he muttered to himself in a disparaging tone, forgetting how many times he had heard that terrible joke. He always hoped, though, that perhaps one day …

Chapter 5

As he stomped into his offices in Reynolds Street, Alexander Law was a very angry man and his obvious fury sent staff scurrying for the shelter of their desks. His sheer size and power would have been enough to ensure he was given a wide berth whoever he was, but coupled with the fact that he was the man who through violence and greed controlled more crime in this city than anyone else, this meant that he was avoided like the plague. Alexander Law was a man who oozed vicious force from every pore and was most definitely *not* someone against whom crime was committed.

Whoever the bastard is who's got my money won't live long enough to spend a penny of it … His thoughts seethed as he slammed the front door shut. 'When I get hold of him …' he muttered to himself, leaving the thought unfinished as he passed through the sparsely decorated reception area towards his own office. He entered the open doorway, ducking slightly and turning his frame to smooth the progress. At six foot seven inches tall, with an eighteen-stone muscular physique, Big Al was an imposing figure; with rage pulsing through his veins, he was terrifying. 'He will feel so much pain that death will be a blessed relief,' he mumbled as he crossed the floor. As he reached the rack beside his desk and took off his trademark camel coat, he shook his head to clear his thoughts. *Enough of that*, he told himself. *There will be plenty of time for that later.*

The money had been a one-off delivery and everyone in

the city knew who these offices belonged to; they were untouchable, or so he had always thought. His blood boiled as he sat down behind his mahogany desk. *Who would dare to do this and how the hell did they know about the delivery?* He had deliberately kept this deal very quiet, because his three inner-sanctum partners in The Institute were unaware of his plans to subsequently expand his own personal empire to the exclusion of them all. Therefore, he had gone external for the financing of this operation and had not involved his bookkeeper or chief of security, as was customary. Partly to keep everything under the carpet, but also because his bookkeeper was a blatant womaniser and in this line of business vital information could easily be given away during some one-night fling with a well placed tart. Consequently, the only other person in the city who knew about the arrival of the money was the security guard who was to bring the bag to his house as soon as it arrived for a cash-in-hand bonus, and so it seemed he had covered all bases because, like himself, Smithy did not like women. Unknown to anyone in the criminal underworld other than the inner sanctum of The Institute, who had been threatened with exile or worse if it became public knowledge, and one member of his personal staff, Big Al was a homosexual.

'Smithy, you little shit ...' Alexander spat the words with contempt, 'yer told someone about the deal!' *Well you're alive for now,* he mused, *but I guarantee only long enough to tell me who it was that stole that cash, and then I'm going to give you some surgery of my own.* He snatched up the phone and dialled a number which was answered on the second ring. 'Do we have any information?' he snarled into the mouthpiece.

'Not yet, sir' replied the male voice with an edge of fear.

'What do I pay you for? Find out!' Without waiting for an answer, he slammed the receiver onto its cradle and slumped down into his chair. Unusually for him, beads of sweat stood out on the forehead of Big Al like glass globules, and equally rare butterflies were starting to flutter around his stomach.

The telephone rang, its sudden noise breaking into his silence, startling Big Al uncharacteristically. He grabbed the receiver, his giant hairless hands almost covering the set. 'Yes?' he practically spat into the mouthpiece.

The voice on the other end spoke meekly. 'No one knows anything at the minute, but we've got everyone out on the street, sir.'

'Damn!' he exclaimed as the line went dead, his fist clenching. It was not simply that the loss of the money would cost him his lifestyle and his reputation, it could cost him his life. Alexander Law started to shake with uncontrollable rage. He barely noticed the muffled crack, until the shaking started to subside and he looked down at his hand and saw the receiver was broken in two. *I've got to get that money back*, he thought as he threw the pieces on the desk and snatched his coat from the rack, causing it to topple over onto the floor. 'Someone will die for this,' he snarled as he left the office, slamming the door behind him. 'And get my bloody phone fixed!' he ordered the startled figure occupying the desk directly outside his office. Alexander Law knew he had to get home. The police would shortly descend on the offices in Reynolds Street to investigate Smithy's beating, and then they would go to the hospital to question him themselves. Not that he was afraid of them; he thought them all to be slow and stupid people, but it would be an inconvenience to have them snooping around his offices, and his ability to conduct business while they were there would be severely curtailed.

Alexander Law had no intention of telling the police about the money. In fact, he had no intention of telling the police very much at all. Coming from the east side of the city, he had learnt early in his career that the bizzies were to be avoided at every turn, for he had suffered more than one cuff round the head from busybody constables who had caught him stealing sweets or breaking windows, before taking him home to his mother. Not that she ever cared – she was normally too drunk or suffering the effects of the latest beau who had taken his drunken rage out on her.

He had been advised when he had started in the protection business at the age of seventeen, 'Never tell the filth anything – let them find out for themselves.' It was a practice he had always stuck to, and as a result he had always walked out of police stations without ever being charged with a crime.

Alexander Law had to get home to make a certain phone call, the thought of which made his throat go dry. It was his fifty-fifth birthday in two weeks, and he was damn well sure he would make certain he was alive to enjoy it.

Chapter 6

As he walked into the casualty department, D.S. Crowe drank in the atmosphere of controlled pandemonium that he was so utterly familiar with, knowing that it wasn't only the police who dealt with the effects of drink or drugs on the human body. Even at this time of day the waiting chairs were filled with the dreary faces of people needing medical assistance, while the nurses behind the counter, in their blue and white striped uniforms, starched aprons and caps, attempted to take personal information from people who were in too much pain to be coherent, in an alcoholic stupor, or reluctant for their details to be made public. Doctors in white coats that seemed designed to flap around their legs, constantly entered and exited the area, with the steady drum of conversation being broken only by the sound of a nurse calling out names of patients. Just like the way his office worked, although it would appear to an outsider that everything was disjointed, he knew from experience just how efficient the system was.

Following a well-trodden path of corridors and ignoring caustic comments from an orderly hurriedly pushing a patient in a wheelchair to an assigned location, he made his way into Nightingale Ward; a large, single-sex dormitory with thirty beds, containing men of all ages and a multitude of conditions and which he knew was run with military regimentation by the matron. Martyn waved haphazardly at the uniformed female seated at the nurses' station in the middle of the ward before he passed through large double-doors situated in the left hand wall, into a smaller more intimate intensive care ward. It was only a short distance from the casualty department, and yet the scene was so different. The general peace and serenity was only punctured by occasional pained moaning: the patients here had to be desperately ill or terminal to be admitted. It was a clinically sterile area that only had two doors, one from which the patient and he had just entered and, hopefully, thanks to the skill of the staff, through which they would also leave, and the other to the ultimate tranquillity of the mortuary, where God waited their arrival.

As Martyn glanced around the small ward he saw that six out of the ten heavy cast-iron beds contained unmoving patients, mostly covered in bandages, between starched linen sheets. A nurse busily dusted the head of one of the vacant beds. Must be preparing for a new tenant, he mused. Then his eyes set upon a starched white cap atop blond hair through the window of a small room to his left. As he neared the room, he saw that the assigned constable was seated, elbows on table, with a biscuit in one hand and a steaming mug of tea in the other, reading the sports section in last night's edition of the *Evening Echo*. Martyn leaned quietly through the open the door and, knowing what would happen, said as sharply as he could, 'Which one is ours, lad?' The result was even better than he had estimated.

In trying to stand up, the constable spilt the tea on his hand, causing it to shake uncontrollably, and sending further hot liquid all over his trousers as he simultaneously tried to speak through a mouthful of biscuit, resulting in him beginning to choke. The young officer finally managed to splutter out, 'Bed six, Sarge,' and visibly winced at the sight of the accompanying crumbs that flew from his mouth in the direction of D.S. Crowe. Martyn sombrely shook his head and tutted, before turning away quickly to hide the grin that was beginning to grow over his face. Cruel, he knew, but he had enjoyed seeing the young constable squirm, and after all, he had not had his morning tea and biscuits yet himself, he reasoned. Still smirking, Martyn turned his attention to the uniformed figure of the nurse, with the dark blue belt, bent over a desk entering figures on a chart.

'Excuse me, Staff ...' Martyn had been in these places often enough to be familiar with the rank of office denoted by the different coloured belts. 'I am Detective Sergeant Crowe, and I'm interested in the man in bed six.'

He followed the nurse who had stood and walked passed him into the small ward, before she turned to face him. 'Is *he* one of your lot?' she asked, using her head to indicate the office they had just left, where the constable was still attempting to clean the tea from his jacket and dry the damp stain surrounding his crotch and thigh at the same time.

'Yes,' Martyn smiled apologetically, 'he's one of ours!'

She continued shaking her head. 'I'll never know how you lot manage to put away so much tea – that's the fourth mug he's had this morning.'

'Oh I don't think he drinks it all, he appears to spill most of it!'

Her young eyes creased at the corners as she appreciated the humour of the remark. Her face, Martyn could see, was lined with the stress and responsibility she carried on her shoulders. They were all highly dedicated nurses who worked in the intensive care side-ward, but how they dealt with all this pain, suffering and often death on a day-to-day basis Martyn would never know. He admired them all very much.

'Have you a name for him yet?' enquired the staff nurse as she walked round to bed six. The name plate on the top of his bed merely displayed 'Unknown'.

'Not yet,' answered Martyn. 'You will know as soon as we do.' He looked down at the patient lying unmoving in the bed, swathed in so many bandages that only one eye and the lips were visible. 'How is he? What are his chances?'

The staff nurse looked at the prone figure with sad eyes. 'Not good – less than thirty-seventy. The damage is all to his head and it's not possible to say yet how badly his brain is affected. The doctor will be round again soon and then perhaps we will know more.'

Martyn looked straight into her eyes and nodded at her sympathy. 'I understand. I'll be leaving the constable here. If there is any news, perhaps you would tell him so that he can let me know?'

The staff nurse sighed as she turned back to her desk. 'I don't know if we have that much tea and biscuits left,' she stated bluntly.

Martyn smiled as he turned to leave. Despite the sarcasm and ribald comments, there really was a lot of respect and goodwill between the nursing profession and the police. As he got to the door, he paused to look back at the figure lying in the bed. 'Poor sod,' he thought aloud. 'What the hell did you do to deserve this?' He pushed his way through the large double-doors and strode purposefully through the main ward, before traversing the corridors towards the exit. He needed fresh air. There was something inherent about hospitals that he didn't like – whether it was the pain and suffering or the pungent smell of bodies and cleaning fluid, he didn't know; he just knew he was always glad to be leaving under his own steam.

Chapter 7

Alexander Law parked his Wolseley 6/80 saloon on the driveway outside his house. Second only to his home, the car was his most prized possession, especially since having the alterations to its engine that increased its top speed by almost twenty miles per hour, compared with the version most favoured by the police. He got out and paused with his arms folded on the top of the vehicle to survey his house. It still never failed to impress him: a Tudor Revival style set back from the rest of mankind by a gated, wooded driveway three hundred yards long, thirty minutes away from the centre of the city, in an area once occupied only by gentry. The three-storey building's exterior features included lavish stonework, five ornate chimneys, half-timbering thick walls and steep rooflines with ridged conical turrets atop white horizontal boarding covering the wrap-around one-storey porch exterior. Slamming the car door shut, he made his way up the steps and across the front portico to the front door, which was opened by some unseen hand that had been watching his every movement since his car had first pulled into the gates.

'Any messages, John?' he snapped.

The valet-cum-assistant answered briskly, 'Only the police, sir. They are sending a man around to see you.'

'Let me know when he gets here.' Law quickly walked towards his large study without waiting for a reply. Using his back to close the door, he peeled off his camel overcoat and threw it onto a large leather chair as he automatically made his way towards the drinks cabinet.

Pouring himself a large measure of expensive single malt, he settled down into his armchair and let his head rest against the cool leather as his eyes wandered around the room. He liked this room, particularly the pink and green hues of the wallpaper and curtains. The fact that his mother had always detested these colours made him like them all the more. She had after all been a great influence on him, for it was the visions of her flabby naked body rutting drunkenly atop any man that paid her attention that had put him off women. Oh, he used them to be seen on his arm in all the right places, because it would never do for his real feelings to be made public; women were all right for looking at, but as for touching … As the thought went into his head he felt the usual shudders of revulsion pass through his body. Nothing, no nothing at all could surpass the feel of a young man's firm but pliant flesh as he took possession of it. Feeling the urges of desire beginning to stir in his body, he stood and drank the remainder of the whiskey in one gulp. This was not the time, he thought – he had a telephone call to make.

Law picked up the ceramic handset from its gold-plated slots and dialled a number, half hoping there would be no answer, but after just two rings the call was connected. He fell silent and stood listening to the deep and malevolent voice on the other end. 'You got the delivery as we agreed. Interest is twenty per cent. Total amount is thirty thousand pounds. You have seventy-two hours!' He had no chance to speak before the connection was terminated, and his whole body was shaking. He replaced the telephone and took out his handkerchief to wipe away the sweat that was on his brow and palms. 'Shit!' *Only three days.* Law went over to the cabinet and poured himself a tumbler full of whiskey and gulped it down, his large hand covering the whole glass so much so that it looked as though the liquid was coming from his hand itself.

He picked up the decanter, moved to sit behind his large desk and pressed the silent bell under the lip of the desktop. Before his hand had returned to the leather-bound top of the desk, his valet drifted silently into the room. 'John, do we know anybody at the hospital who might be of use to us?'

His valet smiled silently at the question; the only people they usually knew at the hospital had been put there under the personal ministrations of Big Al himself. 'I don't know if he could help, but how about that young orderly, Simon? You met him a few weeks ago. Would he be of any use, sir?'

'He might just do,' Law nodded. 'Arrange for him to talk with me as soon as possible.'

'Certainly, sir,' said John. 'Will that be all?'

With a wave of dismissal, Law turned once more to the decanter; he spoke again as his valet reached the door. 'John!'

His valet turned, his hand remaining on the door handle. 'Sir?'

'When the police arrive I will see them next door. Then run a bath for me as soon as they've gone.'

John smiled. 'Very good, sir!' And, as silently as he had entered, he retreated through the door before closing it to leave his boss with his thoughts.

Alexander Law leant back in his chair, still gripping the decanter, and muttered to himself, 'If I can find out who has got my money, and quickly, I might just have a chance.' It wasn't much of a chance, but when it was his life at stake, any chance was better than nothing.

Charlie Morgan replaced the receiver in the telephone box and stood with his head against one of the few unbroken glass panels, sweating profusely as his whole body clenched. 'Shit! Shit! Shit!' he slurred. Word was out on the street already – one of Big Al's boys over at Reynolds Street had had the shit kicked out of him last night and was in hospital, and

Big Al wanted answers about who had done it and quick. The fact that a king's ransom of twenty-five pounds was on offer for solid information had been the sole topic in the Dog and Bucket when Charlie had entered for his lunchtime hair of the dog, along with the fact the guard was still alive and in the hospital. *He should be dead by rights*, thought Charlie. He had definitely hit him hard enough, and hadn't he heard the crack as Smithy's skull hit the pavement? He downed his cheap whiskey as fast as possible and headed out to the phone box on the corner. There was a public telephone at the end of the bar, but today all he needed was the page in the directory listing hospital numbers, which he had carefully ripped out of the pub's copy, and some essential privacy.

'Critical but stable.' *What the hell did that mean? Was he conscious? Was he awake? If so, what had he said?* Charlie could only guess. Upon first connecting with the ward, the call was answered by an obviously junior member of the staff who knew of the 'beaten-up security guard' and was happy to convey the patient's condition. However, no sooner had they uttered that important snippet of information than the phone had been commandeered by a regular nurse who immediately started asking him questions. He had hung up without delay. First she had asked if he was a relative, and then wanted to know a lot of details from him about the guard. *Wait a minute!* If they wanted to know all those details from him, then it was obvious that they knew nothing, not even his name. The relief caused his muscles to relax and he involuntarily farted. Jesus, how could something smell that bad, especially as he hadn't eaten anything in two days? He pushed hard against the door. Why were they always so difficult to open?

He stood outside, grateful for the fresh air, while his hands searched his pockets in the hope of finding a cigarette. Coming up empty, he started to get angry again, 'If I'd got that money, like I should have, I'd be up to my eyes in smokes,' he muttered. He was aware that word was out on the street that whoever had fucked Big Al's man had fucked up. Charlie knew that the majority of people in this area would sell their mother's soul for a fiver, let alone twenty-five quid, and if they even suspected it was him that was responsible, they would be on the phone in a second. His eyes furtively looked up and down the street, checking whether anyone was watching him, but he had no sensation of being scrutinised by the odd couple of stragglers he could see. Although he had initially regretted losing his temper with Smithy, he knew now that he no longer had a choice. Smithy was the only one who could tell Big Al who he was, so Smithy had to die, and soon! That way Charlie would be in the clear from revenge by Big Al and ultimately free to find out what had happened to *his* money. If he couldn't do that, all his planning and scheming had been an utter waste of time.

He was not bothered at all about the police. They didn't know he was responsible, and in the past they'd got nothing from him, even when he'd been caught red-handed. They had no chance with this. No, it was bloody Alexander bleeding Law he was scared of. Had he asked too many questions when setting up the job? Had any of Law's other men seen him with the guard? He had tried to be so careful, but if he had been seen then he had the feeling that Law would already know about it. If that were the case, then at the very least he could expect to wake up one morning with his testicles relocated to a pickle jar. He started sweating again and cursed loudly as more foul wind broke from his backside. He had to think. Slyly and cautiously he began to make his way back to his lodgings.

Barry Bourne woke with a start. It took him a few seconds to come to his senses, but then he remembered and he jumped out of bed, stubbing his toe in the process. Hobbling and cursing, he made his way to the window to pull back the curtain a few inches. The car was still there, and more importantly the boot was still shut and everything on the street looked normal, although that shouldn't have surprised him as there was never any crime in this area where every house was occupied by policemen. He could hear his heart beating in his chest. *What was the time?* He limped over to the table, his toe still throbbing, and looked at his wristwatch: just coming up to ten o'clock. *Damn.* He had only managed about three and a half hours sleep, no wonder he felt so tired. Should he go back to bed? Better not, he decided, today was one day that he couldn't afford to oversleep because Mary was out for the day and there would be no one to wake him up. He would have to make do with a bath to freshen himself up.

He walked towards the bedroom door and stopped to look at himself in the dressing-table mirror. Had he altered overnight? Did he look different to how he normally looked? He had never taken anything that wasn't his before – did it show? He looked down at the photograph of his wife on the dressing-table top. Would she understand what he had done? After all, he had done it for her. Barry shook his head in self-reproach. No he hadn't, and he knew that no matter how many times in the future he tried to convince himself he'd done it *for* Mary, the true reason was he'd done it *because of* her. He stared at the photograph. Although it felt like it had been taken a lifetime ago, it wasn't actually that long after they'd seen the film *Two Weeks with Love* starring Jane Powell and Ricardo Montalban. Mary had had her long blonde locks cut and styled the same as Debbie Reynolds, who was also in the film, within the week. She was beautiful then and so full of life, and even today Barry admitted she was still very pretty. When they had met, he had instantly fallen in love with her with a passion he didn't know existed. His mind wandered to past times of pleasure when she had given him her body so willingly and so often, when she had possessed him and he had loved her so much. Now she had blamed him for their lack of children and their lovemaking had died off, until it had become a pre-booked sort of monthly ritual and felt utterly boring and meaningless.

He snapped his mind back to the present. There was no point in dwelling on the past; he knew he was in a loveless marriage and no matter how much money they had, the lack of children would always drive a huge wedge between them. However, if things went as planned, then perhaps he could find a woman who would let him *purchase* her love on a regular basis, and that way he would get all of the fun and none of the hassle. Depending on how much money there was, there might be no limit to what he could buy; but there would be time enough later for spending. For now, he knew he had to behave normally, if that was possible, and he couldn't break his routine by going to his mother-in-law's before the usual time, which was just after two. He shuffled out of the bedroom towards the bathroom; he would have a nice bath and a few cups of coffee. He was too keyed up to eat, and he knew anyway that he would be having tea at Mary's mother's – it was always the same when he was on nights. However, at least tonight would be different: tonight he would be able to stand the endless chatter and moaning of the two women which normally grated on his nerves. Tonight they could both whinge and crab all they wanted; he had too much on his mind to care.

Chapter 8

Martyn Crowe had parked the unmarked CID car at the end of the driveway to Alexander Law's house so he could have a good look at it on his approach. As he walked slowly up the drive he justified his decision that it wouldn't have been fair to send anyone else to interview Law, for during previous interviews with the police this man had always managed to provoke the officers before they had a chance to glean any information. Every investigating officer had left the interview room frustrated and exasperated, while Law had left without charge and a free man. Today's interview, especially as it was happening on Law's home turf, was something that he had to do himself. Martyn knew he had big enough shoulders to handle any aggravation and not let it interfere with his work, and in addition he had the rank to stand up to Big Al. He could be patient, and it would make his patience all the sweeter if he had the chance to do what no one else had ever done and lock him up in a cell. However, he doubted this would be the occasion for that, Law being one of the injured parties in this case, but information was power and anything he could learn about Law now might be something he could use in the future.

He also wanted the opportunity to have a look inside the house, to see what it was like for himself. There had been a rumour flying about the office and he wanted to see if he also got the impression that it might be true: could one of the kings of crime in this city really be a poofter? Other

42

expressions came into his mind as he tried to dispel all images of a man grovelling up the backside of another, and he suddenly felt so sick to his stomach that he dismissed all further thoughts and reached for the knocker on the door, happy to see it wasn't a phallic symbol. The front door was opened almost immediately by a slim young man in a well-cut, expensively tailor-made dark suit.

'Yes sir?'

'I am Detective Sergeant Crowe from the local CID. I believe Mr Law is expecting me?' said Martyn, holding out his police warrant card for inspection.

'I will see if Mr Law is in,' said the manservant.

As the door was shut in his face, Martyn just stood there calmly. *Don't lose your temper*, he told himself, for he knew that it was tactics such as this that had provoked previous officers. The door opened again and the same man appeared, this time with a smarmy snarl around his mouth. Was the little prat laughing at him?

'Will you come this way please?' Turning without stopping, the valet led him into the spacious hall area. Martyn paused and looked at the grandeur that crime and violence had bought the owner before being directed to the lounge. As he stepped past the valet, the door to the study started to slowly swing open, causing Martyn to stop and emit an involuntary gasp of astonishment, not believing the scene that was opening out before him; it was like something from a nightmare, a grotesque vile nightmare of outlandish depravity. This room, the room of a hard-nosed, violent criminal bully, screamed femininity, and for some reason he compared it to the faces of old women daubed in lipstick and rouge as if trying to recapture a lost youth. The room should have made him laugh, but it wasn't humorous, it was obscene. Everything was in varying shades of pink, green and white, so that it looked like a block of candyfloss set in a field. He remained mesmerised as his eyes amassed all the information and the valet hastily grabbed the handle and almost pushed him into the lounge before exiting and closing the door behind him.

Martyn was still in shock when he saw the figure rise from the chair, and gasped again. He'd heard and talked about Big Al Law, but this was the first time that he'd actually met the man and he just couldn't conceive the size of the individual who confronted him. *Huge … immense!* These words seemed small and completely inadequate. He himself was six foot two tall and he felt that his fourteen-stone muscular frame was more than capable of dealing with any man. His stint of mandatory National Service had always held him in good stead when it came to dealing with trouble and he had seen many shapes and sizes, but the sheer magnitude of the man standing in front of him simply took his breath away. He certainly knew at that moment how David must have felt when he first saw Goliath. The question was, could he find a good enough piece of evidence to put in his sling and knock this man on his arse?

Pulling himself together, Martyn approached Law. The man-mountain nodded in confirmation of his name. 'I am Detective Sergeant Crowe,' Martyn said, 'and I would like to ask you some questions about the security guard who was badly injured last night.'

'I only employ them – I don't hold their hands!' snapped Law.

Martyn continued, 'Could you kindly give us his details? We need some personal information about the man so that we may speak to his next of kin.'

Law moved his hand under the lip of the desk and the door to the lounge opened immediately. 'Get me the details on Smith!' he commanded, without moving his eyes from the face of Martyn.

'Yes sir,' replied the valet, who was already on his way out of the room.

'So the injured man's name is Smith. Do you have any idea

why someone would want to attack Mr Smith?' Martyn pressed on, knowing immediately that this conversation was not going to provide many answers – this man did not like him, and the feeling was mutual.

Without answering the question, Alexander Law falsely yawned before asking, 'Anything else I can help you with, Officer?' He was deliberately trying to antagonise, by using the title of a person of lower rank.

Ignoring this, Martyn decided to plod on as best as he could. 'Was there anything missing or stolen from the premises?'

'Such as?' Law responded a little too quickly. Although he was trying to appear blasé and unconcerned, the question had caught him unawares and he needed to ascertain whether the police knew anything specific or had sent this copper on the usual fishing expedition.

'I don't know – perhaps office equipment or files?' Martyn answered. 'I just wondered if anything had been stolen from the building?'

Alexander Law smiled to himself and thought, *So you're groping in the dark and as usual don't have a clue about what's really going on.* He said out loud, 'No, nothing at all, the only office equipment we have are a couple of typewriters and some telephones, which were all there when I checked this morning.' Law, happy that the police knew nothing, grew cockier by the minute. 'By the way, can I get you a drink?' he asked, reaching for the decanter which had recently been replenished with finest malt whiskey.

'No thank you,' replied the detective sergeant. Just then, following a single rap on the door, the valet entered and without a word handed Martyn a single piece of paper. Anxious to look at it, he instead folded it in half and placed in his right inner jacket pocket; he was determined to look at it outside and not appear clueless in front of this villain. 'So, Mr, Law, what you're saying is that there was nothing stolen from your offices and you have no knowledge why someone would wish to hospitalise one of your security staff?'

'Correct. Is there anything else?' Law was rapidly losing his patience and he intended this visit to come to an end now.

'That's it for now,' said Martyn. 'If you do think of anything else, perhaps you would be good enough to let me know via the station?' Without warning, he advanced towards Alexander Law with his hand outstretched; knowing from past experience that if you do this it is extremely difficult for the other person to refuse.

'Anytime,' said Alexander Law, caught totally unawares as he suddenly realised his hand was moving of its own accord to grasp the policeman's. As he fought the urge to rush outside Martyn was joined at the lounge door by the valet, but he paused and spoke once more to Alexander Law. 'If I do need anything, can I get in touch?'

Law indicated his valet with a movement of his head. 'Get in touch with John, he will fix you up.'

If he's anything like you I bet he would, Martyn thought, but merely replied, 'Thank you sir.' He made his way to the front door and stepped outside as the valet opened it, glad to be back in the real world.

Martyn felt, as he walked down the driveway, that the visit had opened a couple of doors, but none more so than the study door, which had confirmed the rumour: *Big Al was a shirt lifter!* He guessed that the study door hadn't swung back on its hinges by accident – it would have certainly been checked by the valet prior to letting him in, because there was no way that Law would want his darkest secret to become public knowledge, especially to the rest of the criminal fraternity in the city. No, the valet seemed too professional for that, but why had he deliberately unlatched the door, knowing that it would enable Martyn to see beyond? It didn't matter how or why it had happened; that snippet of information was now neatly filed away in the 'pending' tray of his mind for future use.

He arrived at the bottom of the drive and paused, leaning on the bonnet of his car, to let the rest of his thoughts tumble through his head. Big Al may be queer, but he was definitely a cold-hearted bastard. He hadn't asked about the condition of the man who worked for him, who had been so badly injured that he was virtually unrecognisable, but instead had dismissed him as expendable. However, Martyn's instinct told him that Law was nervous about something. *Did Law order the beating himself?* No, if Law had ordered Smith to be taken out, he certainly wouldn't have had it done when he was at work and recognisable by his uniform. So if it wasn't one of Law's men who had done the wounding, it had to be an outsider, but no one in their right mind would attack one of Law's men for nothing. There was a reason for that guard being injured, and Law had answered his question as to whether anything was missing a little too quickly; there was definitely something more to this than met the eye. That being the case, Law would probably already have the word out for whoever was responsible to be found. Although Martyn had a number of his own informants who relied on the money he provided, they would have to be reminded to keep their eyes and ears open for him, for the chances were that Law would certainly get to know who was responsible long before he did. Martyn's mind continued to work. *What if Law cared more about whoever did this than about his own guard's life?* Something had to have been stolen, and whatever it was it had to be important, and there were only two things important to Law: power and money. Unless someone had left the guard so badly injured as a message to Law, which he couldn't honestly see happening, then the chances were, Martyn thought, it had to do with money ... but what specifically? This job would require a thousand questions being answered before the truth finally emerged, and

Martyn knew that Law was aware he had just been scratching around in the dark. That, however, only made him more determined to find out the truth.

He put his hand in his pocket and pulled out the slip of paper that the valet had given him. He read the words 'David John Smith … date of birth 4th February 1930 … address – 3, O'Mara Terrace'. Martyn's eyes flicked back to the date. *Blimey, today's Smith's birthday … boy, that was some present he got.* He stood and glared at the paper. 'You get well, David John Smith,' he muttered, 'you make sure you get well, because if I'm going to solve this I'm going to need to know you a lot better.' He paused as he opened the car door, not looking forward to his next task: a visit to O'Mara Terrace and a chat with the family. He had never been there before although knew the general area, but a quick check of his street index which was always kept in the glove compartment confirmed the location.

As he started the engine, another thought crossed his mine and he was irritated with himself for not thinking of it earlier. What if the beating wasn't just a message job? What if Smith was the intended target all along and whoever it was that had beaten him into next week also knew that he was still alive? They might just be stupid enough to go along to the hospital and finish the job. He needed to make sure his men were properly watching the birthday boy. If anyone was going to try to see him, Martyn wanted to be certain that he knew about it first. *I hope those idle sods at the hospital keep their wits about them,* he thought, and sighed as he engaged the clutch, shifted into gear and pulled out the driveway. He had so much to do, and so little time to do it in. It was two o'clock already – where on earth had the day gone?

Alexander Law stood by the window and watched the retreating figure walk down the drive as he called out to his valet. 'That bastard could be dangerous. Get the word out, no one at all talks to the filth or they will explain it personally to me. Got it? No one! Is there any news from our people or that nurse at the hospital yet?'

'Nothing from the ... *orderly*, sir,' sneered John.

Law stood and glared at his manservant. 'You will take the piss once too often. Now clear out, I want to speak to that *orderly* as soon as. Understood?'

'Certainly sir.' The valet smiled arrogantly as he left the room, gently closing the door behind him.

Law bowed his head in thought; he had to get that money back – it was his debt now and the men he had borrowed it from were not forgiving people. He had to find out who had taken the money. He didn't give a damn about Smith and he really didn't give a rat's arse whether he lived or died in the future; all he really did care about was that Smith was alive now and that he lived long enough to tell him who it was that had taken his cash.

Driving more carefully than usual, not many miles from where Martyn Crowe was hard at work, Barry Bourne was making his way over to Mary's mother's; however, the ten miles from his house to his mother-in-law's detached bungalow seemed to be taking forever. Try as he could to calm himself down, his edginess made him feel that he was driving erratically and would be pulled over by the traffic police. Normally in such cases, a flash of his warrant card would nine times out of ten get him a courteous 'OK, just take it easy in the future,' but there would always be one copper who needed to build up his arrest statistics and so would search his vehicle before writing him a ticket. It would be nigh on impossible for him to explain where the bag full of money had come from, and why he had it.

He had spent the morning at home lost in thought and watching the minutes tick away on the kitchen clock, forcing himself to stay there as long as possible in an attempt to stick to his normal routine, although even now he was still about half an hour earlier than usual. 'Thank God,' he said to himself as he finally turned into the quiet avenue of bungalows without mishap. Normally he would have driven straight into the driveway, but today he planned to back in, to give himself more cover from any prying neighbours. In his state of unease, however, Barry drove too far past the entrance to the driveway to ensure a smooth manoeuvre. 'Shit, pull yourself together, you prat!' he admonished aloud, before turning to look over his left shoulder. With one hand on the back of the passenger seat, Barry used the heel of his free hand to turn the wheel quickly this way and that, reversing up the drive without further incident and getting the car as close as he could to where he knew he could get the canvas bag out of the boot without being seen. He then left the car and made his way to the door at the side – front door for visitors, back door for family was the rule of this house. He paused at the door and as his hand gripped the doorknob, more from relief than happiness, he allowed a slow smile to spread over his face. So far, so good; he had the money he always dreamed of and no one had been hurt. Only Mary and her mother would suffer as a result of his actions, but hadn't he suffered for years with their incessant whining? It would just be him getting his own back.

'Hello Mrs Sharpe, it's only me!' he shouted as he lifted the latch and opened the back door. He had only ever been able to address her formally; although he had been invited to call her Marjorie, he had never felt comfortable to do so. Even the fact that he had lost both his parents in a train crash had still never instilled in him the need to call her 'Mother' or the like. From the start she had been, and she would always be, 'Mrs Sharpe' to him.

'Hello Barry – you're early,' she said as she walked into the kitchen. She was about the same height as her daughter, though plumper and with massive breasts that seemed to stretch down to her middle. With her apron on, she aptly fitted the description of 'homely'. Marjorie Sharpe instinctively picked up the caddy and started measuring spoonfuls of tea leaves into the pot. 'I'll put the kettle on but won't join you as I've got to go and see Mrs Sotcliffe at number 27. Her Ray is off work with stress again. I don't know how she copes – every time he has to do a little work he takes ill, and you know if he doesn't work he doesn't get paid.' Barry felt the relief flow through him; Lady Luck was running with him all the way.

He replied, trying to sound normal, 'That's fine, Mrs S. I'll only be having the one cup anyway as I've got some work to do in the shed, if that's all right?' He knew already that she wouldn't mind; since her husband had walked out on her after the war, Marjorie Sharpe had given her son-in-law the run of the shed and the tools her husband had left behind. She liked having Barry around the house and looked forward to the week he was on nights and came round for his tea – it reminded her of Mary's dad when he was that age and times were happier. At least he would never walk out on Mary, she had thought several times. She took the whistling kettle off the stove and started pouring the hot water into the teapot.

Barry went through into the living room and sat back in his usual armchair, ready to enjoy his cuppa, and began to relax; he could now start to plan his future. He chuckled to himself as he began to realise that it was probably not going to involve a career in the police force – he was not a yes-man and he had definitely left unlicked those things that ought to have been licked. Well, if he was patient and made his plans carefully, the sky was the limit; he sat and let his mind warm to the prospect that his future was safe and secure.

Martyn Crowe, his mind still preoccupied with Alexander Law, turned the car into O'Mara Terrace and was surprised at what he saw. The sight before him was what his mother would have described as a 'well-kept' road, with warm, friendly-looking terraced houses whose front doors opened directly onto the street and those proudly displayed well-scrubbed front-door steps. It all gave the impression that this was a contented and happy place in which to live. The house numbers decreased consecutively by two, so his sideways glance at number 54 had given him a good idea as to where he was aiming for. His next priority was to park his car, which he guessed as he drew into an empty space would not leave him more than four doors away from his destination. He stepped out of the car and, lifting his arms above his head, arched his spine in a stretch, partly to relieve his aching muscles at the base of his back and in his shoulders, but more subconsciously trying to delay the not-so-pleasant task he was about to undertake. He crossed the road and paused outside, taking a deep breath, before reaching forward to avoid standing on the freshly bleached step and rap the gleaming brass knocker, which, in the eerily silent street, seemed to convey his arrival to all. The door was quickly opened by a small, sad-faced woman, made to look starker by her prematurely greying hair pulled back tightly on all sides to the small bun on the back of her head. She stood proudly erect and straightened her clean but worn dress before wiping her hands on the red-chequered tea towel she was carrying.

'Can I help you? I hope you're not selling, as I have something cooking on the stove and I don't want it to spoil.' Her voice was quiet, and although nervous, had that authority that came from a lifetime of anxiety and stress from dealing with insistent salesmen.

Flipping open his wallet to display his warrant card, Martyn went through his opening introduction, which he could, and quite often felt that he did, do in his sleep. Seeing a slight flinch of her body and widening of her eyes, he continued, 'Mrs Smith, can I have a word with you about

David?' She seemed to go immediately on the defensive and appeared to step nearer to the middle of the doorway as if to prevent any intrusion.

'He's not in,' she said. 'Anyway, what's he supposed to have done? He has a good job working nights as a security guard.'

Martyn, trying to use his most gentle and sympathetic tone, went on, 'He's done nothing, love, but I do need to talk to you about him. Can I come in?'

Mrs Smith led the way down the dark hallway into a small but very smart sitting room, containing the usual three-piece suite and formal dark brown sideboards with the obligatory photographs displayed on top. She sat down on the settee, her hands, red and worn from a lifetime of work, resting in her lap as Martyn moved to sit down next to her but paused, saying, 'Do you want to sort your cooking out first?'

She let her face drift into a weak smile and replied, 'There's nothing on the stove. I just use that line to get rid of door-to-door salesmen. Now please tell me what this is all about. My David – he is all right?'

Martyn settled beside her, gently took her hands in his and, as best as he could, explained what had happened to her son. Throughout the description she stared into space, her eyes vacant; recognising the symptoms of shock and disbelief, Martyn rose and made his way to the kitchen, where, after a short search for the necessary items, he was able to return with a cup of steaming hot tea which he placed in front of her.

Looking at him through eyes in sunken hollows, as though this was another of life's blows which perhaps this time she might not recover from, she said, 'I only saw him yesterday ... It was his birthday and I did him a fry up. I even got him a small cake, 'cos he's got a sweet tooth, even though he said he was too old for such things. Is he going to die?'

Martyn knew that the truth, or at least half the truth, was far better than ridiculous optimism. 'He is very seriously ill, that's all I can tell you.'

'Who did it?' As she spoke she looked at him with the look of determination which said, 'If you know, tell me and leave it with me.'

Martyn tried to make his voice sound more confident than he felt. 'We don't know yet, but I promise you we will find out.'

She raised her eyes, but although she was looking at him, it was apparent that she wasn't seeing him. In a far-off voice, she said, 'Since his dad died, he's all the family I've got. I don't know what I'd do without him.'

'How long has he had this job?' Martyn asked.

'Oh, about eight months. It's a very responsible job but it wasn't dangerous – he used to say he was only guarding offices, not the Crown jewels, so I wasn't to worry.' As she spoke her body began to tremble and the tears started to flow, uncontrollable sobbing that racked through her body, and Martyn made no attempt to say or do anything to console her; tears would be the best medicine for her at the moment. After what seemed like an age, she quietly blew her nose and, as she composed herself, said, 'Can I see him?'

Martyn had already made up his mind that he would take her to see her son; he wanted to check on the security arrangements at the hospital anyway. He stood up. 'Get your coat on, love, I'll take you there myself. By the way, do you have a recent photograph of David that I could have?' Mrs Smith gave the detective a puzzled look, but unquestioningly moved to the sideboard and handed him a frame. Martyn looked at the photograph and saw staring back at him a smart, self-assured man in his early twenties wearing a crisp blue security uniform.

The look as she handed it to him showed that David Smith was indeed the pride of his mother's heart. 'It was taken the day after he started,' she commented. Martyn removed the back of the frame and placed the photograph in his pocket, not able, of course, to tell her that her son's face was such a mess now that no one had any idea what he looked like.

'Thanks very much, that will be a great help. I will make sure it's returned as soon as we've finished with it.' He placed the empty frame face down on the sideboard and helped the still dazed woman to lock up her house, holding her arm as they crossed the road to his car. She seemed to have aged at least ten years since they met that short time ago, and she certainly seemed to have shrunk in stature. After sitting her in the passenger's seat, he moved to the driver's side and paused as saw how small and hunched up she looked. Martyn swore to himself that he was going to catch the bastards who had done this, and put them away for a long time. Forcing a smile, he sat down in the driver's seat and started the engine, but remained silent as he turned the car around and began the journey to St Joseph's.

Alexander Law put down the telephone. *Why me? What have I bloody well done to deserve all this aggravation?* He had finally managed to speak to Simon Hunt, the hospital orderly, asking him to keep a very close eye on the man in intensive care. Although he wanted to, Law could not afford to shout and threaten the youth, even though he kept babbling on about the police presence, because Law had had an assignation with him and the last thing he needed was rumours to start flowing about his sexuality. The only thing Law could do was make promises, which of course he had no intention of keeping, such as a cash bonus and a better-paid job on his payroll. All he had been able to ascertain from Hunt was that Smith was still unconscious in intensive care, and there was a police presence in the side-ward. He had however been assured by the young orderly that he would continue to make regular visits and would keep Law informed of any visitors he saw. Big Al knew that he would have to be satisfied with that, at least for the time being. The phone ran again.

'What now?' he snarled as he snatched up the instrument.

He immediately regretted his outburst. The voice at the other end quickly advised him of his precarious new position, almost sending him into apoplexy as he tried to comprehend how they had discovered the problem so quickly, and prompted him that time was running out for him to repay the cash he had borrowed plus interest. 'I may need some extra time to pay you,' he muttered.

The menacing voice droned into the distance as Law recalled their initial conversation when he had originally negotiated the loan, and how he'd confidently assured his backers that nothing could go wrong, it would be so simple...

Law had been introduced to a mousey-faced chemist who had run up a large debt in one of his seedier gambling dens. After threatening to expose him to his family, Law sweetened the coercion by implying that he would consider the debt paid with a little extra for his pocket, if the chemist simply skimmed off a few prescriptions now and then. The chemist had been very happy with the arrangement for the first couple of weeks, until Law's men had upped the ante, forcing him to increase the productivity of his thefts, and finally resulting in hundreds of false prescriptions being written which were now in Law's possession. During the same period, Law had bought off a pharmaceutical supplier who was willing to cash the prescriptions in for a very large quantity of barbiturates, at a price – £25,000. Not normally dealing in wholesale amounts and not wanting to attract the attention of the rest of The Institute, Law was forced to borrow the cash outside of the city, from a crime organisation called 'The Corporation' whose home was in the capital, the big smoke. For a period of three days that he would be charged the ridiculous sum of twenty-per-cent interest, Law would repay these backers £30,000 and their courier would be waiting as prearranged. Law had organised the drugs to be split between three of his biggest distributors, who would each pay him half of the street value, a cool £15,000 each. The sudden influx of that amount of illegal drugs by his boys would be devastating to the rest of The Institute, who would be forced to agree to his demands if they wanted to survive. It was pure and utter simplicity. Borrow the money, buy the drugs, sell the drugs wholesale to the distributors, hand over the money plus interest to the courier, and walk away with the considerable profit of £15,000 and the monopoly of the market, all without having to even break into a sweat. Unfortunately, everything had gone wrong. He knew in his heart that unless he found the money he could not replace it in the time allowed, and as he concentrated again on what the voice was saying, he knew that his three-day deadline was not going to be extended as the voice at the other end stopped and the line went dead. Law remained standing with the receiver held against his ear.

He gently replaced the receiver, as though afraid of offending the person who was no longer on the other end. The bile in his stomach began to rise and he started to swallow quickly several times, trying to rid himself of the offensive metallic taste building in his mouth. Everyone who knew Law would have bet their right arm he was afraid of nothing and nobody, but no one was more surprised than he was himself when he realised that for the first time in his life he was frightened. No, he realised, much worse than that, he was terrified, and had his bowels disgorged themselves there and then over his lime green Persian carpet, it would have been no more than he would have expected.

Chapter 9

Charlie Morgan sat on the edge of the bed and looked at the empty cup in his hand. The fact that it was encased in grime and dirt had nothing at all to do with him hurling it against the far wall – it was his anger that got the better of him again. *Who has the money? Who has my fucking money?* He had been so damned careful, it was a simple one-man job and so he hadn't told anyone else. This entire job was based on the fact that Smithy was a poofter, and although he had loathed meeting him in those places where only 'they' were comfortable, it had meant that they weren't seen together in any of his local haunts and he knew that no one in the places where they had been seen knew him or would ever find him. Plus it definitely couldn't be one of Law's men who had taken the money back, as they would have undoubtedly left him in a worse state than that he'd left the stupid guard in. *Whoever had stolen it would live to regret it.* 'Who the hell could it be?' he growled.

The anger and accompanying red mist in front of his eyes slowly began to clear as he stroked his scar and forced himself to try to make sense of what had happened. He had seen no one at all, and apart from that fucking noise that had nearly scared the shit out of him, he'd heard nothing. Still, at four o'clock in the morning he hadn't expected to see or hear anything, which was undoubtedly why the noise had made him panic, and he knew he shouldn't have panicked.

So if it wasn't one of Law's men … Then maybe it was an

opportunist theft, but there were no tramps or hoboes around there, so it had to be someone who used that area at that time of night. But who? It suddenly came to him – he would have to go back tonight to the same place and same time, to see who was about. It was his only hope. With any luck, he thought, the bastard might just get greedy and come back looking for more. His mind rolled on: *What if there were any coppers lurking about?* He sat and pondered for a moment. *Ah, of course, the old dog lead scam.* While he had been doing his first stretch in prison, he had been talking to his older cell mate about how he had been picked up loitering after a break-in. After receiving the fully expected piss-taking lecture, he had been given a useful piece of advice he now followed whenever he was out on a job at night: he had always carried a dog lead, and if anyone approached him, the lead came out and he would start calling out the name of a dog, any name would do. He had yet to meet anyone, especially coppers, who didn't go soft as putty if they thought you were out in the middle of the night looking for a lost pooch – some of the stupid prats even helped. Anyway, if ever anyone became suspicious, a dog lead swung hard enough could catch anyone a real good clout. Yes it had been good advice and had saved him on a number of occasions, and you never change a winning system. *What to do till then?* He glanced across at his battered portable radio; stolen from the pawn shop a week ago. He'd listen to the news at six as there might be something about the guard. If not, he might yet have to pay a visit to the hospital; he needed to know what sort of state Smithy was in and if he was talking. If the guard pulled round then Charlie would need eyes in the back of his head to watch out for Big Al's men, because if he was caught then at the very least he could expect to have his body parts rearranged in a way nature certainly never intended them to be. He shuddered at the thought, and looked down at his grimy fingers as he involuntarily moved his hand to protect his crotch; if he did visit the hospital he'd have to get cleaned up first. *Shall I do it now? No, sod it, have a kip first and after the news decide on the next move.* He knew that he would have to get things sorted out, and quick – one way or another he had to get away from the city before Big Al located him, and it would make it so much easier if he had the money in his pocket to help him. Time was one thing that was not on his side.

After saying cheerio to Mrs Sharpe as she left to console Mrs Sotcliffe and counting slowly to fifty to make sure that she was at least out of sight, it took Barry only a few seconds to visit his car. He let out a long sigh of relief at the sight of the canvas bag in the boot, before lifting it out, quietly shutting the boot lid and moving back around the side of the house until he eventually found himself surprisingly out of breath just inside the shed door. Standing still, the only sound his heart pounding in his chest, he tried to control his breathing and calm himself down until he felt able to move again. Looking around the workbench, which was littered with bits of wire and tins of mixed screws and nails, along with odds and sods of pieces of wood which were kept in a 'might come in handy one day' pile, he finally saw what he was searching for, and, gingerly picking up the work gloves by the fingertips, tapped them on the bench. Satisfied, he opened each glove to look inside before pulling them on his hands and then located a small triangular wedge of wood which he pushed and then kicked tight under the shed door. He had found out by accident, several months ago, that with a wedge like that in place it was absolutely impossible for anyone to open the door before the wedge was removed. If anyone, and he was mainly thinking of his wife or mother-in-law, did try to get in, he would claim that the wood had dropped there accidentally.

He had spent most of the morning formulating a plan, and now he was in a position to see if it would work.

He was good with wood, and there were plenty of spare boards piled in the corner, next to the large garden roller, and they would comprise the false wall that his new-found legacy could be stored behind. Well and truly hidden. OK, so the inside of the shed would lose perhaps two inches, but with the pile of boards back against it, he was certain no one would notice. He'd make a start later, but first he had one very important and exciting task to complete: he had to see just how much his new legacy actually was – he had to count his money! Barry placed the canvas bag on the workbench, quickly glancing out of the small cobweb-covered window to make sure neither Mrs Sharpe nor Mary had returned early, before moving a sheet of hardboard and placing it against the top of the frame in such a way that if someone should look in from outside they would only be able to see down to the floor, yet it left him with sufficient light to set about his task.

Some time later he leaned back and looked at the workbench. It seemed to be covered in notes. He had arranged them in distinct piles. Those with any marks of blood on them he had put to one side. Those unmarked he had counted into piles totalling one thousand pounds each and stacked them neatly on the other side. Twenty-four piles of those there were, and the neat rows reminded him of his old army days and all those hours of drill and keeping a straight line. He bent forward again and rechecked his figures. Twenty-four thousand, eight hundred and seventy-five pounds, plus one hundred and twenty-five covered in blood. He stood up and rubbed the back of his neck as he tried to comprehend the amount. *Twenty-five thousand pounds! Bloody hell!* He would have to work for over eighty-seven years at his current pay to earn that much. Wasn't it only last week that Mary had been going on about a four-bedroom detached house she had seen closer to her mother's, but had been upset at the asking price of one thousand pounds? He could buy twenty of the bloody things now and still have money left over. He commenced his wish list of what he would buy, or, more to the point, what *couldn't* he buy? He had always fancied one of the new Austin-Healey 100s with the powerful 2600cc engine. *Guaranteed to pull the birds in, that,* he thought as he glanced at his watch and was suddenly startled that it was already past four o'clock. Where had the time gone? Was it already twelve hours since this had all started? He would have to get a move on now; he knew he had taken up so much time that he was not going to get the money hidden properly today. He swore silently under his breath as he placed the small number of bloodstained notes at the bottom of the bag, covering them with his bloodstained handkerchief, before placing all the unmarked notes on top, making sure he had the canvas bag as flat as possible.

He carried the bag to the back of the shed and placed it up against the wall, stacking wood around the bag until it was completely hidden. He looked around and saw what he wanted lying on the floor: a scrap of paper with old measurements from some past project on it. He pushed the paper in between two of the pieces of wood and then with a nail lightly marked the wood, either side of the paper. He knew that if anyone moved the wood, the paper would fall out. If they noticed and tried to replace the paper, the chances of them replacing it so it exactly matched the scratch marks would be very remote indeed. *You can't be too careful,* he mused as he bent down and, using a battered chisel to make sure there were no creepy-crawlies present, scooped up some handfuls of sawdust and dirt, throwing the first lot on top of the workbench and the next on the wood behind which he had hidden the money. He knew it now looked as though no one had recently used the workbench, but it would also tell him when he came in the shed next time whether anyone else had entered in his absence. He stood and dusted himself down as he carefully surveyed the scene; satisfied, he removed the wooden wedge and, leaving the work gloves on the workbench, left, closing the door and locking the padlock. He placed the key in his shirt pocket; having no intention of returning it to its normal place on the nail in the kitchen. If anyone wanted to get inside the shed now they would have to ask him first.

Very pleased with himself, he stood at the back door and glanced back up the garden to give the shed one final vote of confidence before proceeding into the house. After a quick wash in the kitchen sink he felt the need for a well-earned forty winks in the chair until the women turned up in time to prepare his tea. As he crossed into the living room, an idea sprang into his mind and, walking into the hall, he picked up the telephone to make a quick call to the police station. Replacing the receiver, he stood looking at his reflection in the hall mirror. There was no expression of vanity ... or was there? The reflection staring back at him certainly seemed very smug and self-satisfied.

Chapter 10

Martyn Crowe shuffled into the CID office, suddenly feeling very old and tired. He flopped down in his chair and listened as his stomach started to rumble and moan. Aware of his slightly protruding belly, he said out loud, 'You can shut up – I've got enough problems without you complaining!'

The words registered just how hungry he was – he hadn't eaten since breakfast. He hadn't the time to think about food just now, but this was the type of hunger that left a sickly feeling in his stomach. He would phone Rita in a minute to find out how she was, smiling as he did so as he knew that when he enquired 'What's for tea?', she would gently tease him that all he ever cared about was his stomach and that she and the boys were always lower on his list of priorities than his next meal.

Martyn's mind went back to the past two hours. He had taken Mrs Smith to St Joseph's, where he had handed her over to the firm but gentle hands of the sister in charge. He had then checked with the constable who was detailed to watch Smith and impressed on him the importance of the task, being pleased to see it was a different Wooden Top than that morning; at least this one did seem to have a bit of common sense. He had also made arrangements for another officer to be there to back him up, at least for the next thirty-six hours, before returning to the ward for one last look-see. Apart from a hospital orderly fussing around Smith's bed, all seemed to be in order, and he felt that he could leave the hospital content that he had done all he could with the manpower at his disposal. He then made one final call on the doctor, but although he was hoping for some better news, all he got from him was the usual 'As well as can be expected, the next twenty-fours hours will be critical.'

Tell me something I don't bloody well know already, he thought as he glanced over towards Mrs Smith, who was silently sitting by her son's bed trying so hard to will him better that Martyn could almost hear the prayers. *Hope springs eternal.* He recalled some unbelievable messes stretchered into that hospital only to walk out again. What was it they said about only when your number's up? His mind returned to the work on his desk.

Paper seemed to cover every inch, and he was sure that there was more than when he had first looked this morning. He searched and found a blank piece of paper. He had a lot of work for his late-turn officers to do this evening and he wanted to jot it all down whilst it was fresh in his mind. His eyes then caught sight of a message that had been scribbled out on a piece of paper and dropped on the top of his desk. *Where had they learned to write?* His eyes scanned the note: 'Bob Bourne phoned. He wants a meet, will see you in the Chapel at seven tonight'. Martyn sighed. *What the bloody hell did he want?* He hoped it wasn't another depressing marriage guidance session. He would meet him for one drink and that was it. Out of a choice between his missus and Bob, he knew he would not climb over Rita to get to his friend; still, he was a mate. He audibly sighed again as he reached for the phone.

Rita was always the same, no matter how down or depressed he felt, and just hearing her voice on the phone always brought a smile to his lips. He stood for the expected jovial ribbing when he mentioned the food, but noted her silence when he mentioned Barry Bourne. 'Can we make tea about a quarter to six, love?' he asked her. 'I don't fancy going to the pub on an empty stomach, even though I'm only having the one. I'm definitely not in the mood for a moaning mate this evening.' He felt her smile over the phone and knew that her good humour had returned. After assuring her once more that he loved her much more than her sausage, egg and chips he put the phone down and stared back at his desk. The dark clouds of depression returned as he picked up the piece of paper and commenced jotting down the list of tasks.

Alexander Law leaned back in his armchair and scoured the front page of the *Evening Echo* as he listened to the news; the BBC spokesman's monosyllabic tone enlightening the population on the tour of Kenya and other Commonwealth countries by Princess Elizabeth and the Duke of Edinburgh, before detailing how the government had offered farmers five pounds an acre to plough up grasslands for crops. The information he was waiting for appeared as a small stop press at the bottom of the back page, 'A man, whose identity is known to the police, is at present detained in St Joseph's Hospital, having been found by a patrolling police officer during the early hours of Monday morning in Reynolds Street. He is suffering from serious head injuries. Police are appealing for witnesses. Anyone with any information should contact their nearest police station.'

The bland statement made it all sound so unimportant. Law sighed before commenting to the absent writer of the piece, 'It may mean nothing to you, pal, but it's a matter of life and death to me.' He got up and switched off the radio just as the weather forecaster's voice filled the airwaves and he moved over to his drinks cabinet to pour himself a large measure of liquid courage.

His stomach churned as he felt a new sensation rising up inside him. It was fear, and he didn't like it one little bit. He was the one who was used to dispensing fear; he was the one who had the worms of this city quaking in their shoes while begging for a second chance, he reasoned with himself again. Had the money not been stolen, tonight would be the night that the deal was completed and the loan repaid, and he would have been the master of his domain and with a new very lucrative new drugs trade. He knew it was only greed that had pushed him, however, and now he wished he'd never heard of the idea or the name of the person from whom he could borrow twenty-five thousand at the drop of a hat.

He realised as he flopped back in his chair and took a gulp of whiskey that he now had no way of repaying that money. If he tried to borrow again, it would have to be from a local source, and if the rest of The Institute got wind of what he'd done or who he was in trouble with financially, then the vultures would be out for him. He needed a lot more time, either to get some money or to find out who had stolen the last lot. At least that idiot Smith was still alive, and he had better stay that way until Law decided it was time to personally introduce him to his maker after he had found out exactly what had happened and who was involved. This was to have been the biggest, fastest get-rich scheme he had ever conceived, but it had turned into the biggest, fastest bag of shit ever invented, all because of some thieving bastard. *But which thieving bastard?*

Not far away, Charlie Morgan also flicked through the *Evening Echo*. He was sitting across his bed, his feet on what had once passed for a bed cover. 'St Joseph's ' *So the stupid little bastard's still alive?* He involuntarily moved his fingers around the dirty collar about his throat. That was bad news; both for him and for Smithy – now he would certainly have to get over to the hospital. He shuffled off the bed and slouched over to the damaged mirror, still not liking what he saw as he looked upon the face of the man who had panicked and lost him his cash. His chance for a new start had been ruined and if he caught the little shit that had spoilt it for him he would make sure it didn't happen again, but not before he … His imagination began to run wild about the pain he would inflict.

Moving over to the dirty sink, he found the three razor blades lying in the scum. He couldn't remember which one was the badly blunt one that had caused him to cut himself in several places the last time he had shaved, several days ago. He picked them up and, discarding the one that had actually started to rust, flicked the edges of the other two in turn and then carefully fitted one into the safety razor that had been sitting on the window ledge. He had long ago run out of real shaving soap, so he attempted to get lather on his face from a piece of carbolic soap he'd lifted from the pub toilet, but the cold water made the task even more impossible. Settling for smears of greasy carbolic stuck to his greying whiskers, he picked up the razor and cursed loudly as he nicked himself with the first sweep down the side of his face. He swore again as he took the blade out and flung it across the room, where it happened to land close to the broken cup. He fitted a second blade, he persevered with the stinging task of trying to scrape away a week's worth of stubble from a face that wasn't used to soap and water, let alone a razor.

Finally finished, he started to swill the residue down the sink, but soon gave this up as a tedious job and left the shavings to congeal with the other festering muck that nestled in and around the plug hole. He moved to the cupboard, which took up the bulk of his so-called kitchen, and used the end of a dirty finger to scoop up a small amount of lard from an unwashed pan. After smearing it over his palms, he worked into his hair. From his back pocket he produced a comb, and even with its several missing teeth, he managed to trawl it through the grease-ridden mop that now sat atop his head. He wiped off the excess lard that stuck to the comb onto his trousers before he finally replaced it in his pocket. He was quite pleased with his appearance, even though it should really have been Brylcreem and not cooking fat, he pondered. But it would do for now. He wiped his hands down his trousers once more before lying back on the bed, hands behind his head, to formulate a plan without stupidly losing his temper again. He reasoned that he would have to wait until it got darker before he went to the hospital, and he would have to be extra careful as he hadn't any idea who might be looking for him.

He woke with a start. He hadn't meant to fall asleep, and, panicking, rushed over to the turn the wireless on to check what time it was. After a few moments of Johnnie Ray and The Four Lads, the time was announced and he realised he needn't have worried: half past six. 'Shit!' he exclaimed, realising just how on edge he was and that he had panicked more in the last few days than he had previously in as many years. *Time to move*, he thought, as he took one last look in the mirror to make sure his rest had not affected his shiny appearance before opening the door.

He was at the top of the stairs when he remembered. 'Damn, I'd forget me bastard head if it wasn't screwed on,' he mumbled as he returned to the room and after a couple of minutes' searching, reappeared on the landing with dog lead in hand. He smiled to himself as he stomped down the stairs. *When a scheme works well ...*

He stood at the entrance to his lodgings and looked and listened to the sounds of the street. Old missus fat-arse, the Greek lardy from number 36, was screaming at her apparently no-good husband, while the kids from the tenements were kicking an old football against the wall of the building, somehow just missing the windows of the lower floor. Everything appeared to be normal – if the police were anywhere near, the place would have been silent – so, satisfied that all was as it should be, he skulked off into the shadows of the evening towards the hospital.

*   *   *

Barry pushed back the chair from the dining table and belched loudly. 'Manners!' recriminated Mary with disgust. Ignoring this, he rose to clear away the crockery from the tea table. He picked up his plate and looked admiringly at the L-shaped bone which was all that remained of the pork chop, garden peas and potatoes, as he sucked at his teeth in an effort to dislodge the small scrap of meat that always seemed to get stuck in the space between his upper back teeth. The enjoyment he nearly always got from this tussle was spoilt immediately by the loud 'Tut, tut!' which emanated from his wife. He stopped and looked at Mary, who, as usual, was by now taking no notice and carrying her cup of tea from the small dining table to the side of the sofa. She remained quite attractive, with pert breasts, a firm, peach-like rear and shapely legs, and probably still having enough sex appeal, he knew, to draw many knowing glances and unspoken innuendoes from his colleagues at one of the rare official functions they attended. He tried hard, as he watched her back disappear towards the settee, to remember what had happened to the spark that had caused such sexual excitement that he had hoped, once, would last for ever but had already gone out. There were still times during their monotonous pre-planned sexual rituals when he would feel the spark beginning to return, only to have it extinguished by the complete lack of interest shown by his wife. *Would it have been different with children? Probably not!* He turned in the direction of the kitchen and felt, with a sigh of relief, that children would have undoubtedly complicated his current situation; at least now he wouldn't be abandoning his kids. Carrying the plates towards the sink, he managed to further irritate Mary, who was now looking at him through the doorway, as he was not carrying out the task as she had previously instructed.

'Barry, how many times do I have to tell you? Wash the cutlery first, and then the dishes and the pans last!'

'Stuff you,' he mumbled under his breath, before remarking that he was going to leave the pans to soak and do the cups later. Standing at the sink, looking at his reflection in the darkening window, he could visualise Mary and her mother after he had done a bunk, blaming men for all the troubles in the world, little realising, and certainly never admitting, that women, with their bossy, moany, nagging attitudes, were probably responsible for starting the trouble in the first place. He let the thought drop from his mind as he continued to wash the grease off the plates. He had once tried to put forward this point of view but had let it drop, never to be mentioned again, when their knowing looks and raised eyebrows told him exactly what they thought of his comments. He had realised then that in the matter of men he would never win against Mary and her mother, so he had given up. *Was that why Mary's father left? Perhaps he couldn't stand to live with two masters?* He didn't know the actual reason for her father's departure, and had never before felt the need to ask.

He wiped his hands on the tea towel and took a deep breath in anticipation of the imminent displeasure. 'I don't want to stay too long tonight,' he called through to Mary. 'I'm meeting Martyn at the Chapel at seven.'

His wife couldn't contain the anger in her voice as she blasted back, 'Why?'

He thought quickly. 'He phoned me here this afternoon and asked me to meet him. I forgot to mention it to you when you got in.' The twisted lie came out so easily – he knew that any request from Martyn always got a sympathetic hearing from his wife.

'Well,' she grumbled, 'don't drink too much – remember you're on nights!' She was in truth not particularly bothered whether he drank or not, as his visits to the pub always left her with time to herself, which she much preferred these days. Her only worry was that because of drink he might lose his job, and she knew that the house went with the job.

Neither spoke during the fifteen-minute journey home from her mother's, not because either one was angry with the other, simply because there didn't seem anything at all to say. As he drove, Barry could feel the shed key nestled in the top pocket of his shirt; he glanced at his wife from the corner of his eye. *If only you knew ...!*

He parked their car in its usual spot and he and Mary made their silent way through the front gate and up the short garden path towards the front door. As he navigated the two small steps that began the path, Barry glanced in the direction of the window three doors away, where he saw Rita Crowe busying herself while she awaited Martyn's return. As though struck with a bolt of lightning, he realised that he envied Martyn, for his wife, his family, his lifestyle and his promotion. Mary also noticed Rita and raised a hand in greeting when her friend looked out of the window to see if she could see her husband approaching. She returned the wave. Mary had, upon their first meeting, quite fancied Martyn and it had seemed he had quite liked her, but as she got to know them better she had realised that for all his teasing and friendliness there was only one woman in Martyn's life and it was the woman who had become Mary's best friend: Rita Crowe.

They proceeded into their small semi-detached and once inside, went off in different directions, still without a word being spoken. Barry headed up the stairs to get himself ready for the night, preceded by his visit to the local. As he changed into his uniform he decided he probably wouldn't bother coming back home from the pub before heading out to the nick for his shift.

Mary, meantime, had gone into the sitting room and lit the small gas fire in the centre of the room. She kicked off her shoes and crossed the carpet to switch on the small mahogany-cased Bakelite television set; only the second person in the road to have had a set, she treasured it as it had been the very last present given to her by her father. As she knelt in front of the screen the BBC tuning signal slowly appeared as the set began to warm up. She tweaked the knob on the right to adjust the controls to get a clearer signal, all the while thinking how much she missed her dad. Satisfied that the picture was as good as she was going to get, she moved to the kitchen to make herself a mug of cocoa. She didn't bother to ask Barry if he wanted some, as he would shortly be going to the pub. When ready, she took her steaming mug of cocoa and a couple of digestive biscuits back into the lounge, and settled down in the settee to watch *What's My Line?* presented by Eamonn Andrews, who she had always thought was ruggedly handsome.

A short time later she heard Barry coming down the stairs. After raising her cheek for the customary peck and accompanying non-committal 'See you' to which she could only nod, the front door slammed and she was left alone with the terrible solitude which would last all night. Mary was locked in her box; no one cared if she was lonely or miserable. She picked up her cocoa, holding the warmth of the mug for comfort in both hands, and became conscious of the solitary tear which slowly rolled down her cheek until it hung at the corner of her mouth. She flicked out her tongue and wiped it away, before moving her hand to pinch any remaining tears from her eyes.

'I don't care. I just don't care any more,' she stammered as she nestled further into the warmth of her cocoa and chair. The trouble was that she did care, and no matter how hard she tried the tears flowed unchecked down her face and chin as she tried to focus on the television.

*   *   *

Martyn Crowe parked his car behind his friend's, and noticed how both cars were getting past their best, in parts showing signs of rust and equally with odometers that betrayed the years of miles they had achieved. However, he had spent a lot of time and a fair amount of money trying to keep the bodywork of his car free from the ravages of the elements, which was more than could be said for Bob Bourne. He glanced out of the window at his friend's house and thought he saw Mary crossing the sitting room to the kitchen. Taking out his door keys, he walked three houses along and made his way up his front path to his own 'castle'. He opened the front door and was immediately hit in the face by the welcoming warmth; it was not the heat from the gas fire, but the glow of a family that were ready to greet his homecoming. He quietly closed the door and paused briefly as he inhaled the smells of cooking and listened to the sounds of the scurrying hustle and bustle taking place behind the closed kitchen door. After removing his overcoat and placing it on the vacant hook by the door, he turned to see the face of his wife as she appeared from the kitchen, with its full beaming smile. She always gave him that smile whenever he walked in, however she felt, and he quickly reached out to pull her towards him and kissed her full and hard on the lips.

'I love you,' he said, staring deep into her eyes when the embrace finally ended.

'I must try doing that again sometime!' she responded with a giggle as she wriggled free of his arms and bustled back into the kitchen to check on the food.

He turned into the sitting room and was greeted by the sight of his two sons in matching blue-and-white-striped pyjamas, sitting on a rug front of the fire. Both noticed their father's arrival simultaneously, and their pink freshly scrubbed faces lit up as they yelled 'Daddy!' continuously, and struggled to their feet to run to him and smother him in what was a daily ritual. The crescendo, which now included Martyn's laughter, didn't stop until he managed to get an arm around both and carried them to the settee, dropping them with the rough gentleness that can only come from a father to his sons.

'Well, what have you two scamps been up to today?' was followed by both, in full gusto, detailing their own exploits in the usual volume where Martyn could understand neither. With a bit of tickling and lots of hugging, he eventually managed to calm them down and after a couple of kisses each, both boys settled back on the floor to complete the jigsaw puzzle they had received from Santa Claus.

Martyn rose and made his way into the kitchen. 'How's tea coming along, love?' he enquired as he paused behind his wife, his hands around her waist and his head nuzzled into her hair.

'It's going to be later than I thought, I'm afraid,' she said. 'Is that going to throw you out?'

Martyn held her a little closer and smiled as he replied through her hair. 'No, don't rush. It'll probably suit me better to go for a drink now, then.' Give me a good excuse to get back early. Sure you don't mind?'

Rita turned in his arms, 'Off you go then, and be good ...'

Martyn pulled her close again and after squeezing her waist and kissing her nose, finished her sentence for her: '... but if you can't be good, be careful!'

Rita didn't mind at all about Martyn going for a drink. She knew that his friendship with Barry 'Bob' Bourne went back to when they were doing National Service together, and she knew he felt a genuine brotherly concern for his friend, but she also knew that the troubles between Barry and Mary got Martyn down.

Martyn paused at the sitting-room doorway and stared

lovingly at his two sons playing contentedly together. He felt his heart stir and knew that indeed he was a very lucky man. 'Shan't be long,' he called to them, their reply lost as pulling on his overcoat he went back out through the front door.

Chapter 11

Charlie Morgan waited in the darkness of a doorway and stared across the road at the entrance to the hospital. With lights on in every window, it had the appearance of an ocean liner sailing in a sea of darkness. From his vantage point it looked very warm and secure and he wondered what his next move should be – wander around inside the hospital until he found the ward and bed Smithy was in, or be direct and try and bluff his way through reception? On the one hand, if he was caught wandering in an unauthorised place he could encounter trouble; but on the other, he really didn't fancy walking up to the well lit reception area and placing himself in open view. *If only I knew which ward the little bastard was in.* He could have been in and out faster than the blink of an eye, but the place was huge and it might take him all night to find him, especially as he couldn't risk being questioned too closely by any of the staff. Finally he made up his mind: he would have to discover which ward he was on, and that meant bluffing his way in. Reception it was, then.

He stealthily moved through the large open doors of the hospital and into the brightly lit scene, concentrating so much on creating a plausible cover story that he didn't notice the two men standing around the canopied entrance having a crafty smoke.

The rather large and pompous female behind the desk scrutinised his approach and looked him up and down suspiciously as he stood in front of her. 'Yes?'

He knew that his appearance might attract suspicion and had worked out a fairly reasonable cover story, but at the sight and tone of the receptionist he simply blurted out, 'Can I see a mate of mine? He has been hurt badly. It was in the *Echo* earlier.'

The receptionist stared at him with disbelief and distrust. 'You are not a relative then?' He simply shook his head and looked to his shoes as she continued, 'Wait there, don't move. I will go and check.'

Charlie watched her depart, struggling to believe that she was indeed only one woman and not two roped together, as she wobbled her bulk into a back office and started talking quite animatedly to someone he couldn't see, continually glancing in his direction. Suddenly alarm bells started ringing in his head as he realised that things were not going as planned and, never one to ignore his instincts, he turned quickly and moved quietly away from the desk and back through the large doors into the security of the night – not towards the main road, but around the outside of the hospital to where the shadows were longer and darker.

He had no idea why he had taken this path, as he walked below the lit windows of the first storey, until he saw a door with the sign 'Intensive Care Ward. Emergency Exit. Do Not Block'. He climbed onto a large dustbin and carefully peered through the window. The room inside was swarming with nurses, doctors and visitors administering either medicine or sympathy to the inhabitant of the bed they attended. There were rows of beds, and at least half of them were occupied. 'Shit!' Charlie whispered. With all the swathes of bandages that seemed to cover every inch of every patient's skin in there, there was no way that he would ever find Smithy; he was wasting his time. He carefully climbed down and quickly made his way through a grassed area. Guessing correctly that he was now at the rear of the hospital, he crossed the car park and moved off into the night.

Unbeknown to Charlie, his instincts had served him well once more, for had he decided to return the way he had come he would have bumped into two large plain-clothes policemen searching long and hard for him.

The lights of the Church Tavern shone brightly and seemed to throw a happy welcome into the night. Consisting of a small public bar and a smarter lounge area, with the landlord's living quarters covering the top floor, each room had its own dedicated regulars who rarely ventured into the other section of the pub. Even the separate toilets outside had their own regulars. How the Church Tavern became known locally as the Chapel was lost in the annals of folklore, every one of the older regulars having their own version of the tale. However, one thing was certain: should a stranger ask for the Church Tavern they would be answered with blank stares, but if they asked for the Chapel they would be directed with a beaming smile.

Barry had arrived first and gone as usual into the lounge – none of the occupants of the police houses in their street used the public bar. The other locals – those who weren't involved, either legally or illegally, with the police – tended to use the public bar. There were exceptions, but that was the general rule of the establishment. The landlord, of course, welcomed the use of his pub by the police; he could always guarantee a trouble-free evening, and if it meant staying open later than his normal hours for a lock-in to accommodate the seemingly unquenchable thirst of the law, then so what? The security and peace of mind it brought him were worth it, never mind the extra takings in the till.

Picking up his pint glass, being careful not to spill the overflowing frothy head, Barry walked over to the corner he normally occupied to await the arrival of his friend. Contrary to what his wife imagined, he had no intention of drinking too much, not because he was about to go on a night shift but because tonight he needed a clear head to ensure he could turn the conversation around to work-related matters – namely, the money – without arousing any suspicion. Work was not a subject usually mentioned in the pub – in fact, it was a kind of unwritten rule that the job was never mentioned outside of work. Barry knew, however, that if such a large amount of money as he'd found had been stolen, then the chances were that Martyn would be involved and might casually mention it, especially if prompted, in the course of conversation – after all, it was more money than any of them would ever see in a lifetime of saving.

He sipped the froth off the top of his glass as he looked around the lounge. The log fire, on the far side of the room, had been lit and it sparkled and cracked greedily in the hearth, sending a glow around the room that was caught by horse brasses of every shape and size that hung from the walls. The new idea of having piped music through the rooms seemed to be working; when first introduced, it had of course been criticised for being either too loud or too quiet, but it was now accepted as part of the atmosphere and in fact was missed by the patrons when switched off. The padded seats, laid out in half-moon shapes, tended to split the room into smaller areas; the design had worried the landlord at first, but he soon came to realise that policemen and their families tended to congregate in small batches and this was another reason they preferred the lounge over the bar. Anyway, it never appeared to stop a good sing-song on a lively Saturday night.

Barry's musing was interrupted by the sight of his friend entering the room, and he called over, 'The money's behind the bar – you've only got to order.' Martyn lifted his hand in acknowledgement but didn't reply. The landlord had seen him come in and was already pulling his pint, which he handed over with a smile. Martyn nodded his thanks and picked up the drink, then made his way over to where his friend was sitting.

He raised his glass in front of him as he approached in a form of salute. 'Cheers Bob,' he said, and took a sip before dropping into the padded seat and placing the drink on an awaiting beer mat, then shuffling his backside along the leather of the seat until he was a hand's length away from Barry.

'How are things, Bob?' Martyn asked. 'I got your message – anything wrong?'

Barry shook his head. He had long ago got used to answering to two first names. His nickname, along with thousands of other monikers, had been created in the Army. Most of the others based on surnames, though his of course came from his initials. Those named White were called 'Chalky', Miller's became 'Windy', Bell converted to 'Dinger' and even Martyn had been called 'Scary' for the period of his National Service. The only problem arose for Barry when he was in mixed company, and he had long tired of trying to explain when he saw the confused look on some people's faces why his colleagues and friends called him Bob, while Mary and the other women called him Barry; as a consequence, it just didn't matter to him any more.

Barry took a sip from his drink. 'Been busy mate?' he enquired.

'Bloody well have, me old son – but what can I do for you?' Martyn lifted his glass and took a long drink, wiping the remnants of froth from his top lip with the back of his hand. His mind was still trying to analyse the day's events – his visits to Law and the hospital – and the last thing he wanted to do tonight was to chat about it until he had organised his thoughts. What he really wanted to do was to go home, eat tea and cuddle up to Rita on the sofa. He could even feel that the half pint he had consumed was going straight to his head, because of his tiredness and his now gurgling empty stomach.

'Nothing really – I just fancied a chat.'

Martyn grimaced. 'Bad day at home then?'

Barry, his relief almost evident that Martyn wasn't becoming suspicious, replied, 'Yeah, but I don't want to talk about it. Tell me about your day instead.' He leaned forward with his elbows on the table between them in a movement that feigned interest.

Martyn sighed and settled back in his seat, turning his pint glass slowly around on the beer mat. 'Had a savage wounding this morning – he's in bad shape and if he snuffs it, it will be a sod of a case to crack.'

'Got any ideas?' Barry enquired as he lifted the glass to his lips.

Martyn started to voice his thoughts as he tried to piece them together. 'Well, the injured bloke was a security guard for Big Al Law, and that's where the problem lies. Nobody is going to talk to us about anything, are they?'

'Anything else?'

With a look of bewilderment, Martyn retorted, 'Piss off will you? What else do you want me to say? I've been working like a prat all day in and out of hospitals, and you know how much I love them! Interviewing that bastard Law and getting absolutely nowhere, plus consoling a woman whose son had the shit kicked out of him – there's not a lot to discuss!' With that he drained the remainder of his beer and picked up Barry's empty glass before sliding along the seat to stand up. 'Another?'

Barry nodded his head, slightly stunned at the unexpected outburst, and sat in silence staring at the beer mat on the table, until Martyn placed a full glass in front of him. 'Sorry mate,' Martyn apologised. 'No more for me. I'm knackered and I'm starving. Tell you what; we'll have a proper evening out with the girls when we get time.' Without waiting for a reply, Martyn turned and walked out the door.

Barry stared at his newly replenished glass. Perhaps it hadn't been such a good idea to have asked Martyn for a drink – he wasn't sure his friend had swallowed the story about him not wanting to discuss with him his troubles with Mary, but at least he was now fairly sure that Martyn didn't know anything about the money. He would definitely have been involved if twenty-five thousand quid had been reported stolen or lost – that amount of money would have been the talking point of the century. However, he could always see if there were rumours floating round the station later. Feeling good, he relaxed and momentarily toyed with the idea of going back home again for the two hours or so that remained until his night shift started, quickly comparing the imposed silence, with its unspoken exasperation, there with the open warmth and friendliness of his current surroundings. With a contented sigh, he leaned back and lifted the glass to his lips. Smiling, he wondered just how many pints of beer he could buy with twenty-five thousand pounds, but arithmetic had never been his speciality, so he settled for the satisfied thought that he could buy enough to remain inebriated for most of his remaining lifetime.

Charlie Morgan let himself back into his dingy little room and dropped backwards onto the bed, to stare vacantly at the grimy ceiling. 'That's that,' he said to himself, 'the hospital is definitely out – too bloody dangerous.'

He wasn't worried about the rotund receptionist; even if she went to the police, by the time they got there she would only be able to provide a general description, unsure of what he looked like or what he was wearing. It never failed to surprise him just how bad and varied people's memories could be, or that the descriptions were always so bad that the police were ever able to use them to find the culprit. But although he had tried to keep the right side of his face more prominently in her view, she got a fairly good look as he was walking in and undoubtedly would have seen the scar, which was one thing she wouldn't forget to tell them.

He was reasonably satisfied with his decision to go to

reception rather than stand the chance of being caught wandering inside the hospital; however, he reflected, it may have been a mistake to return to his digs. If the police got a description of a man with a large scar down his face, then it wouldn't be long before word was out on the street, and Law would definitely recognise the owner of his own handiwork. The thought of what Big Al might do to him caused his stomach to churn and produce another involuntary fart, so loud it startled him.

'Fucking Jesus!' Charlie got off the bed, the aroma too much for him to handle, and suddenly realised how hungry he was. He searched his pockets before scouring the top of the cupboard for loose change. Just enough for a pie from a stall at the market. Then he silently berated himself that everything had gone wrong. He should have been away by now: he should have had enough money in his pocket for thousands of pies. Instead, he was still in this shitty room, with no smokes, no booze and nothing to bloody eat. Life, with its recent promise of wealth, was quickly becoming a real bag of shit!

Like so many times in the past when he was hungry, Charlie forced his mind to think over what he had to do. He would stay where he was for a while and then, like a predator, he would enter into the night, which was his territory. Like all habitual villains, he had learned to use the resources that nature provided, and none was better for clandestine activities than darkness.

He was not ready to give up on his dream of wealth and luxury just yet – he would find that bastard and ... well, that would come later. But first, with a possible description of him already circulating on the street, he had to stay safe before he was ready to make his move. Using the only chair he had left, he jammed the back under the handle of the door and made sure that the rear window was open – if he did have any unexpected visitors, he intended to give himself a bolt hole for escape. He went back to the bed to lie down and rest until it was his time to join the other vermin loose on the streets in the dead of night.

Martyn Crowe closed his front door gently, knowing his sons would definitely be in bed but probably not asleep. His wife stuck her head around the kitchen door and gave him a loving smile. 'You were quick. Was he there?'

'Yes love, he was there,' Martyn replied absently, as he removed his overcoat for the second time that evening.

Rita paused before returning to the kitchen to administer to her culinary delights. 'Was he all right?'

'I don't really know,' said Martyn as he hung up his coat and loosened his tie. 'He said he just wanted a chat and I presumed he and Mary had had another barny, but all he seemed interested in was what I had done at work today. Anyway, after one pint I'd had enough, so welcome home your lord and master.'

Rita rushed out of the kitchen with a smile to give her husband a big hug. As he held her in his arms, Rita felt, as always, utterly contented and so safe. She had been so lucky to have found him. If it hadn't rained that day, if he hadn't broken his normal routine and popped into the café for a cup of tea, if she hadn't been doing someone else's shift as a favour … The 'ifs' were endless, but she was very, very happy.

The smell of the food from the kitchen woke her from her reverie and, pulling away, she enquired, 'Have you upset him?'

Martyn grimaced, half for her having left his arms, and half for her question. 'How can you upset someone like Bob, unless, of course, you're Mary? No, I don't know what it was tonight, I can't put my finger on it, but it just didn't feel right.'

'You're probably imagining it,' sang the soft lilt from the

kitchen before adding, 'Dinner in about fifteen minutes – that OK? Sorry it's late.'

'Not a problem, darling,' countered Martyn as he headed for the stairs. 'I'll just check on the boys.' He started climbing the stairs two at a time and finished at the top in a single weary step, before turning right and moving along the landing to pause at the bedroom door of James Barry, who was named after his maternal grandfather and godfather, and who was hard and fast in prayer. Leaning closer to the door, which was ajar, he tried to pick up the words; it seemed to Martyn that his eldest son was obviously in dire need of salvation, as probably were the entire class at Gilmore Primary. Deciding not to interrupt him before he was finished in his spiritual petition, his mind drifted back to his own childhood and recalled that for years, after mishearing the second line of the Lord's Prayer, he thought that God's name was Harold, for he had recited 'Our Father who art in Heaven, Harold be thy name ...' He blushed with embarrassment as he remembered his juvenile error, and entered the small box room which was occupied by his youngest son, John Martyn, who was named after his paternal grandfather and father, and who was lying half asleep diagonally across the bed. Martyn managed with some success to negotiate the minefield of toys strewn across the floor without serious mishap and, pulling down the bedclothes, he attempted to adjust his son into a sleeping posture of some normality. He knew it didn't matter – by the time he checked his son once more before going to bed, he would undoubtedly have returned to another seemingly impossible nocturnal position. Brushing his son's blond hair from his forehead, for which he received a semi-unconscious smile, Martyn bent and kissed him before tucking in the bedclothes and quietly retreating from the room.

The silence from his eldest son's room encouraged him to enter, and he found James lying on his back trying to give the impression of reading the book he was holding. At six years of age he was able, with encouragement, to read simple words, but his attempt to convince his father that he was easily coping with the *Boys' Annual* without problem brought a smile to his father's face. 'All right there, son?'

'Fine thanks, Daddy,' came the attempt at a grown-up voice. 'Just having a read, it helps me sleep.'

'Don't be too long then,' said Martyn softly, and he leant over and kissed him on the forehead before tousling his auburn hair with his hand. 'Good night James!'

'Good night Daddy, I love you.'

'Love you too son,' answered Martyn as he closed the door of the bedroom behind him. He paused on the stairs, hand on the banister, and stared silently at the two closed bedroom doors. *I love you both very much*, he thought as he softly descended before being brought quickly to reality by the harsh sound of the telephone ringing in the hallway.

Sighing as he moved towards it, he heard Rita mutter a stifled 'Oh no!' as she popped her head around the door frame, just as he lifted the receiver to his ear and pronounced, 'Crowe.'

Rita watched as Martyn listened to the caller and nodded before finally raising his thumb in salute: good, that meant he hadn't got to go back to the station. She smiled as she retreated to the kitchen with the thought she had got her husband to herself for the whole evening, and a tune started to come from her lips, as she sang her own rendition of 'The Loveliest Night of the Year', recently recorded by Anne Shelton, while she returned to the steaming saucepans on the stove.

Martyn soon joined his wife in the kitchen. 'Trouble?' she asked him. She wasn't being nosy, just showing interest in her husband's work.

'Somewhat,' he replied, absently realigning the cutlery on the table already set. 'That was the nick. We had a nasty wounding today – bit complicated, but no real problem. The injured man is in St Joseph's and the station just rang me to let me know that some scruff bag was asking after the victim. It may be nothing, but you never know.'

'Is that the man in the *Evening Echo*?' enquired Rita, who was trying not to burn his chips.

'I suppose so. Although I haven't seen it, I knew we were going to make an appeal for witnesses. Fortunately I had placed a couple of blokes at the entrance to the hospital, but unfortunately they couldn't find him to ask him any questions.' He moved over to the sink to be next to her, before saying, more to himself, 'Someone is definitely interested in our man.' He made the decision then to call the station once more before he went to bed.

At that point the aroma of the food that had been put on his plate, and that now awaited his arrival at the table, reminded him just how hungry he was. He sat down and gazed admiringly at the victuals before him. *This is going to be one of the most pleasant demolition tasks ever*, he thought, as he added some salt and a dollop of ketchup before picking up his knife and fork. 'Thanks love,' was the last words he spoke for the next twenty minutes as he eagerly devoured what had been his only meal of the day.

Chapter 12

'On parade!' It was quarter to ten, and with the rest of his shift, PC Barry Bourne stood to attention, glancing out the corner of his eye along the line at the other eight members of his watch. There should have been nine, but PC 'Chalky' White was having his usual extra day off. Not long ago they had started a new system whereby you could have up to three sick days off consecutively without having to provide a doctor's note, and Chalky was the one who had seen fit to abuse the system; in reality, according to the rumour mill, he was checking up on his missus …

Barry jerked himself back to reality, standing ramrod straight with his left hand holding his pocket book, handcuffs and first-aid pouch, while his right displayed his truncheon upright at right angles to his wrist, together with his whistle connected by a silver chain to the top jacket button of his uniform tunic. These five items were called 'appointments', and because they were an essential part of the officer's needs during a shift, they had to be produced for inspection before proceeding on duty.

Although the inspection was merely a formality compared with the inspections of his service days, he still felt relief when his turn was over and his attire and appointments were found to be correct. The inspector progressed along the front of the line before going behind the officers, but only when it was very long or untidy was a comment passed about the state of an officer's hair. Barry remained staring forward, shifting his weight only very slightly from one foot to the other out of habit from his Army drill days, to help stop his calf muscles cramping.

'Appointments away!' commanded the inspector as Barry and the rest of his shift returned all the items to their allotted pockets, with the exception of their notebooks, which they simultaneously flicked the restraining elastic band off that was there to keep the small indelible pencil safely attached to the notebook's edge. The eight men now stood at ease as the inspector droned on, their pencils poised to note down any information pertinent to their particular area. On a separate slip of pink paper kept inside their book they also annotated the dozen or so stolen vehicle number plates they were aware of before each shift.. Barry knew that if he were to look back through the pink slips amassed at the rear of his notebook there would be hundreds of numbers, and he recalled when he had first started how he had conscientiously checked every number plate he saw against those written down on his pink slip. It was different now – he knew the majority of vehicles and their owners on his beat, and where they were usually parked, so he found little occasion to refer to his pink slip.

As he listened to the rest of the briefing he realised there was nothing of interest to affect him tonight and noted that his meeting time with the sergeant was the same as on the previous shift – no doubt the inspector and sergeant had planned on an early evening of snooker and the times had been arranged to accommodate this.

Barry had come to work a little earlier than usual, ferociously sucking two mints just before he arrived in an effort to disguise the odour of beer on his breath, never sure which was worse – the smell of beer or the aroma of mints and alcohol mixed. Having checked the usual books and message sheets, listing all the serious crimes, and having found no mention of missing money, he had managed to get a quick look at the offences received from other divisions that had been filed away for information. There was nothing to tell about the money, but he had noted there was a lot of paperwork regarding the serious wounding; all stated that DS Crowe was in charge and most requested information and further enquiries. He had also been careful to listen to the general chat around the station, and had heard no word of the missing cash; from experience he knew that had there only been the slightest whisper or suspicion, the station would have been awash with rumour in no time. Barry often thought that the men he worked with were the worst gossips and rumour mongers he had ever come across – they were far, far worse than women. If anyone knew anything or even thought they would be the first to spread it around, then it would travel through the grapevine in a flash.

There was nothing! So where had the bloody money come from? Whose was it? *Someone* must have lost it! *Well, finders keepers,* he thought to himself; he had it now and he was going to make sure it bloody well stayed his.

The parade over, the eight officers were lined up once again after donning their topcoats and then marched by the sergeant in line from the station to the first corner, where they would individually peel off and move towards their respective patrol areas, parting with the usual ribald, inane comments. Barry moved gratefully off on his own into the cold night air; he had a full eight hours in front of him, and he wanted his own company.

The intensive care side-ward of Nightingale Ward was quiet, with only the gentle moaning of one of the patients breaking the silence; the strategically placed night lights casting a strange unearthly radiance across the ten-bed ward. Mabel Docherty, the night-duty nurse sat at her desk at the end of the ward monitoring the sounds, which told her that currently everything was well. She hoped it would continue that way until morning, looking involuntarily at the button on the wall, which, if she pressed it, would bring people scurrying as if from nowhere to assist in saving someone's life.

Glancing up from the papers on her desk into the eerie glow of her ward, she caught sight of the mother of David Smith, whose small, frail figure curled hunched up in a chair in the ante-room, where so many relatives and loved ones sat and prayed. From experience, Mabel knew that only half of all patients admitted into this ward got out alive and that God probably played as big a part in their recovery as the expert skill of the surgeons. Mabel stretched long and hard, to release the tension forming in the small of her back, before rising and quietly strolling over to the ante-room, where lay the promise of a hot cup of refreshing tea. Quietly entering the room she stepped past the restful Mrs Smith towards the back, where the two uniformed police officers were dozing in chairs. 'Why should Britain tremble?' she muttered to herself as she lifted the kettle off the small hob and shook it; smiling as its contents swished with enough water for a cup of tea. With deft movements, she lit a match from the box on the side and turned the knob on the stove. The whoosh of the gas igniting extinguished the match which she dutifully dropped into the metal waste bin, before placing the kettle on the bluish flame, minus the whistle attachment. After swilling out the small teapot, she dropped in two teaspoons of tea from the caddy and then removed a clean cup from the shelf and added a splash of milk from the bottle in the cool box. The whole procedure took less than two minutes.

Suddenly, alerted by nothing more than instinct, Mabel looked back into the ward to see an orderly she recognised bent over bed six with his ear by the patient's mouth. Moving to investigate, she noted as she approached the bed that the patient appeared agitated and his breathing laboured. Just as she was about to confront the orderly, he turned and scurried through the doors leading to the mortuary. Pausing until she was content that things were back as they should be, she gave up on her cuppa and settled once more into her chair.

What was all that about? And what were you doing Simon Hunt? Well, you come around my ward again tonight and I'll tell Matron and she will personally make sure you need a bed!'

Alexander Law lay on his back and stretched. His naked body had been satisfied and felt good between the silk sheets, before a movement next to him caused him to turn and look at his bed companion, a fair-haired youth in his late teens. *What was his name?* Shrugging his shoulders, Alexander thought, *What do I care?* He had been very stressed and there was only one thing that relieved what he was feeling – he needed a sexual outlet. But he'd done something he didn't normally like doing – he'd brought back a past conquest, and he didn't like that because he didn't want to give any of these nancy-boys the impression they had a hold over him. He knew, however, that last night was different; he hadn't wanted any strangers in his house until he had sorted out his problems, and besides, he had enjoyed his night companion. No playing around, jut straightforward raw sex and no worries afterwards.

His cravings satisfied for the moment, Alexander lay his head back on the cool pillow and let his mind wander over the last twenty-four hours. *Why had it all gone wrong?* He had never dreamed, even in his worse nightmare, that this could ever happen to him, but it had.

Suddenly hearing an unusual noise in the night's silence, he felt a rise of panic in his chest. *What was that?* He finally identified it – it was the telephone downstairs. For the first time in his life, Alexander Law was nervous. *Who the hell could it be at this time of night?* He looked at his watch: eleven thirty.

No one ever dared to call him at this time of night ... unless. His thoughts were interrupted by a gentle tap at the door, followed immediately by his valet entering the room, not in the least bit bothered by the naked juvenile male next to his boss; he was paid well enough to work for Big Al not to judge his morals.

Arriving at Alexander's side of the bed, John whispered, 'It's that orderly at the hospital. He says he will only talk to you!' John held out a light green dressing gown, and as Alexander Law pulled his bulk out of bed and stood with his back to the valet for him to help him dress, the latter noticed the stains on the sheets, sighing at another job he would have to do in the morning.

Alexander descended the stairs two at a time and snatched up the receiver that had been laid on his desk next to a freshly poured tumbler of whiskey. 'What?' he shouted down the phone. A small smile started to form at the corners of his mouth as he listened, downing the whiskey in one satisfied gulp before replacing the receiver in its cradle. 'Got you, you little bastard! Pirate, you're mine, and this time I won't be so lenient!'

He paused for a few seconds before again reaching for the phone to set in motion the wheels that would bring whatever fate to Charlie Morgan that Alexander could finally dream up for him. All he knew at this moment was it would involve pain, lots and lots of pain. He smiled, not sure whether it was the phone call, the drink or the expectation of violence, but something had stirred his body and he felt his desires starting to well up inside him as made his way back up the stairs.

Barry Bourne found the night dragging. He had started off by going over the plans in his head, but until he was happy with the arrangements in the shed and, more importantly, until he knew where the money had come from, he couldn't relax. He was on the third tour of his beat and was heading once again to the area where he had found the money when he glanced at his watch: twenty-four hours – had it only been twenty-four hours since he had relinquished his principles and turned his back on his own code of conduct? It seemed a lifetime ago.

Time for a smoke-o, he thought, and reached for his cigarettes as he moved towards the corner of the alley. It was then that he saw the man standing in the shadows. Not thinking the man had seen him; Barry stiffened and moved cautiously forward, noticing a dog lead hanging limply from the man's hand.

'Are you all right, sir?' he asked, moving his fingers from the cigarette packet to the strap of his truncheon. Seemingly startled, the man replied, 'Sorry, officer, you made me jump. I've lost my dog.' As he spoke he looked down and lifted the lifeless dog lead in his hand.

Barry stopped himself saying, 'Well it's certainly not at the end of that,' and instead replied, 'What sort is it? I certainly haven't seen any dogs around here tonight.'

The man let out a long sigh. 'It's a spaniel called Bess. She's getting on and I don't want to go home without her – the wife would be heartbroken.'

Barry thought, *What you really mean is you don't want to go home to an ear bashing from your missus,* but continued, 'I haven't seen her – mind you, that isn't unusual – there's not normally anyone or anything around at this time except me. I'll tell you what, let me have your details and I'll make sure they get to the desk sergeant. You never know, the dog may be found somewhere and reported.'

Smiling gratefully, the man replied, 'Max Barnett. The wife Jessie and me live at 24 Crown Road. Thanks very much for your help, Officer, but I had better keep looking.'

Barry stood and watched the man move off, and hearing him occasionally call out the name 'Bess' forlornly. He certainly was a scruffy-looking and smelly bloke. *But I suppose it takes all sorts*, he thought. As the man disappeared from view, Barry realised where his fingers had remained throughout the encounter: on the strap of his truncheon. Laughing, he took out a cigarette and lit it before starting to write down the details in his pocket book.

Charlie Morgan had seen the policeman long before he himself had been noticed, having been standing in that spot for some time, after checking the surrounding area for the bag and its contents. It had been a surprisingly mild night and as a result he was starting to sweat from his excursions. But when he had first sighted the copper he had made sure his hands weren't slippy, wiping them on his trousers first before getting a good grip on the dog lead.

After the conversation, Charlie had moved off, conscious of the eyes following his movements but satisfied that he was not going to be followed. The scam had worked like a charm; funny though, the copper had seemed nervous. Perhaps it had been the unexpected sight of him. There was definitely something nagging at the back of Charlie's brain though – something had been said, but what the hell was it? He was still calling out the made-up dog's name and casually turned into an alley, where he stopped and craftily peered back round the corner to where the copper had been, to see the red glow of a cigarette in the shadows. 'Lucky bastard!' he muttered, remaining still until the policeman moved off. He guessed that if nothing untoward happened that would be the last he would see of the flatfoot that night, but he still wanted to see who else was about.

Christ, he was hungry though. Reckoning the time to be just after four o'clock, he decided he would stay another hour – by then the market tea stall would be open, he thought as he slipped the dog lead back into his pocket, while racking his brain for whatever it was that had been said that he couldn't quite remember.

*   *   *

Alexander Law woke with a start and glanced at his watch: twenty past four. That was enough rest for him; he jumped out of bed and, disregarding his dressing gown, made his way to the bathroom. He was about to run a bath when he was joined by his valet. 'Get rid of him,' he commanded, his head indicating the bedroom. 'Give him some cash off the table, John. Give it to him and get rid of him. No excuses necessary,' he snarled.

Lying back in the warm, scented water, his head resting on a small pink towel at the end of the bath, his mind became active once more. What if they didn't find Morgan? What if he had already done a bunk with the cash? How would he pay back the money? Alexander knew that what he needed to do was to sort this problem out, one way or another, and sort it out now. *What if I disappear for a while? All I need is time,* he mused. They would get their money back from him, but just not yet. *Get yourself some breathing space, give yourself more time.* With that thought, he allowed himself to sink deeper into the water, letting the luxury of the warmth seep into his body and temporarily wash his problems away. *That's it,* he decided as he sat upright. If they found Charlie Morgan and the money, then he would be OK; if not, then he would have to do a bunk himself for a little while. He picked up the soap and began tenderly lathering some very sensitive places.

Chapter 13

The glow of the morning sun was just beginning to break through when Charlie moved from the vantage point of his overnight vigil and worked his way through the alleys and back streets of the city, his destination the market area which was already alive and throbbing with activity while most residents were still asleep. A place where the day's work was just ending at the time when most normal people's commenced, its public houses, cafés and food stalls all licensed to open at four thirty in the morning to satisfy the thirst and hunger of the traders, who spent their unsocial working hours moving produce from farm transport to warehouses to await the daily arrival of the shopkeepers and hoteliers who scurried around, bargain hunting. The entire area only occupied three or four streets, but for that short time in the early morning, six days out of seven it buzzed with enough activity and excitement to fill several football stadiums.

Charlie moved from the receding shadows to the back of a dirty-looking stall. The smell of hot, greasy food emanating from it threw his hunger pangs into frenzy, but he instinctively decided to wait until the small queue of traders it had already attracted, diminished. His stomach audibly growled contempt for the delay as Charlie, ever vigilant, spotted a full, undamaged cigarette which had obviously dropped unnoticed from someone's packet behind the adjacent tea stall. Knowing that a welcome blast of nicotine would temporarily pacify his appetite, he picked up the smoke and was searching his pockets for a lighter when he heard his name.

Charlie froze, all his animal instincts coming into play as he tried to merge with the background while searching for a way out. The voices were coming from the front of the tea stall.

'Charlie Morgan,' said a gravelled voice.

'Who the bleeding hell is he?' replied another, while making chinking noises, obviously stirring his mug of tea using the spoon which was chained to the stall ledge.

'Known as Pirate, he is – a greasy little shit with a scar down his face,' rasped the receding voice. 'All I know is Big Al wants him badly, and like yesterday.'

Charlie knew he wasn't going to be able to hear any more of this conversation, and anyway he had heard enough already. The word was out. Big Al wanted to get him. Smithy must have grassed him up. 'Bloody Shit!' he exploded under his breath. *Why didn't I hit him harder?*

He slunk away from the busy market area, knowing his own lodgings were now a no-go area, and headed to a part of the city that was comprised mostly of derelict buildings. It was a throwback to the Second World War that had finished nearly eight years before, an area of bomb damage that still awaited its turn to be demolished and rebuilt into one of the new-look council estates. It was an area he knew well, having grown up there; it was where he started his somewhat unsuccessful criminal apprenticeship; it was where he had met Bobby, whose 'career' had been cut short by Al Law; it was where he could hide if in trouble; it was where he could lie low and think.

Once out of the market, the streets now quieter, Charlie knew he could get to his sanctuary quicker by keeping to the main streets rather than skulking through the maze of alleyways and back streets he normally used. The only opposition to this plan was made by his stomach, which growled and complained at being denied its morning nutrition the whole thirty-five minutes it took Charlie to get there.

He found the building he was looking for, his old school, and checked the boards of the fence that was designed to keep the public out. Finding one loose, and with an agility that would have surprised anyone who knew him; he wriggled his way through the gap and swung the board back into place. Charlie crossed the dilapidated ground and quickly moved to the rear of the school, removing the lower of two boards that had been nailed to the frame of the back door to deny access. A single sharp kick just above the door handle ensured that the door flew back on its hinges to reveal what had once been the caretaker's storeroom. After pausing briefly to confirm he hadn't been followed, Charlie bolted through the doorway of his rat-hole and scurried into the darkness beyond.

Martyn Crowe arrived at the station early again, regretfully leaving his wife snuggled up in their warm bed fast asleep, knowing he had got to catch up with some of the outstanding paperwork mounting on his desk before giving his full attention to catching the villain who had caused the horrendous injuries to David John Smith. He'd shivered in the cold morning air as he unlocked his car, realising he had just missed speaking to Bob as he caught sight of him disappearing through his own front door after his arrival home from his night shift. Even with the windows up and his overcoat buttoned to the neck, Martyn hadn't stopped shivering during the drive to work because the car hadn't yet heated up during the ten-minute trip.

On his arrival he had received the expected comments from the uniform division and provided the accepted replies to the ribald comments about his early appearance there.

No, he hadn't shit the bed. No, he hadn't had to jump unexpectedly out of his lover's bedroom window. No, he hadn't forgotten to go home, and yes, his wife did know where he was. All cheerful early-morning banter that he didn't object to, knowing that at a later date he would be able return the compliment. He groaned upon entering the CID office and seeing the paper amassed on his desk. He was sure one of the others was giving him their share as well – it couldn't possibly all be his. Before starting the drudgery of paper shuffling and filing, he telephoned the ward, expecting and dutifully receiving the news that there had been no change – at least the poor devil was still alive. The sister didn't think it necessary to inform him of the orderly's visit or the brief agitation of the patient, but pointedly told him that the two policemen were indeed awake and that she was contemplating sending a bill to the Chief Constable for the amount of tea and biscuits being consumed. Satisfied that all was as well as he could expect, he picked up the first bundle of papers and opened the cover, spending the next hour engrossed in diligently checking reports, making notes to investigating officers, signing off overtime expenses and filing completed cases. So intense was his involvement in his labour that when the telephone rang he literally jumped in his chair. He glanced at the office clock as his hand moved to the receiver: seven thirty two a.m. *Who could this be?*

He picked up the receiver. 'CID office.'

There was a momentary silence and then a serpent-like voice slithered down the line, 'Mr Crowe?'

Martyn stiffened. 'Yes. Who's that?'

The whisper turned into a soft Irish brogue as the voice continued, 'Paddy Riley, Mr Crowe. I've got something I think you'll find interesting.'

Martyn relaxed and smiled. Patrick George Riley, known as Patrick to the unfriendly, Pat to his wife and Paddy to his friends, had for a long time been an informer of his. As a criminal who had been treated fairly well by his arresting officer, Martyn, and more through luck than judgement escaped a likely prison sentence, he had become an informer when a subsequent bond had developed between him and Martyn. A mutually beneficial deal had quickly been reached: money for information, the bartering of which was discussed over many a pint.

Paddy had been arrested for theft by Martyn, then a young PC, and would have had a long jail sentence had Martyn not spoken up for him in court, explaining that he had a young wife and three kids to feed and wasn't considered a 'bad lad'. By sheer good fortune, the politics of the day had been for fewer prison sentences and more rehabilitation, and so he had been let off – although his punishment was actually six months' probation, to Paddy Riley and his family it was the same as being let off. As a result of the probation he had obtained a steady job with the council and kept his nose clean ever since, and from that day on Paddy had given Martyn snippets of information, not, it seemed, for the money, which he took anyway, but more to try and repay a debt he felt he never could.

'What's up, Paddy? Are you in trouble?'

'Begorra, no!' replied the Irishman, giggling. 'I'm OK Mr Crowe. I'm down at the market, doing a bit of casual like.' That meant he was doing a second job in the mornings, fetching and carrying vegetables, for which he was paid cash in hand and so didn't feel the need to pay any tax on that income. 'Thought you'd like to know Big Al has the word out for some bloke called Pirate, real name Charlie Morgan.'

Martyn froze. 'Paddy, keep your ears open, but don't get involved. Anything involving Alexander Law means big trouble.'

'Don't worry, Mr Crowe,' Paddy assured him, 'Big Al doesn't know I exist, and anyway I'm more frightened of Molly than him, but it certainly sounds like he wants this fellow bad 'cos there are a dozen blokes asking after him and he's offering big money.'

Martyn smiled at Paddy's reference to his wife Molly, who fervently kept him on the straight and narrow and still found time to look after their seven children. 'Listen, Paddy, I owe you for this one and there'll be a couple of quid in it for you.'

'Mary, Mother of Joseph!' exclaimed Paddy. 'It must be important! Listen, I've got to go, Mr Crowe, I'll see you later.'

Martyn sat listening to the dialling tone with the receiver against his ear for the next few seconds, realising that if Big Al wanted Pirate this desperately, there had to be more to the wounding case than was being admitted – he definitely needed to find this man before Law. Martyn shook his head, feeling totally inadequate; it still never failed to amaze him how fast the criminal grapevine worked, but thankfully at least he now had the information as well, and when it came to finding Charlie 'Pirate' Morgan, he mused, may the best man win. With that thought still in his mind, Martyn replaced the receiver and, scraping the chair back on the floor, moved across the office to use the internal direct line to the Criminal Records Office. This phone had no numbers on it and only a single call button, as it was designed to stop outside unlawful callers having access to criminal records.

He picked up the phone and pressed the button. *Let's find out exactly what we know about you, shall we, Mr Charlie Bloody Pirate Morgan?* When the phone was answered, Martyn spoke urgently and rapidly to the person at the other end before absently drumming his fingers on the desktop as he awaited a reply, eventually sighing with relief as the records officer verbally relayed the details and promised to teletype the information to his office immediately. But Martyn had already got all the information he needed to start the wheels in motion on the process that would place one 'Charles Henry Morgan aka Pirate' on the 'urgently wanted' list of every police force in the country.

*   *   *

The current topic of conversation on both sides of the law, Charlie Morgan sat back amongst the dirt and grime of Mr Jenkins' decrepit storeroom-cum-office, listening to the scratching and scurrying sounds in the darkness around him which competed with his audible stomach pangs. He suddenly felt like he had a lot more in common than he'd previously thought with the scavengers that called this place home. Shutting his eyes, he gently rocked back and forth as a moan of desperation escaped his lips. What was he going to do now? Where was he going to go? For he knew that go he must – his life depended on it – but not until it was safe to do so, and it was safest when it was dark, when there wasn't normally anyone around … His brain finally snapped the missing piece of the jigsaw into place. '*That's* what that fucking copper said,' he blurted out, making the unseen vermin scurry for cover. '"There's not normally anyone or anything around at this time except me."'

The answer had been in front of him the whole time: all night long, Charlie had only seen one other person, *the copper*; the place was all office buildings, garages and empty shops, and there had been no one else. 'That copper! *He's* got my fucking cash!' he roared with a rage previously unknown that sent him cold with anger. 'And if *he* hasn't got it, he'll soon tell me where it is.'

Charlie spent the next thirty minutes calculating his future and caressing the pink mark slashed across his face, making up his mind to stay put for the day before returning to the same spot where he had conducted last night's vigil, to await the arrival of that flatfoot. He now instinctively knew it was the copper, it had to be. Right time. Right place.

'Bloody coppers,' he commented to himself. 'You can't trust anyone nowadays!'

Settled with his plan, he lifted his hand and flicked away

the insect that was searching his face, as his stomach continued to growl for attention. He still had the coins in his pocket but couldn't afford to be caught out on the streets now; this was going to be a long wait. He settled back, ignoring whatever it was that was nibbling and pulling at the dried stale food lodged in his trouser cuffs, and drifted into a slumber in which he dreamt happily of the pain that would be suffered by the policeman at his hands.

Chapter 14

The clanking and banging of the dustcart woke Barry with a jolt and he immediately leaned over the bed to glance at his watch: twelve o'clock. He had slept better than normal, having crawled straight into bed and totally ignored his wife's complaints about cold feet, before drifting into unconsciousness immediately his head touched the pillow. He yawned, stretched, got out of bed and headed into the bathroom for his usual ablutions, the exertions of the dustmen audible as they slammed the bins onto the side of the cart to empty their contents, before dropping them back outside the appropriate house and clanging the lids back on. He wiped the steam off the mirror over the sink with the butt of his hand and inspected the pronounced stubble that shadowed his face; he never bothered to shave at this time in the day when on nightshift, as it would only mean he would have to remove his five o'clock shadow again before work, and shaving once a day was enough for any man.

He donned jeans and a shirt before heading downstairs to make tea and toast. It would soon be time to go over to his mother-in-law's, in this tedious routine that was his life. Mary would arrive later, they would all eat tea together and the evening would grind on until they returned home so he could begin his preparations to go to work. It was all so boring and monotonous – and Mary never asked him what he was going to do, and he wasn't the slightest bit interested in what she did.

There had been a time when they had been courting when, instead of the cinema, all they could afford was a bag of fish and chips and they'd sat on the town hall steps sharing the food, happy just to be in each other's company. Now, though, it seemed that either would do anything to avoid the other.

He took his cup and plate into the kitchen and washed and dried the two items, placing them carefully in their allotted places in the cupboard before folding the tea towel and hanging it on the handle of the cooker. Had he been conditioned to do this? Yes, he decided that he had been, but he was only acting out of self-preservation: it was never worth the scolding he would get if he didn't leave the house looking as though no one lived there. Well, no one really did *live* there – it was just a place to exist in, Barry mused, demoralised. Then he smirked and the smirk quickly developed into a beaming smile as he realised that today was different, today he was going to complete the task of hiding the money, and then he could sit back and see what developed before making his move. *Not long now, be patient.* Nothing at all could go wrong, he felt confident about that. He left the house whistling a tune.

Alexander Law flopped back in a chair, the sweat seeping from his forehead. He knew that his next move had to be carefully planned. There was no way that The Corporation would let him off paying back the money or give him more time – to do so wouldn't enhance their reputation as no-nonsense businessmen, and they were much more likely to put a bullet in his head than say, 'No problem, Alex, take your time.' To them he was an expendable liability. He wondered if he was being watched.

Wiping his brow with his handkerchief, he picked up the phone and dialled a long-distance number, spoke for some ten minutes and then replaced the receiver. His plans were under way; he had confirmed his hideaway destination, somewhere he was certain they couldn't find him, and as he relaxed, his old anger began to reassert itself; now he wanted results. He was paying enough money to enough people – surely they could find one poxy individual! Oh, the frustration of having to rely on others! The telephone rang. He gingerly picked up the receiver, wary as to who the caller might be, but relaxed as he recognised the voice. After less than two minutes the call was over and a long, drawn-out whistle escaped from his lips. The police were looking for Pirate as well, were they? Alex knew that once word was out on the street, some weasel would tip off the coppers; they would probably only earn a fifth of the twenty-five quid his blokes were offering. *Well, Pirate, you're definitely in the shit now.*

He smiled contentedly as he considered how surprised that smug-looking detective sergeant would be had he known that the last call was from one of his own men. Alexander had happened upon the policeman in a betting office, had paid off his fairly mediocre accumulated debts, and subsequently had a tame informant in blue. It was indeed very useful to have a bent copper in your pocket, but an added bonus when that copper worked in the Criminal Records Office. *Ah! Whoever said money doesn't talk was oh so wrong!*

He buzzed his valet and told him to prepare for an early-morning departure.

'Location and duration, sir?' John enquired, adding quickly, 'so that I may pack appropriately, sir.'

'I will give you all the details later, but pack at least three suitcases with both casual and formal,' replied Alex, 'and make sure you keep a watchful eye out – that nosy bastard of a copper is bound to show his face again.'

'Certainly sir.' John exited the room to start on the packing.

Alex was in reality less concerned with the detective

sergeant, and more bothered about any elements from The Corporation poking their nose round his place – he knew he couldn't be too careful. But the bastards to whom he owed money would have to be up very early indeed if they wanted to catch him.

Chapter 15

The bell on the wall burst into life, startling the two policemen relaxing with yet more cups of tea. The day-shift nurse had pressed the panic button to alert the doctor before quickly marching across the ward to a patient both the policemen knew. She was quickly joined by a group of four others, two doctors and two staff nurses. Each, without uttering a word, took up their positions around the bed of David Smith and as they were doing so the day shift nurse gently took the arm of Mrs Smith and guided her back to the small ante-room with a firm embrace of her elbow and remained with her as she continually enquired, 'What's the matter? What's happening?'

The two policemen now stood at the doorway and watched the scene around the bed unfold in front of them, until one of the nurses drew the two sections of white screen around it to afford their patient some privacy.

The silence of the next few minutes was only broken by curt instructions from the senior doctor, which were carried out without question and with the utmost efficiency and urgency. After a prolonged flurry the activity stopped and the five people, who such a short time ago had moved with expectancy and hope, now exited the bedside in a much slower and more sombre fashion. Through the gap in the screen caused by the departure of the dejected people and the subsequent lack of necessity for discretion there could now be seen an immobile figure shrouded in a white sheet pulled up over the head. The fight for the life of David Smith was over.

A staff nurse moved away from the bed and followed the senior doctor into the small ante-room, where the doctor gently explained what had happened, as the nurse drew the stunned mother gently but firmly away from the sight of the bed and her deceased son.

The two police officers suddenly realised that they had been staring open-mouthed at each other throughout the medical emergency. The senior of the two then indicated to his colleague to remain where he was, while he telephoned the station and informed the detective sergeant of this turn of events and that his only witness was dead.

Detective Sergeant Crowe replaced the phone. *Sod it! Bloody well sod it!* He turned and announced to the office in general, but to no one in particular, 'The guard snuffed it!' The murmurs from those present began to increase until the office sounded like it was under attack by a huge swarm of bees. To them it was good news: there would now be lots of lovely overtime, especially for those currently in attendance, for they would be chosen to be on the investigating squad, and within thirty minutes the rest of the staff would be squabbling for jobs like ants round a picnic.

Martyn didn't take any notice of the excitement his words generated. He reached into the bottom right-hand drawer of his desk and removed the folder labelled 'Suspicious Death', the contents of which told him precisely what procedure he was now to follow. As he opened the folder he sadly realised that a murder was one of the easiest crimes to investigate, not in respect of the actual act but because more resources were readily available, including as many extra officers as he would need, all of them suddenly eager for overtime. He inwardly hoped that the enquiry wouldn't last too long, not so much for the sake of the victim or his family, but because as long as the Chief Constable authorised the overtime then the men would work all the hours God sent, but if the enquiry dragged on and budgets were overstretched, the overtime would be decreased and there would suddenly be requests for time off or men would declare themselves unavailable to do extra hours.

He forced his mind back to the task in hand, and after rereading the list entitled 'Things to be followed', he picked up the phone sure of one thing: now that David Smith had died, unless they got hold of Charlie Morgan and he talked, then whatever involvement Alexander Law had in this case would never be discovered and he would get away scot-free again. He therefore had to ensure that they intensified their search for Morgan; he was now their only lead. Dialling the number for his next course of action, he listened to the ringing at the other end of the line as he began to jot down a list of names in a notebook, fully aware of, but pretending not to notice, the faces that were milling about trying to attract his attention.

Charlie Morgan woke with a start, his neck and back screaming in agony due to his nocturnal posturing. His hands pushed against the small of his arched back as he tried to remove the knots in his neck by rotating his head slowly before attempting to move to a more natural position; but the cramps that suddenly attacked the muscles in his legs made the whole act of rising impossible and he flopped back into the dirt, causing unseen creatures to scurry noisily back into their own holes. He gave in to the pain until it subsided of its own accord. He could hear high-pitched, excited shouting coming from somewhere outside the school. Realising that it was just a couple of youngsters playing, he began to think about what he had been like at their age but quickly stopped himself. *Just concentrate on what's going to happen next.*

112

Charlie stirred again and moved his legs, the pain slowly dissipating as he stood and stretched every muscle and fibre. He wondered whether it was worth calling Big Al and telling him that the copper had the money and letting him sort it out, but he knew he was too deep in the shit for having nicked the money in the first place for Law to forget him. *No!* he told himself. *Keep your mouth shut and sort this out yourself!*

Barry smiled as he let himself into his mother-in-law's house. They each had a key to the other's home, supposedly for emergencies only, though he half suspected the real reason was to allow the women a good chance to nose around the other's place if either were away. *All women, after all, are inherently nosy sods.* He didn't have long, he realised, to complete the work required to secure the cash in the shed, for once he had finished on nights he wouldn't just be able to pop over, as that wasn't the normal routine, and if he did, the inquisitiveness of one or both women might get the better of them. *I'll get it done right and then sit back and relax until it's time to enjoy the luxury I'll be able to afford,* he thought, *unless the shed catches fire …* He immediately scolded himself for tempting providence. Still annoyed that he should entertain such ridiculous thoughts, he entered the kitchen to find a note pinned to the tablecloth from Mrs S promising to he home in plenty of time to make his tea.

He went immediately to the shed and let himself in, pausing in the doorway to look for signs of tampering. Content that nothing had been disturbed in his absence, he put on his work gloves and began to toil quickly and efficiently. First he removed the money from the bag so that he could measure the bundles stacked together and build a corresponding area at the back of the shed to be hidden by the end of the workbench and a few well-placed scraps of planking. The money returned to the bag, he carefully cleared the area adjacent to the door to enable the workbench to be moved the three and a half inches required before he selected the oldest and most worn planking to form the cover for his homemade vault, cutting the appropriate number of lengths to size for joining together later. Using the leftover creosote from last year's renovation of the shed, he then painted the planking, and, when dry, the addition of encrusted sawdust would create a perfectly matched camouflage to the remainder of the interior. So engrossed was Barry with his labours that he was utterly startled by the cry of 'Barry! Fancy a cup of tea, dear?'

'OK Mrs S, I'll be along in a minute,' he shouted, knowing there was no chance of him continuing any more that afternoon, and so he set to work replacing the bag of money behind his original makeshift hideaway. With a final glance at the replaced scrap of paper nestling between the planks, he removed his gloves and left the shed, making sure it was locked securely. *Another couple of days like today,* he thought, pursing his lips to silently whistle a tune, *and it'll be finished. No stopping me now!.* He went in through the kitchen door.

Martyn Crowe was finally able to put down the telephone. The fleshy part of his ear lobe felt red hot from being pressed to the receiver for hours, and he tried to rub some life back into it. He leaned back in his chair and looked down at the carbon copies of the various lists he had two-finger-typed in between phone calls on the office's shared Remington Model II, sending the originals to the detective inspector for approval before displaying them on the station notice board. Martyn knew that the large number of officers allocated to the investigation team would upset more colleagues than it would please, but he wouldn't lose any sleep over it; he had broad shoulders, and after all, he was paid to make decisions and not to win popularity contests.

He was still studying his copies, wondering if he had chosen the right balance, when the phone rang again. He

114

immediately snapped back to reality at the sound of the DI's calm voice at the other end. 'Martyn, I've just double-checked the list you sent me and I've had to remove two names, Jennings and Gough. They're both on a course in ten days' time and I don't want them to have to start the enquiry only to hand it over.'

Martyn responded, equally composed, 'Yes sir, I had considered that when I selected them, but they are both excellent officers and I wanted them on my team. With the information we have, I had hoped that it wouldn't take that long to conclude the investigation, but I take your point and I'll find two other names.'

DI Hopgood smiled to himself: he should have known that Martyn would pick up on a fine detail like that and that he hadn't in fact slipped up. The DS would soon be ready for promotion if his work ethics continued, he mused. 'Pick a couple of uniform chaps, will you?' he told him. 'That will keep them sweet. Let me know the names and I'll square it!'

'Thank you sir, I'll get on to it right away,' replied Martyn, thinking with horror, *Wooden tops!* He didn't intend to have any idiots mess up his enquiry, and he moved over to the wall to study the list of the uniformed shifts pinned on it, scanning down the names. One caught his eye, a chap who had been on the CID team of another division before dropping into the brown sticky stuff. He might be worthy of a second chance, so Martyn wrote his name on a scrap of paper before he caught sight of his friend Bob Bourne's name. *Why didn't I think of him before? He could always do with the money and he's always as keen as mustard for a chance not to have to go home,* he thought. With the two uniformed officers' names thus selected, he returned to his desk and made the call necessary for his boss to sanction their temporary transfer into plain clothes for the duration of the enquiry.

Martyn then took the opportunity to call Rita, and after listening to how her day had progressed and telling her he didn't know what time he would be home, he asked her to pop over to Mary's and give Bob a bit of advance warning of his plan.

'That your idea or from above?' she enquired.

'A bit of both, love,' he replied. 'Everyone could use the extra money, but I thought it might give them both a welcome break from the constant bickering. Get Bob to call if there is a problem, but remind him that although it came ultimately from on high, I want him!'

'Take care darling!' was his wife's parting comment as she hung up the phone, smiling at her husband's thoughtfulness and modesty at not taking credit for looking after his friend.

Martyn replaced the receiver and tidied up the loose papers on his desk. Looking down at the stack of finalised dossiers ready to be filed, he felt motivated enough by what he had achieved so far that day to move off to the Murder Incident Room. This room would now become his base of operations for this investigation and he knew it would be a few days before he returned to his desk and more new case files. He cast a parting thought of sympathy for the two detective constables who had been left to cover the day-to-day business in the absence of the people who now made up the murder enquiry team. He was fully aware from past experience that it was an ideal opportunity for some to pass over all their dodgy jobs that couldn't be completed, knowing that they would never have to accept them back. However, he also knew that if you clear all your workload onto someone else, then when they are seconded to a murder enquiry the favour will be returned, normally ten-fold.

Chapter 16

Barry was sitting at home in his favourite chair by the side of the fireplace, watching the glow of the coals and the odd spark making a break for freedom from the inferno below; he was wondering whether he could get out to the pub again tonight for a quiet pint and a pleasant chat with the landlord, or whether he would have to sit it out in the house until it was time for him to go on his night shift. It hadn't been too bad at his mother-in-law's; his concealed excitement at having progressed with the hidden vault had occupied his mind so much through tea that he had hardly noticed the incessant bitching, as they ate, between his wife and her mother, that they called a conversation. He was still amazed after all this time that even though they saw each other practically every day, there was always a topic on which they could unerringly complain; in his good spirits he had even managed to consume the liver and onions, which, despite being constantly advised was good for him, he detested more and more with each serving. However, it wasn't too much later that his contentment waned as he received his belated daily reprimand from his wife for not washing the sink.

'How many times do I have to tell you? Wipe out the sink after you've emptied the bowl. Look, just look at the line of grease there. Wipe it down or it will leave a permanent ring!' scolded Mary, under the watchful eye of her mother. *So what?* he mentally retaliated as he picked up the cloth and rinsed it under the hot tap before carefully wiping around the sink, as he had been instructed.

Throughout the twenty-minute journey home and the subsequent silence as he nestled into the armchair in the sitting room, his thoughts recounted the incident of the dirty sink over and over, but each time he replayed the event in his mind he retorted with a quicker and wittier comment. So engrossed was he in his task to relive the moment and so successfully have the last word, that the sudden knock on the front door made him start. As he started to rise he heard Mary making her way down the stairs and so contentedly flopped back into the chair, as she uttered loudly to herself, 'No, don't you bother getting up. Just sit on your fat backside and I'll go!'

Curiosity pricked at who could be calling at this hour, and he listened intently, trying to make out the conversation that was just too low to be understood, until the talking suddenly stopped and the door to the sitting room opened with Mary's announcement, 'Barry, it's Rita for you. She's got a message from Martyn.' Rita entered with a smile on her face that would brighten anyone's mood. Barry had liked her from the first time they'd met and had been immediately attracted to her sexually – if he'd thought he had a chance he might have tried to seduce her, but Martyn was his mate, and as they always said, 'If you ever shit on your own doorstep, don't knock and ask for paper!' The thought made him smile as he looked up expectantly.

'Martyn wanted me to pass on a message,' said Rita 'He's after you.'

Barry's face immediately took on a reddish glow and grew hot. *How did he find out about the money?* The feeling of guilt seemed to envelop his body. 'What the bloody hell do you mean?' he blurted, puzzled. The look of astonishment on Rita and Mary's faces combined with 'You all right, Bob?' from the soft-spoken Rita broke the embarrassed tension in the room caused by his unexpected response, and he replied, 'Yes, fine thanks. It must be these nights, I never have got used to them. So what does the old bugger want?'

Rita relaxed once more and smiled. 'Whatever job he has been on has turned into a murder. He says to tell you he wants you in the Incident Room at nine o'clock in the morning – that all right?'

Barry stood, his guilt dissipating quicker than it had arrived, as his thoughts instantly passed to the shed and his unfinished task which he wouldn't be able to complete tomorrow as planned. 'Have to be, won't it?' he snapped, before jerking himself back into the present as he saw the shocked expression on Rita's face. Trying to make amends, he smiled and, rubbing the back of his head with his hand, said, 'Sorry love – yes, of course. Tell Martyn I'll see him in the morning at nine.'

Mary, who had stood quietly behind her friend, spoke up as Rita turned round. 'Time for a cuppa?' she asked.

Rita looked pityingly at Mary's sad and dejected expression as she shook her head. 'Sorry love, I'd love to stay and chat but I just popped over to give Bob that message. The boys are on their own and I told them I'd only be a couple of minutes. I'd better get back.' Both women walked slowly to the front door, where Rita paused and, putting her hand on Mary's arm, said quietly, 'If you feel like talking, how about tomorrow? I can make it after I've dropped the kids off to school.'

Mary smiled at her friend's comforting smile and touch. 'I would like that. At the café at, say, ten?'

Rita smiled reassuringly. 'That would be great. I'll look forward to a girly gossip,' and she quickly made her way along the path and towards her own house.

'What the hell's the matter with you?' Mary yelled in anger at Barry after closing the door and marching into the sitting room.

Barry, who had sat back down, looked up innocently and

answered, 'Nothing – why, what am I supposed to have done wrong now?' He knew he had been unnecessarily short-tempered with Rita, but her remark had been unexpected and caught him off guard. He'd have to be more careful in the future, watching not only what he said and who he said it to, but more importantly how he said it. This money business was making him jittery and he was more on edge than he had realised. Mary looked miserably at her husband and shrugged her shoulders despondently before turning towards the kitchen. There was a time, she thought to herself, when she would have cared, when they had been able to talk to each other, to talk out their problems and worries, but that had been a long time ago and now she just didn't care. She knew being on the murder investigation team would mean more money, but also it took him off his night shift, and she had wanted to be on her own tonight. Although her deepest wish was that it could be different; more importantly she dreaded the thought that he would want her sexually and she felt the beginnings of the headache that would readily become her excuse.

Barry stared once more into the fireplace. Normally he would have been delighted at the prospect of working in plain clothes and breaking the monotonous routine of trudging the beat, but this time he felt frustrated. He didn't like the feeling that he wasn't in control of his emotions, as that disastrous episode with Rita had just proved, and he certainly didn't need the extra money – he had more than he could have ever dreamed of – all he had to do was work out when the next opportunity would arise for him to finish the job properly. However, he knew that it would raise huge suspicions in his wife, in Martyn, and in the rest of the lads down the station if he didn't jump at the chance to be on the murder enquiry team. No, he had to appear eager, and after the enquiry he would complete the task of hiding the money.

More settled in his mind and making a mental note to

apologise to Rita when he next saw her, he started to work out an appropriate excuse for Martyn in the morning by blaming his brusqueness in responding to Rita on Mary. He started to get up from the chair before suddenly remembering he was no longer on nights, and immediately his moodiness was heightened by the thought of having to spend the whole night with his wife. *God, I hope she doesn't take this as another opportunity to try for a child*, he thought. He definitely wasn't in the mood for sex, and if she started any shenanigans tonight he would claim he was too tired.

The euphoria of the afternoon was gone and his mood seemed to be getting blacker by the minute; even the thought of spending all that loot couldn't raise his spirits. Making sure the fireguard was in place, he picked up the paper and began to read, his mind in such turmoil that although his eyes were scanning the words, he was not in fact seeing anything.

Rita Crowe stepped inside her house and leaned back upon the closed door, her neck tilted upwards so the crown of her hair rested against the wood, and she closed her eyes as if trying to erase the memory of the atmosphere inside the house she had just left. *How on earth can Mary live like that?*

Lost in her sympathy for her friend, she suddenly noticed the pad of tiny feet approaching and opened her eyes to look down at her eldest son, standing still in front of her with a look of concern on his young face. 'You OK, Mummy?' he asked earnestly.

'Perfectly all right, darling!' she said as a look of devotion passed between them, before she turned him round and fondly patted him on the backside to direct him towards the sitting room. 'In there, trouble,' she rebuked jokingly, 'I want to have a quick word with Daddy!'

'Can we say hello?' came the united chorus of both boys.

'No promises. We'll just have to see how busy Daddy is,'

replied Rita, trying to calm them down as she picked up the phone and dialled the station, her voice familiar to the answering officer.

'Hang on, Mrs C,' he told her. 'He's about somewhere.'

She waited for a few seconds before hearing the click, indicating the call had been transferred to Martyn's location, before the dulcet tones answered, 'Murder Room, DS Crowe.'

'Hi darling,' she crooned, 'I've obeyed the instructions of my lord and master, and passed your message to Bob. Terrible atmosphere though, I'm certainly glad it's you working with him and not me.'

'Thanks love,' replied Martyn. 'Sometimes you try to help people and it's not worth it. Everything else OK?'

Rita hesitated, not wanting to get her husband into trouble or hog the phone line. 'Don't suppose you've got time to wish the boys goodnight?'

'Always time for the important things,' said Martyn, 'but it'll have to be quick – put them on. Love you, hope to see you later.'

'Same here, sweetheart,' she replied, and with pleas to not be too long, she passed the telephone to the waiting boys, as she moved off into the kitchen to prepare their warm milk. She smiled as she heard her eldest enquire, 'Caught any bad men today, Daddy?' She felt sure they would go to bed tonight without any trouble.

Alexander Law sat at his dining table also deliberating about the coming night, having made up his mind that if he didn't have his hands on Pirate by ten o'clock, he and John would leave the city in the early hours of tomorrow morning. He preferred to leave at sunrise for two reasons: the lighter traffic would make travelling easier, and it would also make it easier to see if anyone was following them. He stared down at the barely touched meal that adorned his plate; it was a beautifully cooked and very expensive sirloin which, under normal circumstances, combined with the mushrooms, onions and potatoes, was a meal he would have relished eating. However, his usually voracious appetite had deserted him. The only thing acceptable to his stomach was the deep red claret, as proven by the empty decanter next to his place setting; he didn't even have a desire for any of the desserts he knew John kept a ready supply of. He dropped the silverware he had been holding onto the plate with a clatter and, pushing back the large carver chair from the table, strolled over to the desk, which he leaned over and rang the bell that would alert John that he was required.

Alexander was well aware of the look registering on the face of his valet as he entered the room to clear the table and saw the majority of the food he had so carefully prepared still remaining on the plate.

'A large brandy in the lounge please, John!' he requested, avoiding the disapproving scowl.

'Certainly sir. Anything else?' enquired John, managing to keep a civil tone in his voice.

'Yes, it's settled. You and I will depart no later than five tomorrow morning, so you can go and pack now as per my previous instructions.' John simply nodded to each statement, mentally noting each point, as Alexander continued, 'You will take all the phone calls tonight and I will remain incommunicado, unless it is to hear that Charlie Morgan has been located. However, and this is the most important thing, *do not* inform anyone else of our excursion. Make sure the house is secure, and remember only you and I are to know of our impending venture.'

John once more nodded his accord to this emphasised point. 'Certainly, sir. Destination?'

Alexander smiled. It was one of the things he liked about this man – no wasted time, just a simple, direct and logical question.

'North initially, then I will direct you en route,' said Alexander dismissively, as John moved towards the drinks cabinet to collect the cut-glass decanter and glass before following his boss into the lounge.

Alone again, Alexander warmed the tulip glass in his enormous hands, allowing the heat to transfer across to the cognac, gently swirling the golden brown liquid before savouring his first sip. He was Alexander Law and he would not be dictated to or threatened by anyone, not even the heavies of The Corporation. He marvelled at the titles criminal organisations gave themselves, as if to justify their place in the world of business; his city controlled by 'The Institute', London by 'The Corporation', Glasgow by 'The Firm' – all nameless companies made up of the biggest criminals in the country.

Although he had every intention of paying them back, due to circumstances beyond his personal control, remuneration would now be under his terms and he felt clever enough to outwit anyone who came against him, confident he knew what he was doing. He leaned back in his armchair and allowed his senses to soak up the colours and decor of the room. He had no idea how long he would actually be away, but it didn't really matter – he could easily control his piece of the action from where he was going to and still impose enough fear to have his orders carried out without question. He would show them all that he was still Big Al and still someone to be reckoned with.

Martyn Crowe stood up quickly and unceremoniously from his chair and roughly massaged his right, painfully cramping calf. His actions caused him to hop unsteadily away from his desk and curse under his breath at the pain.

The violent discomfort eased almost as quickly as it had arrived, as the detective sergeant glanced up at the office clock and saw that it was just after eleven. *Can it still be the same day?* He rubbed his face and squinted back at his desk, his eyes aching from reading the three large piles of paperwork he had cleared from his in and pending trays during the last sixteen hours at work. His head started to spin with all that remained to be done to complete the investigation. In particular he was not looking forward to attending the morning's post-mortem, a task normally assigned to the higher-ranked detective chief inspector; however, the duty had been delegated back to him with the accompanying well-worn excuse that the DCI already had a pre-planned meeting with the Chief Constable. *Bloody hell,* thought Martyn, *I'd have gone and seen the Chief and you could have had the pleasure of having to watch the world's worst operation.* Still, he mused that every cloud has a silver lining, and during an earlier visit to the hospital he'd had the pleasure of conveying to the young police constable who had stayed with the body there that he now had to formally identify the deceased to the Home Office pathologist, in order to provide what was known as continuity of evidence. The startled young officer had called this dubious honour something entirely different as he realised that what he had previously thought of as a favour – being left to guard the body – was in fact nothing more than passing the buck.

Sod it, thought Martyn as he recalled the shocked officer's expression, *I don't know why I'm smiling – I'll be stood next to him.* He hoped for the young PC's sake that Professor Webster wasn't booked to do the post-mortem; the first one you attended was always the worst, and the sight of a cigar-puffing chain-smoker letting his ash drop into the intestines of a cadaver was something that would never be forgotten.

Knowing he was really no good to man or beast when this tired, Martyn stacked the three piles of dockets into one and carried it across to the uniform sergeant's desk for filing, before turning to finally check the three large boards arranged on the wall of the Incident Room.

The left one was entitled 'David John Smith' and contained the photograph provided by his mother and all personal details obtained from official sources – date of birth and death, the results of the CRO search, bank account details and next of kin, plus a few scraps of uncorroborated data.

The middle board carried the details of any known associates that the deceased may have had, including friends, colleagues and girlfriends, in addition to any other information that may lead to an arrest.

The right-hand board was for any known or possible suspects. Only one photograph was currently displayed, which Martyn knew that he was bloody lucky to have; the inscription below it read 'Charlie Morgan'. Remembering he had still to settle up with Paddy, he walked over and pencilled a note on his jotter to that effect, before returning to face the right-hand board and reread the facts. Charles Henry Morgan, alias Pirate, was born locally on 4 April 1907 and Martyn hoped he was still local, although his last known address had already been checked and had proved negative. Not yet in possession of his military service record, Martyn skimmed over the rather lengthy criminal record, noting the fifteen convictions for theft and violence-related offences; Charles Morgan had spent thirty-one of his forty-five years incarcerated either in prison or in juvenile detention. *What a waste to have spent over half your life behind bars!*

Martyn moved closer and spoke directly to the pock-marked and scarred face in the photograph: 'Where are you, Mr Pirate?' Half expecting the suspect to answer him, he continued, 'Did you know David Smith? Did you kill him? If so, why?' He suddenly realised what he had been doing and cast a self-conscious glance around the office in case someone had entered and heard him. Shrugging his shoulders, he addressed the image once more. 'Someone knows you and they know where you are, and when we find them we'll have you!'

126

He decided not to ring his wife and let her know he was leaving – not that Rita would curse him, for she would wait up for him no matter what time he called it a day, but she was probably asleep in an armchair and it would be a shame to wake her before he got in. He paused at the office door and out of habit had a last look round; the room was quiet but felt ready, like a giant predator preparing to leap on its unsuspecting prey. He switched off the lights and made his way out of the building, pausing at the station steps to pull his collar up against the cold night air as he heard his stomach growl; although it was very late he was hungry. Hoping that Rita had plated up some sandwiches for him, he marched off to his car.

Chapter 17

Two o'clock in the morning saw four men in different locations lying awake, each deeply concerned with their own problems and unaware that in their respective ways they were responsible for the lack of sleep in the others.

Martyn Crowe, although not able to sleep, was trying to lie as still as possible so as not to wake his Rita, who had, as he suspected, been asleep in the chair when he finally got home, but had been happy to see him and eagerly served a warmed-up dinner; both of them laughing at the dried-up gravy which had formed a skin on the plate. His mind was far too active to let him sleep as thoughts tumbled uncontrollably, giving him the nagging sensation that he had forgotten something. He went over the procedures and facts one by one before his thoughts drifted to the main suspect, Charles Morgan, trying to imagine what sort of a man he was and deciding on the best way to conduct the interview when they got hold of him. Then his mind jumped to Alexander Law and raised questions as to his true involvement in the case. He reflected that however much control he, Martyn, thought he had over Charles Henry Morgan, Morgan would always be more scared of Alexander Law than of him. He began to fantasise about finally apprehending and successfully prosecuting Alexander Law, and as a smile crossed his face he finally drifted off to sleep, with the vision in his head of Big Al looking out of a barred window and wearing an arrow-motif jersey.

Barry Bourne lay just three doors away with his hands clasped under his head staring at the ceiling. He too was trying not to wake his wife, not out of any anxiety over her welfare, but rather because of not wanting criticism about how he was keeping her awake. He was concerned whether his money would be safe until he could complete the job of hiding it; he could report sick and finish the task, but how would he justify visiting his mother-in-law during the feigned illness? He could ask to be withdrawn from the enquiry team and continue his night shift, but how would he justify his reason to Mary or his colleagues? He definitely didn't want tongues to start wagging or any nosy parker to discover the true reason by accident, so he was just going to have to bide his time as part of the murder enquiry team. At least that way he would be in the right place to pick up any snippets of information about the money, as there was no better grapevine than the police force. If the money was stolen or hot in any way it would be the main topic of conversation and he could organise an escape route; if it wasn't stolen, then he had no worries. His mind raced as he endeavoured to decide which country he should move to. Was his passport in order and still valid? Come to think of it, where *was* his passport? He tried to slow his thoughts as he moved carefully onto his side with his back to Mary, keeping as far away from her as possible without falling out of bed, before succumbing to tiredness. *You could get a regiment of soldiers between us,* he thought. *Or better still, how about a regiment of naked land-army girls?*

Alexander Law, propped up in bed listening for any unusual sounds, had no interest in or intention of sleeping, his mind flashing from one notion to the next as he went over the steps taken to cover his tracks. He knew he had to stay one step ahead, and the person who owned the house which was his intended destination did not know his true identity – indeed, they had only met during a holiday and their friendship had grown out of that one brief sexual tryst. Alexander, as far-sighted as ever, knew that one day his safety might be in question and had seen the potential of remaining in touch with this man by phone, always initiating the call, and now he was about to reap the benefits of his wisdom. The only sounds he had heard were the muffled tones of his valet on the phone, and he presumed the person at the other end was giving all negative reports regarding the sighting of Morgan, who, he went on to picture, with a great deal of displeasure, was going to have every protruding part of his body cut off when he caught up with him. He shuffled down the bed and lay back, his head sinking into the cool silk-covered pillow. He knew his disappearance would piss off his unwary backers, but if he eventually repaid them with a sizeable addition he might just get away with it. And if he did indeed get away with it, it would undoubtedly boost his reputation within the inner sanctum of The Institute and then they would certainly have to recognise him as the kingpin. He began going over the plans in his mind again, step by step; there would be enough time to sleep when he was safe.

All the fourth man, Charlie Morgan, wanted to do was sleep. His eyes felt heavy and gritty and he was only able to keep them open with a concerted effort. Although desperately tired, he knew if he allowed himself the luxury of sleep he would miss his rendezvous with the copper, and he had an awful lot he wanted to say and do to him for all the aggravation he had suffered in the past day or two. He lay back and stared through the small crack in the ceiling above to watch the night sky. He had spent so many years in prison staring at the sky through the bars that he could almost calculate the time within thirty minutes. *Not time yet!* He deliberately moved his spine onto the edge of a brick, knowing that each time he moved, the brick would dig into his back uncomfortably: he was not going to fall asleep tonight.

Four o'clock in the morning and Martyn Crowe was sleeping the dreamless and happy sleep of the just. Barry Bourne dozed on and off, waiting for time to pass and the workday to start. Alexander Law lay soaking in a hot bath, knowing he would soon be on his way and then perhaps he could breathe a little easier. Charlie Morgan stood in the darkness awaiting the arrival of his quarry, having earlier urinated against a nearby wall, marking his territory like the animal he was.

In the blackness of the night, Charlie moved his right foot slowly until it gently nudged the empty bottle. There was no time for the dog-lead deception tonight – he wanted something simple that would cause the most damage but had a perfectly innocent meaning if it was seen on the floor next to him. He could ignore it if necessary but use it to devastating effect in one fluid movement, and that is what he wanted to do; he wanted to render the bastard semi-conscious with a blow to the back of the head below the helmet, and then if he didn't get the information required, the broken end would make an excellent job of rearranging the face. 'Where the fuck are you?' he swore under his breath, his feet so cold he was not certain they were going to respond when he tried to move them. He had tried wiggling his toes, but they hurt too much and he couldn't risk making a noise. Then he heard the distant rattle of metal on metal and the tramp of booted feet as they approached. *How the hell do they ever surprise anyone, let alone catch 'em in the act?* He listened carefully, following the footfalls before seeing the approaching shadowy figure in a cape occasionally checking door handles or locks, giving the impression of a giant lumbering bat struggling to take off.

Certain that the officer had passed his concealed position without noticing him, Charlie picked up the bottle and moved out of the shadows to sneak silently up behind his victim. The adrenalin surge through his body had eased the movements of his joints and he crept slowly ever closer. Whatever the reason, because he was never to know the truth, when he was just about to strike, the policeman spun round to face him and Charlie felt his jaw drop.

For a split second his mind went numb as he uttered, 'You're not him!' The face that looked him square in the eye wasn't the same. *It was a different copper.*

Police Constable Anthony Blakemore detested the strangeness of the streets when patrolling someone else's area, preferring his own beat where things were as they should be and a quick glance could soon alert or calm his nerves. But for some inexplicable reason he hated this patrol route more than any other; it wasn't anything specific, simply that the area had no life in it at all. Even when he had last worked here on day shift, it seemed to consist of continual office blocks and warehouses with nowhere to nip in and have a chat or cadge a crafty cuppa or smoke; on nights the smoke was no problem, but there was definitely no chance of a cup of tea. However, tonight he was particularly pissed off as Bob Bourne had plucked the easy task of a murder enquiry because his big pal was running it, and he had been clobbered with Bob's shifts. *It's definitely who you know and not what you know in this job,* he mused. He was determined to bring it up at the next Police Federation meeting, although it wouldn't resolve matters, as the federation wasn't a union and the reps didn't want to upset the apple cart and miss out on the chance to attend the annual national conference, an all-expenses-paid, wife-free week at a popular seaside location.

Constable Blakemore paused to allow a seed of inspiration to gain strength inside his head; a list of names from which each enquiry team was picked was a bloody good idea. He would put it on paper, so no sneaky bastard could pinch his idea, and he would present it at the first opportunity. He had always desired to be elected as a federation rep as it was a really cushy post and certainly better than walking the streets in the freezing cold of the night. His mind was still mulling over his idea when some inner sixth sense had him spin round. It may have been a strange noise or his unfamiliar surroundings, but the instinct that kept many a policeman alive now saw him less than four feet from a lean, dirty-looking fellow gripping a bottle by its neck, who reeked of body odour and fear. He tried to concentrate on the man's face to be able to provide a description in his report later, but his eyes were hypnotised by the bottle, held up apparently ready to be smashed down on his head.

As though time stood still, both men remained motionless, PC Blakemore's eyes transfixed on the bottle and Charlie Morgan's on a face he hadn't expected to see, until the policeman mechanically moved forward his right hand to draw out his truncheon and Charlie uttered, 'You're not him!' before dropping the bottle as he turned and ran. The sound of the glass shattering on the concrete startled the officer into action and he began to chase the fleeing figure, blowing on the whistle he had pulled from his pocket, already losing ground.

As predator turned quarry, Charlie's whole being was at that point focused on escape; he could sort out what had gone wrong later, so he simply hurtled down streets and darted through alleyways in a desperate attempt to flee, still hearing the shrill of the whistle, which did not seem to be getting any closer but was not going away either. In his initial few steps of flight he had bolted for the nearest dark alley, but he quickly regained his bearings and recognised the area as he began to compose the best route back to the disused school and relative safety. He had to go to ground before the baying pack, hard on his heels, caught him and tore into him. The quickest, but by no means the safest, route was through the market, and although this route would bring him out in the open for a short time he didn't care, for once through the market it was a stone's throw to the demolition site and he would be safe.

Charlie seemed to sense rather than know that there was now more than one copper on his tail. He was only a short distance from the busy activity of the market, which ultimately spelled freedom, when he became aware of the pain in his chest which felt as though his heart was about to burst from his body. As he got within one street of the market he allowed himself to pause in the darkness of a doorway to catch his breath. He tried to calm his gasping but soon could hear three distinctly different whistles, as well as the urgent running of booted feet at the furthest end of the alley in which he now sheltered.

'Shit!' he muttered as he turned and ran straight across the road directly towards the entrance to the market. However, in his haste he had not seen the lorry barrelling down the road. The driver, late in arriving and in a hurry to find a place to park, slammed his hand down on the horn, which blared its warning far too late. Charlie Morgan stopped in his tracks and turned to face his new attacker, but was unable to move as he became hypnotised by the head-lights, while the horn continued blaring. Charlie raised his arms and covered his eyes to blot out the powerful beams as the lorry struck him full on; the initial agony he felt was accompanied by an intense blinding white flash, momentarily followed by the sensation of floating through the air before total and inevitable blackness engulfed him. A wild, terrified scream escaping from his throat, Charlie Morgan landed some thirty feet away from the lorry, his life and worries no more.

Police Constable Tony Blakemore exited the alley only two seconds after Charlie hit the ground like a rag doll hastily discarded by a child, and rushed to stoop over the lifeless remains of his quarry. Unable to speak, bent over with his hands on his hips, he wheezed and tried desperately to draw fresh air into his tortured lungs. He slowly felt the pounding of the blood in his head and the mist in front of his eyes clear as a whistle-blowing colleague joined him, also gasping for breath.

Finally able to focus his thoughts on the incident before him, PC Blakemore tore his eyes away from the mangled figure at his feet and started the difficult job of processing the scene. He moved towards the lorry, its engine still purring, as his colleague used his authority to enlist the help of the market traders who had come to gawp. As he wondered what the fascination was for viewing such a scene, he looked up to see the white face of the driver staring through the windscreen mouthing something, the eyes mesmerised by the remains of the figure that had just catapulted off the front of his vehicle. Reaching up to open the driver's door, he saw the movement in the corner of his eye of his colleague directing two men who gingerly moved forward and covered the body with a tarpaulin.

Hearing the driver stammering, 'I-i-i-t wasn't my f-f-f-fault – he j-j-j-just ran out. Honest to G-g-g-god, i-i-i-t wasn't my f-f-f-fault!' PC Blakemore took him by the arm and gently but firmly pulled him down from the cab. He could hear the distant bells of the ambulance racing to the scene as the first tears began to flow down the driver's face. 'No hurry, old son,' he said silently to the ambulance driver, 'nobody here is going anywhere in a hurry.' He helped the driver sit in a chair that another of the onlookers had provided, with his back to the body, and then reached up to turn the key and stop the engine before joining his colleague. As they waited for more help to arrive they both knew that this was going to be a long night.

Chapter 18

Alexander Law sat in the back of his Wolseley in excellent spirits, a blanket wrapped around his legs. In such a good mood was he that he graciously accepted the small hip flask from his valet, by way of apology for the few neatly wrapped packets that were on the seat beside him for which there was no room in the boot. He held it up, shook it and found it to be full. *Well done, John.* He raised the flask in a mock salute behind of the head of his valet who now occupied the driver's seat. It was good to have one person on whom he could rely and trust.

As the car slid silently forward he turned in his seat and looked longingly through the rear window at his house, wondering just how long it would be before he returned. He knew that he would miss its luxurious splendour, but at least he was safe and able to plan his future and eventual return.

Law spent the next fifteen minutes regularly glancing behind until he was satisfied they were not being followed, but then his mind was jerked back to the present by the blue lights and clanging bells of an ambulance as it flashed past them. *Some poor sod in the shit!* Realising he was still holding the hip flask, he unscrewed the cap. *Waste not, want not,* he thought as he gratefully took a deep slug of the alcohol and settled back to enjoy the journey.

It was just before six o'clock when Barry Bourne, bathed and shaved, entered his sitting room clutching a mug of steaming hot tea, having managed easily to get out of bed without disturbing his wife. He had long given sleep up as a bad job, but was sure he would sleep better tonight; it was probably the change of shifts, he tried to convince himself. He automatically switched on the wireless, followed by a mad scramble to turn the volume down without spilling his tea or waking up Mary. He finally sat down with a distinct sigh of relief. He heard the pips marking the hour and lifted his watch to synchronise it with them as he paused to listen to the news. Nothing but trouble and aggravation the whole world over, he thought, before catching an obviously distressed announcer read out a newsflash …

'It was announced from Sandringham at 5.45 a.m. today, February the 6th 1952, that the King, who retired to rest last night in his usual health, passed peacefully away in his sleep earlier this morning.'

Poor old George! God rest you, sire! Barry toasted the wireless with his tea, before the weather forecast told him to expect rain sometime during the day. *Thankfully I should be indoors for a while*, he thought.

The music of the ensuing light programme wafted gently around the room, when movement in the bedroom above causing him to freeze. Had she woken up? Was she coming down? *Another half hour, please. Just stay where you are for another half hour.* The noise stopped and he again relaxed back in his chair.

Martyn Crowe was also up but in no position to listen to the news – his two sons, who seemed to think that sleep was something only grown-ups did, were making an unholy row. He had stumbled into each of their rooms in turn, intending to be angry, but as usual when they had both looked at him, any bad feeling just melted away. He had taken them both downstairs, in the hope that his wife might be able to get a bit more sleep. However, his attempt at refereeing the cereal selection failed miserably and he was just about to give the whole procedure up as a bad job when his wife walked into the kitchen and sanity once again settled on the Crowe household.

Martyn moved to the kitchen window and pulled aside the net curtains. 'It's going to be a dirty wet day,' he said, half to himself and half to the world in general.

Rita smiled as she asked, 'Breakfast, Martyn?'

Pausing for a moment he replied, 'Just toast I think, love – I've a post-mortem this morning and there'll be enough over the floor anyway without your breakfast as well.'

Rita smiled again, 'One slice or two for my super hero?'

Martyn grinned. 'Two please,' he said, and he gave her a gentle pat on the backside as he went past her on his way upstairs.

Fifteen minutes later, ready for work, he sat munching his toast and listening to the supposed torture his sons thought they were being subjected to by the application of soap and water. *Once that damn post-mortem is over I can get on with sorting things out*, he mused. He loved a challenge and could never quite put into words the satisfaction he got from solving a case that he had been involved with right from the initial complaint. A successful outcome, he knew, was seventy per cent hard work and thirty per cent luck.

Even the best policeman always needed that slice of luck. He rubbed his hands together as much in keen anticipation as in an attempt to rub off the marmalade that had stuck to the side of his fingertips, while he moved into the hallway to collect his overcoat. As he looked through the drawn curtains of the sitting room he saw his friend coming out of his house and, opening the small side window, he called out, 'Hang on, Bob; I'll give you a lift. No sense in taking two cars.' His shout acknowledged by the wave of a hand, Martyn closed the window.

His second piece of toast firmly clamped between his

138

teeth, Martyn put on his coat and shouted his departure to his wife as best he could through his clenched teeth. The normal response of 'Watch how you go!' was accompanied by unintelligible roars from his sons, as he went out of the door, making sure it was shut behind him.

Barry turned to face his colleague as they sat in the car, 'Thanks Martyn! Not just for the lift – I'm grateful for the chance to go plain clothes, plus the overtime will please Mary.' Over his morning cup of tea he had reasoned that any other comment might invoke curiosity, and friend or no friend, he wanted no unnecessary probing into what he had been up to.

Martyn, wiping the last of the toast crumbs from his mouth and jacket, responded, 'I thought it might help, although Rita was a bit concerned – she thought she had upset you last night.' They had both been friends long enough for straight talking.

Barry replied, 'Yes, I know. I was a bit short and I will say sorry next time I see her. Mary has already given me a rollocking over it. I was miles away at the time.' He continued talking, intending to change the subject. 'Anyway – what's on? Something to do with that security guard you mentioned to me in the Chapel?'

Martyn sighed. 'Yes, the poor sod popped his clogs yesterday afternoon.' He briefly stopped talking as he negotiated a zigzagging cyclist who seemed to have a death wish.

'Any idea who's responsible?'

'I can tell you unofficially. I had a call from a snout of mine. You had heard that the dead man worked for Alexander Law?' Looking at Barry, who nodded, Martyn pressed on, 'Well, Big Al has put the word out to have someone picked up for the job, so I reckon if we can find him first we'll have the right man.'

Barry was about to say something, but could only close his

eyes and gulp as Martyn shot over an amber-turned-red traffic light. Once sure that nothing was going to happen, he continued, 'Anyone we know?'

'I don't think so – even though he's a local man, one Charles Henry Morgan, aka Pirate.' Barry shook his head; the nickname meant nothing to him. Martyn swung the car violently around a corner as he went on, 'I know there isn't a lot to go on, but I'm giving you the job of finding him.'

'No problem,' Barry replied, deciding to keep quiet in order to let his friend concentrate on driving, and anyway, he knew that he would find out everything he needed to know from the briefing.

Alexander Law was very comfortable sitting in the back of his car. The journey was going well and he had enjoyed the passing scenery, and now that they were well on their way, the immediate danger had passed. He went to raise the flask to his lips again, but found that it was empty. He had drunk more than he normally did at this time of the day but he felt extremely relaxed, and anyway, he was on holiday; besides, wasn't a man in his position entitled every now and again to have one too many? Mind you, he was glad there was no more alcohol left as he was beginning to experience a fuzzy feeling at the back of his head – a combination, no doubt, of too much drink and lack of sleep. He leant back and closed his eyes, expecting it would soon pass.

Chapter 19

'You lucky bugger!'

Barry, who had walked into the police station a few paces behind Martyn, turned to see who had spoken and saw the inane grinning face of Police Constable Jonathan 'Windy' Miller, who subsequently moved up to stand in front of him. PC Miller was another who had gained his nickname during National Service in the Army; behind his back, though, he was also called 'Olympic Torch' because he hadn't been out on patrol ever since being elected as the local Police Federation representative; he had been re-elected three times.

Barry looked at his colleague. 'Who, me?'

'Yes you, you jam-strangled git!' accused Windy.

Barry spoke resignedly. 'Listen, Windy, I didn't ask for this job – it was given to me.'

Windy initially looked surprised but quickly cottoned on to the fact that Barry didn't know what he was talking about. 'No, not the enquiry, what went off last night.'

Over Windy's shoulder Barry watched Martyn disappear upstairs and knew that he would have to hurry along for the briefing. 'What the hell are you on about you, stupid bugger? Don't muck me around; I've got a briefing to go to.'

Windy, ever the station gossip, gleefully forged on, 'Tony Blakemore was covering your pitch last night and a bloke tried to bottle him – but lost his bottle instead.' He paused to laugh at the joke he had just made up, making a mental note to leave it in when he embellished the story later. Regaining his composure, he continued, 'Anyway, a chase takes place, with Blakey after this geezer, who only goes and gets himself wiped off the face of the earth by a three-ton lorry full of spuds.' He paused for effect. '*He's* certainly had his chips!' Windy started to laugh again, his story getting better by the minute. 'Anyway, they're still on shift with the stiff in the mortuary.'

Barry interrupted. 'Tony Blakemore all right?' He had no particular fondness for the chap, but he was a policeman, and a policeman who had been attacked.

'Yes, not a mark, unless you count his underpants.' Windy proceeded to go off into fits of laughter, but was hastily interrupted by the voice of the first watch inspector, who snapped, 'Bourne – my office – now!'

Barry had only time to reply, 'Sir!' at the retreating figure of the inspector. Did he know anything about the money? He tried to shake off the feeling of guilt as he made his way to the inspector's office.

Inspector Crow turned round to face Barry from behind his desk. He was, Barry knew, a totally self-opinionated bighead whose only reason for ordering him into his office was a show of authority. No relation at all to Martyn, Inspector Crow was completely different from his much popular and more respected namesake.

Leaning forward over his desk, his fingers resting on the short stick that was the official badge of his authority, the inspector said officiously, 'Heard about the fatal?'

Barry gave a hidden sigh of relief. 'Yes sir, PC Miller was just telling me.'

The inspector continued as though irritated by the interruption. 'It happened on your patch and Blakemore doesn't know who he is. I want you to go to the mortuary and see if you know him, immediately!' He looked down and moved his fingers forward in dismissal; he was surprised when Barry spoke.

'Sir, do you want it done now or, as I am on the murder enquiry, after I have booked in?'

Inspector Crow frowned. The question had put the responsibility back on him and he didn't like that. If he told him to go to the mortuary now he could be in trouble for delaying a member of a murder squad enquiry, but if he said go later it would seem his authority was being usurped. He knew he had no real choice after all, though. 'All right – get upstairs and book in, but then do it.' With that, and trying to restore his lost authority, he picked up his stick, placed it under his arm and turned his back on Barry to stare out of the window, indicating that as far as he was concerned the conversation was over.

Barry left the office, closing the door none too gently behind him. 'Silly prat,' he muttered to himself as he climbed the stairs two at a time to get to the Incident Room. Martyn was standing at the door.

'Where have you been? The briefing's about to start.'

Barry, always formal at work to his friend, replied, 'Sorry Sarge, I got caught by "Namesake".' When the inspector had first heard the moniker which compared him to the more popular Detective Sergeant, he had gone berserk and forbade anyone to use it, which, of course, was a fatal mistake, as it guaranteed that from that moment on the phrase stuck. He would have been completely mortified had he known that the chief superintendent also referred to him in the same manner behind his back. 'There was some trouble on my patch last night and a chap got killed in a road accident,' Barry explained. '"Namesake" wants me to have a look to identify the body.'

Martyn replied tersely, 'OK, but make it after the briefing – the gaffer is on his way up now. Get in there and sign on!' With that, Martyn pushed Barry through the door and turned to greet the detective chief inspector, who was walking up the stairs.

Barry didn't learn many more details from the briefing than Martyn had already described in the car. The only task he hadn't completed because he had been running late was to look at a photograph of the suspect pinned to the board. When the briefing came to an end he was caught up in the general chitchat of those present. The main topic of conversation, especially among the uniformed officers, was not about catching the suspect but, as usual after every initial briefing, about making sure the enquiry lasted at least seven days in order to milk the overtime and expenses to the full. Although having it drummed into them by the DCI that the expenses account wasn't a bottomless pit, all the men knew that as far as the boss was concerned, if they got a person charged with the crime within the time limit then their extra money was as good as in the bank.

Barry eased his way through the small groups of men until he stood facing the boards at the end of the room. As he looked at the black-and-white photograph on display, he realised that looking back at him was a much younger version of Charles Henry Morgan. Barry suddenly became aware that he had seen that face before and racked his brains until he remembered where: it was that bloke who had lost his dog. He looked again at the photograph, harder this time, and saw a man with a full head of hair, looking well nourished, but the puckered line from eyebrow to lip was clearly visible and an immediate giveaway. Although the man he had seen in the alley was thinner and had less hair, he was certain it was the same man. He turned and after a few moments, as he flipped through the pages of his notebook, he caught the eye of Martyn, and indicated that he wanted to speak.

'What's up?' asked Martyn.

Barry indicated the photo of the suspect with a toss of his

head. 'I've seen that bastard recently on my patch. Night before last looking for a lost dog.' His eyes flicked down to the page he held open. 'Gave give the name Max Barnett of 24 Crown Road. Although I wouldn't hold out a lot of hope over the address, I will check him out.'

Martyn looked hard at his colleague. 'Are you certain it was him?'

Barry nodded. 'One thousand per cent sure – I'll get on to it as soon as I've got this mortuary business over for "Namesake".'

Martyn stood and looked at the retreating figure of Barry as he made his way to the door, his mind in a turmoil. *What the hell was a man who had supposedly beaten seven bells of shit out of a security guard, and was being hunted by both sides of the law, doing in the back of bloody beyond looking for a sodding dog?* The whole thing was utterly absurd; he was going to have to be a cross between Sherlock Holmes, Sam Spade and Hercule Poirot to work this one out. *Just what the hell was going on?* He groaned slightly as he got to his desk. He still had the post-mortem to go to yet. God, how he hated them.

Chapter 20

Alexander Law woke up from his nap, the drone of the powerful engine confirming that they were still on course, and couldn't understand what was happening. Here he was sitting in the back of his luxury car; his mind was working, he could see, he could hear and he could smell, but the trouble was, he was completely unable to speak or move a muscle. He tried to look around, but his head was frozen in position on the headrest; he was only able to frantically flick his eyes around the interior until they finally came to rest on the hip flask which had fallen out of his now useless hand and onto the leather seat next to him. Aware that his bottom lip was sagging and the lower part of his face felt as if it was drooping down, he desperately wanted to attract John's attention. He knew he needed help quickly, and became so frightened that his bladder started to empty.

As his fear reached new, previously unknown heights, he felt the car begin to slow until it finally came to a rest and a surge of relief coursed through his veins. *Thank God! When John sees me he'll know something is very wrong and get help.* The back door next to him opened and he tried but failed to frown inquisitively as John's arms pulled his torso forward to gain a better grasp under his armpits before pulling him out of the car. His feet flopped out of the door frame before he was dragged along the gravel of the road.

He was leant up against something but immediately slid to the right as John's released his hold. A snatched grab and heave propped him securely back in place – against what, he had no idea, as he looked down and saw his hands lying uselessly by his sides. He could only follow John with a look of utter bewilderment as the valet returned to the open door of the car, removed the parcels, blanket and hip flask from the back seat, and placed them in the seemingly empty boot. After slamming the lid, he walked back, stepping over the motionless limbs and dropping to his haunches to look his employer square in the eyes. The appearance of the valet had completely altered. Gone was the meek, subservient expression, replaced by a granite-like face with steel grey eyes that burned into Alexander's soul, and a deep, accented voice so different from the one he had grown accustomed to hearing.

'Do you know what is happening?' John snarled. 'You're about to die – in fact, you only have a few minutes left.' Alexander tried with all his might to speak but his vocal cords wouldn't respond and he found it harder to focus his eyes. Seeing his victim struggling so ineffectually, John sneered, 'Don't waste your time. The Corporation knew of you and your greed for control of The Institute long before you'd heard of them, and they sent me to watch you. You shouldn't have tried to cheat them, Mr Law – they're very displeased with you.'

Alexander tried harder to address his assailant but only managed a gurgling sound from deep in his throat, as John continued to explain his actions. 'This is nothing personal, just business. If you'd been allowed to get away with it, what would that have done to The Corporation? Everyone would try and put one over on them, so for their reputation's sake you had to be taught a lesson – you can understand that, can't you?' Alexander looked on helplessly as this man whom he had trusted completely continued to justify his impending death. 'It was a drug in the flask and it paralyses the body but leaves the brain until last. A bullet would have been quicker but they wanted to make sure you knew why – shame really, because I quite enjoyed working for you.' John shook his head in disapproval. 'If only you had realised that they were far bigger than you could ever imagine and hadn't tried to cheat them.'

Finishing his vindicating speech, John gently patted Alexander's face twice before standing up and turning his back dismissively on the dying man to walk back to the car; already planning to return to the Law house and ensure everything was ready for the police, who would undoubtedly be calling eventually to break the news of the unfortunate demise of his employer.

Alexander felt himself begin to slide sideways, the gentle pat from John all that was needed to dislodge him from his precarious perch against the steel tube of the road sign. Gravity then took hold and he fell heavily so that his face rested on the ground and the fluid oozing from his scalp began to be soaked up by the earth. Gravel from the turning car sprayed his face and he blinked helplessly as the noise of the changing gears disappeared, leaving him in quiet solitude. He inwardly sobbed. *I don't want to die*, he pleaded, before his mind began to empty and total blackness through loss of consciousness slowly consumed him.

With one final strangled gasp, Alexander Law went into the unknown to join Pirate, who knows where.

Chapter 21

Barry Bourne stepped out into the open air and gave an involuntary shiver at the cold, damp chill that greeted him when he left the warmth of the police station. Walking down the steps and turning left, he set off on the short journey to the mortuary, conveniently situated in a side road behind the Coroner's Court. He strolled past the giant iron gates that marked the rear entrance to the main Criminal Court, the main entrance being a hundred yards away on a parallel street. Through these iron gates was an intricate Victorian system of white-tiled and well-lit passageways, giving underground access to those due to appear in court away from the prying eyes of the public.

As Barry passed the Coroner's Court building and turned right up the cobblestone alley which led to the mortuary, he wondered whether it had been more by luck than judgement that the Victorians had made the alley just wide enough to allow an ambulance or hearse to pass through. Parked by the mortuary entrance, such vehicles were, tactfully, completely obscured from public view.

At the top of the alley Barry was greeted by the sight of a small, glass-fronted office, the Chapel of Rest, where relatives were taken to officially identify the body in a very tasteful environment. However, he knew that the area he was aiming for was anything but tasteful, as he approached the Coroner's Office, positioned so as to deliberately ward off anyone who accidentally entered the alley. He withdrew his warrant card ready to show whoever was on duty today, and saw through the doorway that it was someone who had once been a member of his shift but volunteered for this duty to while away the last few years of his service. Embarrassingly, Barry couldn't remember the man's name.

Barry hesitated just inside the door as the acrid odour hit him so hard he could almost taste it. He'd never been sure whether it was the mixture of disinfectants, formaldehyde and cleaning fluids or just the smell of death, but he was certain that whatever caused the stink would cling to his clothes and his hair. Whoever he met for the rest of the day would give him a wide berth; even fellow police officers would recognise the smell and move away.

With one final gasp of fresh air, he stepped inside the office and turned to face his older colleague. With a look of repugnance Barry saw the open brown bag containing sandwiches on the desk behind the counter, although why it had disgusted him so much he wasn't sure. 'Why would anyone volunteer to work in a place like this?' he muttered silently to himself.

The coroner's officer looked up and smiled. 'Hi Bob, what can I do for you today?'

Still unable to recall the man's name, all he managed to splutter was, 'How are you keeping?' as he visibly searched his surrounding for some indication of the officer's identity. Seeing nothing, he continued, 'I've been sent down by Martyn Crowe's namesake to have a look at the stiff from Tony Blakemore's road traffic accident. It happened on my patch when Blakey was covering and Namesake wants me to see if I can ID him.' Just as he finished explaining his presence he noticed a sheet of paper sticking out from under the sandwich bag headed, 'For the Attention of PC 643 Michael Jones, Coroner's Officer', and inwardly breathed a sigh of relief.

PC Jones indicated towards a single door with a flick of his

150

head. 'Help yourself, there are only two in there and yours is on the far slab.'

Barry smiled and said, 'Thanks Mike,' noting the officer's satisfaction that his name had been remembered. As Barry Bourne strode down the one step into the post-mortem room he curled his nose up at the all-consuming, completely obnoxious stench.

The room contained four white post-mortem examination slabs lined up in the middle. Barry could see the middle two slabs were occupied, with the pathologist and mortuary assistant standing between them to enable them to turn from one corpse to the other with the least inconvenience. The walls and ceilings were completely tiled, while the floor was constructed of smooth concrete; drainage channels criss-crossed the floor to allow any waste products swilled off the slabs, either solid or liquid, to run along to the main drain outlets situated in each corner, although the floor seemed to be continually awash with water. Tables were set against three of the walls, and on them were empty specimen bottles ready to be dispatched as necessary to the forensic science laboratory.

Barry stepped inside as the door swung closed behind him silently. Though he didn't mind dealing with death on the streets, he was deeply uneasy here, but didn't want to display any signs of apprehension that the coroner's officer could use to make fun of him around the station. He looked at the two examination tables on which were displayed recently deceased bodies; the nearest slab contained a naked blonde female who was apparently unmarked, the mortuary assistant feverishly holding out stainless silver bowls for the pathologist each time he lifted his hand out of the gaping cavity in the cadaver chest.

His vision of the second body was impaired by the meticulously efficient medical team, but his head-only view of it confirmed that this was who he had come to see – he had been to too many road accidents not to recognise the horrific injuries that they can cause.

The right side of the face he was looking at was no longer recognisable – it was simply a mass of grinning exposed jawbone and teeth caused by the skin bursting open like a melon as the skull and jaw shattered from impact. The eyeball had popped from its socket with the energy of a cork bursting from a bottle, snapping the optic nerve so that it was no longer connected to the body.

He moved closer, approaching the two occupied slabs from the feet end to gain a better vantage point. He stopped at the end of the slab containing the body that he was interested in and took a deep breath in revulsion. The force of the lorry as it hit the man and propelled him through the air had pushed the right shoulder and chest inward and upward; breaking the collar bone and ribs so that the skin now looked more like a flapping sail than a rounded trunk and the right arm flopped brokenly, two inches shorter than its left counterpart.

Barry continued his slow circumnavigation of the figure, finally stopping to look down at a face, which on the side he was looking at now was comparatively unmarked. He couldn't believe what he saw.

'Bleeding hell!'

Disbelief took over from fear as Barry bent down until his face was about a foot away from the victim, whereupon he found himself looking directly at the man who had tried to injure PC Blakemore; this, he realised, was also the bloke who'd claimed to be looking for a lost dog and obviously the bastard they wanted for murder. He stepped back in amazement and caught the heel of his police-issue boot in one of the drainage channels crossing the floor. Instinctively his hand shot forward in an effort to steady himself and he found himself gripping the arm of the deceased, which moved towards him mechanically. He felt his stomach churn as if his breakfast was making a move to reappear and as he snatched his hand away the arm flopped back onto the slab with a sickening slap.

He swallowed hard and moved backwards away from the table before marching briskly towards the outer office. Without a word to Mike Jones, even before the steel door had closed behind him, he picked up the phone and dialled the number of the Murder Incident Room. Martyn Crowe had barely started to recite his rank and name when Barry interrupted: 'I'm at the mortuary – you'd better get down here!'

Rita Crowe had arrived early at the Coffee Pot and taken a seat at a table near the window. Having placed her shopping bags on the only other vacant chair, she held the warm mug of coffee as she watched the hustle and bustle of life outside. She had become so engrossed in her daydream observations of the various passers-by that she literally jumped as the bags on the chair next to her began to move and a splash of coffee landed on her hand. She started round and saw Mary Bourne's smiling face as she placed the bags on the floor in order to sit down and asked, 'Penny for them, Rita?'

Feeling her cheeks starting to blush, she turned in her chair in order to directly face her friend, nervously giggling, 'I'm sorry, Mary – I was miles away watching that lot out there.'

Mary Bourne was really quite a pretty woman, decided Rita, her hair always tidy and her skin glowing with health; it was only the jerky movements of her hands and the continual chewing of her lip that told Rita that Mary was unhappy and living off her nerves.

'Did Martyn get off all right this morning?' asked Mary.

'I think so – I was upstairs with the boys and heard him go. I think he gave Bob – sorry, I mean Barry a lift. I sometimes wonder who he is, with Martyn calling him one name and you another!'

Mary paused and looked at her friend, her eyes full of sadness. 'There could be more truth in that than you know. I've started to wonder who he is and where we're going myself. One minute everything's fine and the next he's snapping my head off.' Mary took a sip of her drink, pausing to remove the small piece of milky skin that had formed on the top of her coffee and stuck to her lip. 'I had such hopes not long ago.'

Rita looked her straight in the eye. 'I don't know what's going on either, but I'm sure it's not another woman. You know what the gossip is like at the station, and I can promise you I've heard nothing of the sort – I'd tell you if I knew anything.'

Mary sighed. 'No, I don't think it's another woman either. Perhaps if it was, at least I would know what I was up against. I just don't know what it is – he doesn't seem to want to spend any time with me and I just hope and pray that we don't go down the same road as Mum and Dad.'

Rita leaned over and placed her hand on top of her friend's. 'Any more news from the doctor's?' she enquired, knowing that what Mary wanted more than anything else in this world was a baby, and she was waiting for the results of her recent examination.

Mary smiled. 'He told me to come back in three weeks and he should have the answer. I used to think that if we had a baby then everything would be all right. I know when we got married we said "for better or for worse", but this is far worse than anything I ever imagined it could be.'

A silence descended on the table as both women became lost in their own thoughts, sipping their coffees as they faced each other but actually gazed straight through one another, as the minutes slowly passed until they both finished their drinks and paid their automatic visit to the ladies' before leaving the café.

Normally happy to spend the rest of the morning together,

today although neither wished to be rude, both desired to be on their own. Mary wanted to be at her mother's, where she could keep the subject of Barry alive, and Rita simply wanted to escape the depressing attitude of her friend.

It was Rita who spoke first. 'Where do you fancy shopping today?' she asked, holding her breath until her friend pleasingly replied, 'Well, to be truthful Rita, I half promised my mum I'd go over and help her with her hair.'

Each knew it was a fabrication, but it was a lie that suited them both, and after a brief peck on the cheek, Rita and Mary happily parted to go their separate ways.

Martyn Crowe stood alongside Barry in the post-mortem room looking down at the two corpses on their respective slabs. The preceding autopsy now complete, the female corpse had been replaced by the body of a blond-haired youth with obvious head injuries, who Martyn knew was David Smith, and whose post-mortem he would shortly be attending. *Ironic*, he thought to himself as he looked down at the unidentified body on the right, *if this does turn out to be Charles Henry Morgan. Murderer and victim lying together.* He moved to get a better look at the mutilated face, the neck supported by a wooden block, and as he passed by the exposed jaw and teeth, he contemplated that even in death the corpse seemed to be laughing at him.

'What do you think?' Barry asked his boss, who remained silent as he took hold of one of the dead man's hands and turned it over so that the palm faced him.

Speaking slowly, and looking down at the blue-stained hands which showed that the fingerprints of the deceased were already in the process of being checked, Martyn replied, 'I think so, I think it's him, but let's wait until we get the results back from Fingerprints.'

After moving back into the office, both men stood leaning against the wall, Martyn having already phoned a senior fingerprint expert, explaining what he wanted and why it was urgent. He'd given him the extension number of the Coroner's Office, where he was now waiting.

Barry kicked his heels against the wall as Martyn, to no one in particular, said, 'What was that bastard doing? What had he been playing at?' Before he could continue the telephone rang and he strode to the desk to answer. 'Mortuary – DS Crowe?' He listened carefully to the caller and let a slow drawn-out whistle escape from his lips as he replaced the receiver. 'This is getting bloody silly!'

'Is it him, Sarge?' Barry enquired.

'Oh yes, it's him all right – Charles Henry Morgan, or what's left of him. But the story doesn't end there – there's also been a message from our friends in the Shropshire force who've gone and found a body, and are asking for our help in their enquiries.'

'Shropshire?' questioned Barry. 'Who the hell do we know who'd be dead in Shropshire?'

'Only Alexander Law, Alexander bloody Law found dead as a sodding dodo!'

Martyn turned to Barry. 'Go on Bob. You'd better leave a contact number with Mike Jones and get back to the nick before anyone else in this case dies on us.' As Bob left, the young PC who was present at the hospital walked gingerly into the room. With a curt, 'Come on son, let's get it over with,' Martyn and the constable walked towards the body of David Smith to formally identify him, before the scalpel moved to slice the corpse from collar bone to pubis.

Detective Chief Inspector Kelly stood in the Incident Room looking at the enquiry team standing in small groups, either openly curious as to the reason for the unexpected summons or chatting about what they knew or thought they knew. The steady hubbub of gossip and rumour required him to bang loudly on the desk twice to get the silence he needed to speak.

'Will you lot shut your mouths? You're like a load of old washerwomen. For the next twenty minutes or so, I will do the talking and you will do the listening.' Satisfied that he had gained their undivided attention, he continued, 'What I will tell you first and what DS Crowe tells you second will not be unsubstantiated rumour, but facts, so pay attention.'

The DCI paused to let his words sink in, and everyone waited expectantly.

'Item number one,' he continued, looking down at his notes, 'our murder suspect, Charles Henry Morgan, is now lying peacefully alongside his alleged victim, David John Smith. That's the easy part. The hard part is now you lot have got to prove it.' A buzz of surprised excitement flew round the room until the DCI continued, 'It needs to be proved for both the coroner and HQ, which won't be as difficult as having to prove it to a jury, but nevertheless it is still going to take some hard graft.

'Now to item number two. Our beloved top villain, Alexander Law, has turned up his toes in answer to a summons from on high.' Immediately astonished muttering began but this time, with a wry smile, the DCI let it continue for a few moments before speaking. 'This means that for the next few weeks there will be a lot of jockeying within the criminal fraternity to take his place. There will undoubtedly be power plays taking place as we speak, and it shouldn't take long for us to find out who is likely to be his successor as top dog. However, it will also give us a chance, if we play our cards right, to pit one off against the other and rid ourselves of some more scum off the streets. Keep your eyes and ears open – I want to hear about every snippet of gossip, no matter how irrelevant you think it might be.' He paused before raising his voice, concerned that what was about to be said was not misunderstood. 'Listen, all of you. Now that Big Al is dead, no one – and I mean *no one* – is ever going to become that powerful in this city again. This is our chance to be on top of the criminals and we are going to grab this opportunity firmly by the balls and hang on no matter who squeals. Have I made myself clear?' He stopped and, noting the nodding movements of everyone present. 'Martyn?'

DS Crowe stood up and exchanged places behind the podium with his governor. He stood silently to accentuate the words just spoken by the DCI before emphasising the importance of what they had just heard. 'What the gaffer has just said is vital. We have got a long-awaited chance and we mustn't waste it. Get amongst the scum, stir as much shit as you can and turn them all against each other. Get your snouts working for their money; spread the word about Law to whoever you think will listen. More importantly for this enquiry, while they are all twitching I want statements taken there and then about anything to do with either Smith or Morgan. We need that vital link: find me that and I will do the rest.'

Martyn paused again, then said, 'I am going to reallocate your jobs and duties. I want you to get out there and, for once, get this job done quickly. Don't drag your heels for overtime. If I find any of you trying that one on, you will be off this squad and never chosen for another. Clear? Now get some results for the DCI.' He looked at his watch. 'Get yourselves off to the canteen and get some food down you, then let's see what you're made of. Don't think of coming back in until you have a result.'

Martyn stepped down and watched the collected officers begin to leave the room. Instead of boredom there was a keen anticipation on all their faces. He exchanged smiles with the DCI; they had done their jobs well, and now it was up to the men.

Chapter 22

Alexander Law's valet had managed to arrive back at his deceased employer's house without being seen. He had reversed the car into the garage, leaving the large wooden doors open, in the hope that the gusty wind whipping around the house would assist in cooling down the engine sufficiently to avoid awkward questions when his expected visitors arrived.

He had contacted his underworld bosses immediately upon his return and it was obvious from their comments that they were very pleased with his work. He knew that the criminal grapevine worked even quicker than that of the police, and by lunchtime all the major criminal players in the country would have heard of Alexander Law's indiscretion and untimely death. John Vincent was also aware that his actions and knowledge did not make him immune from retribution in the future. Not interested in the slightest about what the police knew or thought they knew, as long as he remained useful to the men he worked for, he was safe. However, the moment those men suspected he had become a liability, he would be made to 'disappear'.

As instructed, he had collected all the papers he could find within the Law house and placed them in two bags by the front door, from where they were due to be collected within the next fifteen minutes. He wondered what his bosses would have said had they known about the three sheets of paper folded inside his jacket pocket. By the end of the day, they would join the other items in his safety deposit box. They were his insurance policies, not for money, but for his life.

The bags duly collected, he commenced the task of wiping furniture and glasses free of fingerprints as he patiently awaited the arrival of the police.

Barry pulled the chair closer to the desk he had been allocated and started to study the papers laid out before him. He had been assigned the tedious task of searching through all the background records and discovering anything ever printed about Charles Morgan, and he spent the next hour either on the telephone or operating the teleprinter machine. People were so untrusting nowadays, he grumbled to himself, there was a time not so long ago when all you had to do was telephone a station, request information and it would duly arrive on your desk. Now if you telephoned for a statement, unless it was immediately followed by a written request over the teleprinter, you could either wait for ever or forget it.

He stared at all the notes and sheets of information that cluttered his desk and tried to piece together the reasons for Charlie Morgan's reported movements during the last few days of his life: Smith had reportedly recently been sighted in a couple of downtown poofter dives in the company of a scruffy, rank-smelling bloke with a scar; Morgan had form for violence; Smith had worked for Law and had been done over; Morgan had been seen at least twice in an area five hundred yards from Law's offices – once by Blakey and once by him; Morgan had tried to attack Blakey; Big Al had put the word out for Morgan for some important reason.

Suddenly his task was made much easier by having in his possession a single piece of the jigsaw not seen by another living soul. After re-reading the data for the umpteenth time, the piece of the jigsaw suddenly fell into place and, like a fruit machine hitting the jackpot; bells started sounding in

160

his ears. *The money! Charlie Morgan was looking for the money I found! He must have dropped it.* Barry's mind delved further. *Morgan, together with Smith, must have stolen the cash from Alexander Law, and, being greedy, Morgan belted Smith to keep it all for himself. The missing-dog story was cobblers, but somehow he must have guessed that I had it and went looking for me, but found Tony Blakemore instead.*

Barry sat back in his chair and quietly contemplated what he had discovered. That meant that with the deaths of David Smith, Charlie Morgan and Alexander Law, everyone who knew about the money was gone. The slow smile that had started to work its way across his lips suddenly burst into a wide grin. *They were all wonderfully and marvellously bleeding well dead.* He was safe! The money was all his and no one could spoil his future now.

Martyn Crowe walked up the drive of Alexander Law's house for the second time in as many days, and knocked on the door. Although he had already identified himself to the occupant of the house, as he waited for the door to open, his right hand automatically moved to his top pocket and by the time his knock was answered he had his warrant card on display.

When the door opened Martyn saw the same man he had seen on his last visit.

'Sir?' the man enquired.

'I don't know if you remember me – I am Detective Sergeant Crowe from the local CID and I would like to have a few words with you.'

John Vincent, having resumed the persona of a subservient valet, immediately countered, 'I am sorry sir, Mr Law is not at home.'

Martyn gave a weak smile. 'I know. Can I come in please and speak to you in private?'

The door was opened wide and Martyn stepped inside. 'Is

there anyone else in the house?' he pressed on as they both stood regarding each other.

With no indication that this conversation was going to take place anywhere else but the hall, the valet replied, 'No sir, I am here on my own.'

'May I have your name, and do you have any other address?' asked Martyn as he removed his notebook from his jacket pocket.

'My name is Vincent, sir. John Vincent, and this is my permanent address. May I ask what this is all about?'

Martyn assumed a compassionate role as he gently guided the man to a side room where he broke the news about the death of his employer. He explained that he was only there to make preliminary enquiries, and because the body was discovered in another county, he should expect the arrival of a detective from that police force to take a full statement.

John Vincent, having already requested permission to sit down, asked, in an assumed shaky voice, 'How did he die, sir? What happened?'

Martyn, full of sympathy for this loyal servant, replied, 'The full details are not yet known. When the other officers get here in a couple of hours, they will be able to tell you more.' Noting the meek nod of acceptance, Martyn continued, 'When did you last see Mr Law?'

'Last night, sir.' John Vincent paused for effect, as if trying to collect his thoughts, and in a quiet, respectful voice, gave a prepared account of the previous evening. 'Well, he had dinner as normal. He then informed me that I was not required for the remainder of the evening.' Upon seeing the raised eyebrows of the detective, he explained, 'That is not unusual, sir. My room is at the rear of the house and only if I am required do I remain in the pantry until Mr Law retires for the night. After being told I was not required, I prepared his bedchamber and spent the rest of the evening in my room.'

'Then what happened?' prompted Martyn.

'Well, not a lot really, sir. I rose as usual this morning and went to enquire what Mr Law wished for breakfast. I saw that his bed had been slept in and the bathroom used, but upon coming downstairs I realised that he was not in the house.'

'Was that unusual?' Martyn interrupted.

'Mr Law does, I'm sorry, *did* what he wanted. He never thought fit to inform me of any of his plans except when it involved the preparation of his meals,' replied John Vincent officiously.

'What are you going to do now?' asked Martyn, somewhat irritated by the supercilious tone of the valet.

'I don't know, sir; I will have to wait until I get instructions from Mr Law's solicitors.'

'Oh, he did believe in something legal then,' blurted out Martyn, immediately annoyed with his complete lack of professionalism.

John Vincent made as if to save his embarrassment by replying as though he hadn't heard the sarcastic remark. 'Oh yes, sir, Mr Law had many professionals working for him.'

I bet he did, thought Martyn. 'Do you know the name of his solicitor?'

John Vincent looked bewildered for a moment. 'I'm not certain, sir. I think it was Fairbrother and something. I know they have offices in that building next to the telephone exchange.'

'One more thing, Mr Vincent – did Mr Law have any relatives you are aware of?'

The valet paused for a moment, as if trying to recollect. 'I'm not really sure. I think I heard him mention a brother once … or was it a sister? I am sure his solicitors would know. Was there anything else, sir?'

Martyn looked at the deadpan face in front of him. 'Yes. Make sure you are here when the other police officers arrive. They will want to take a formal statement.'

'Yes, sir,' replied John Vincent meekly, as he escorted the DS towards the front door, which he opened immediately.

'John Vincent. That sounds very English, but do I detect an accent?' asked Martyn as he paused to look back through the open doorway.

Allowing the first smile of the interview to cross his lips, John Vincent replied, 'How very astute of you, sir. My mother is English but my father, God rest his soul, was Italian – perhaps it is that?'

'Could be,' replied Martyn from the doorstep as the door was closed gently on the conversation. *Well, you didn't say a lot, Mr John Vincent. I wonder what our Criminal Records Office has on you?* He was aware that the Shropshire lads would find Mr Vincent very interesting and they would give him a far harder time in questioning him than he had. Martyn set off to walk down the drive towards his car, well aware as he went that there was a pair of eyes watching his every step.

John Vincent, or, to give him his birth name, Giovanni Vincento, immediately moved to a window upon the departure of the detective, where he stayed until the officer was completely out of sight and his car had been heard to leave the grounds. He did not have long to complete his final tasks before he must leave, not having the slightest intention of being within fifty miles of the house when the other policemen arrived. He spent the next thirty minutes finalising his cleaning operation, ensuring as far as possible that he obliterated any trace of his presence in the house. The entire building was spotless – even the hip flask was thoroughly washed out and back on view in its allocated place in the display cabinet. There was no reason for the house to be examined, but even if it was, then they, whoever they might be, would find nothing at all.

John Vincent made one final cursory check of the house and then left by the back door. He crossed the large gardens at the rear and passed through a small gate leading onto an adjoining park, which he crossed to get to the lock-up garage that he anonymously rented by the week. The owner of the lock-up had never seen him, the transaction having taken place over the telephone and the payments by post always having been made in advance. He placed his small bag containing his belongings on the floor and, using the small crowbar hanging on the wall, he carefully removed the driver's-side rear hubcap and took out the set of keys from their hiding place. He replaced the hubcap and hung the crowbar back on the wall before unlocking the car and placing his luggage in the boot, and then backing the vehicle out into the fresh air.

He re-locked the garage and pushed the keys under the door, as previously arranged when he had paid the bill for the forthcoming six weeks, and then returned to sit in the driver's seat and revved the engine before proceeding on his way. He was never going to return to this place, and after he had made a few simple alterations to his appearance, anyone enquiring about John Vincent would have to work extremely hard and be very lucky to end up finding Giovanni Vincento.

Chapter 23

Over the next ten days, the city's police were overwhelmed by the floodgates that appeared to have opened in terms of criminal activity following the demise of Alexander Law. On the one hand, the fear of revenge having been removed, the interviewing of witnesses became a lot easier, while on the other, the spate of petty crimes had risen to vast proportions. Normally, members of The Institute would have commissioned and approved nearly all the crimes committed, but now, with each side vying for control and small-time villains trying to become the next Big Al, there was no honour amongst thieves. Houses, offices and businesses were all being attacked and violence and injury had become commonplace, particularly between those who were striving to become the next crime boss.

Detective Chief Inspector Kelly could not believe what was happening. He knew that every one of his officers was working flat out, and he summoned Martyn for an update. After the usual greeting, they stood side by side looking at the urban wall map displaying the entire area under their command. Coloured pins gave a visual display of the current crime rate and the location of incidents; red pins indicated crimes committed, while blue indicated those solved. The red pins outnumbered the blue ones by nearly five to one, giving the impression that the situation was rapidly getting out of control.

The DCI spoke whilst looking despairingly at the map.

'Martyn, you would not believe the number of times in the past that I had wished Alexander Law dead. I have even dreamed of it, so perhaps this is a fitting punishment on me. I know that it is an utterly stupid thing to say, but at the moment I think we'd be better off if he were still alive.'

Martyn remained silent. He knew that his boss was being given a hard time from headquarters, but although it didn't seem like it at the moment, he was certain that if they stuck at it, it would all work out to their advantage in the end. They had both known that this could happen. He was about to speak words of encouragement when Kelly asked, 'How's that murder enquiry going? I could really do with some of your men back on the streets.'

Realising just how stretched they were for manpower during this crime spree, Martyn replied, 'No problem, sir! It's going well – in fact, I can shortly let you have most of the team back. With the statements we've got, I've been able to place Morgan and Smith together in a couple of dodgy dives and at least one restaurant, plus a bloke has come forward who knew Morgan well, and he will swear he saw him being let into the offices in Reynolds Street in the early hours of the morning that Smith was found battered outside. I shall soon be ready to put the papers in – just a couple of loose ends to tie up now.'

Martyn turned to face his boss – they both liked and respected each other – and continued, 'The only sticking point in the enquiry is … *Why?* If I could only find out the answer to that I could close the case now, but the only three people who can answer the question are all lying in the morgue. To be honest, I was coming to see you when you sent for me; I just don't see how we can go any further.'

The DCI, who had complete faith in Martyn's instinct and abilities, said, 'OK Martyn, it's been two weeks – wind up the enquiry, submit the papers to the coroner, and for Pete's sake let me have some manpower back to sort out this lot.' As he spoke, he waved his hand dejectedly in the direction of the wall map.

Martyn felt very concerned for his boss. 'Don't worry sir. Give it a chance. We will get on top of this, I promise.'

Martyn waited in the briefing room until all his team were present, pondering over what had happened to John Vincent and where he had disappeared to. He had already spoken to the senior officer of the Shropshire force, whose men were all over the station and none too pleased that he hadn't held onto their witness when he had the chance. It didn't matter that he had no reason to hold Mr Vincent – his attempts to justify himself simply fell on frustrated deaf ears.

The last of his enquiry team now present, the door was shut and they listened intently as he told them how far the Law enquiry had gone and of all the problems that had occurred since his death. He went on to say that he thought the Morgan/Smith murder follow-up had gone about as far as it could go and that he had been instructed to wind up the enquiry and submit all the papers to the coroner. He requested all outstanding paperwork connected with the case to be on his desk by eight o'clock the following morning.

Amid mutters and murmurs, thinking the briefing ended, they started moving towards the door, but were stopped by the sound of the DS's voice addressing them once more. 'Just a couple of final things. Thanks to all of you for your help and hard work – it has not gone unnoticed. You have all done a damn fine job.' He knew they deserved praise and would appreciate hearing it from him. 'All CID officers return to your respective areas please – the lads are snowed under, so get stuck in straight away.' He was interrupted by the good-humoured muttering of, 'Poor sods can't do without us.' Martyn shouted over the banter, 'I want to speak to the two uniform lads who have been helping us in plain clothes. The rest of you can go, and thanks again.'

He paused to wait for the room to clear before approaching Barry Bourne and the ex-detective, PC Steven Jackson, and speaking to both, 'The same thanks apply to you two as well – you have both done a grand job. I have checked upstairs with the governor and he agrees – you can both have a couple of days off before you start your respective shifts again.'

He was disturbed by the shrill ringing of the telephone. As he answered it, he felt extremely annoyed at the interruption as he saw both men walk out of the room, as in particular he had wanted to express to PC Jackson what sterling work he had done and tell him that he was going to mention his name to the DCI during their next chat. PC Jackson would be a very useful asset to the department. He spoke into the receiver, 'Murder Room, DS Crowe.'

Barry left the room with mixed feelings. He was glad of the opportunity to complete the work in his mother-in-law's shed, but he knew just how much he had enjoyed being part of a busy team again. He hadn't had time to think of anything else these past days, not Mary and not the canvas bag, until now. He had really enjoyed the pressure of the job and knew that it had been the sort of work he could get real pleasure out of. He felt like he was buzzing with adrenalin – it was just a pity that he wouldn't be staying in the police force, especially if there were going to be more opportunities to work in the CID. He looked at his watch and realised that he would have time for a couple of well-deserved pints in the Chapel before going home. He was still full of excitement and he didn't want it spoilt by one of Mary's moods. Yes, he thought to himself, a couple of pints would go down really well, especially as he could have a full day in the shed tomorrow.

Mary Bourne had been really surprised by the genuinely good-humoured mood that her husband had been in over the past couple of weeks. She had heard through the wives' grapevine that they were all functioning under a lot of pressure and working long hours, which meant a lot of overtime money, but it wasn't that. For the first time in a long time Barry seemed to be really enjoying the work and even thriving on the pressure it entailed; what's more, he was enjoying coming home and was very happy when he was there. Perhaps, just perhaps, it could be just like old times again; she was very content with the prospect.

Rita Crowe sang as she waited for Martyn to come home for his tea. Although she worried about him and how tired he was looking lately, she knew he relished the pressure, even if it came from two different directions – from the enquiry and from Headquarters. Mind you, she was always worried. Still, she could pamper him when he got in by making sure his food was ready and that she was always there with a shoulder for him to lean on. She was looking forward to their first day off together, whenever that would be – even if Martyn spent it fast asleep in bed. All that mattered to Rita was that Martyn was safe and well.

Chapter 24

Martyn was making his way to Symonds Avenue to assist one of his men by visiting a house that had been broken into, the morning after the murder enquiry had been wrapped up. *Why did the name Symonds Avenue seem so familiar?* It nagged at his brain, but he simply couldn't recall how or why he knew it.

Earlier that morning, after completing as much of the paperwork on the murder as possible, and while still waiting for statements to be typed, he had gone into his old office to catch up on what had happened in his absence. He knew that all his office personnel were working to full capacity, so when a uniformed officer entered the CID office with what was obviously another crime to be dealt with, he took it on himself. It was a report of another breaking and entering, in a well-to-do area, too. He knew he could have ignored it and one of the DCs would have got round to it eventually, but if he was seen by his staff to get stuck into the workload and help them out, they would jump at the chance to repay the debt if he ever needed assistance in the future.

He had told the uniformed officer to record him as the officer in charge of the case, and after booking out, he left the station to make his way to investigate the scene of the crime. He had wanted a bit of time on his own anyway to mull things over, which he did during the drive over. He had managed to catch hold of Paddy Riley and pay him his money, but was slightly disappointed that his informant hadn't any new info; mind you, with policemen swarming all over the city no further news wasn't exactly surprising, even though Paddy had promised to keep in touch should any crop up.

Martyn had gone over the murder case many times, and had not slept well because his mind wouldn't stop asking the same questions: *Why? Why had Morgan beaten Smith to death? Why had Morgan tried to assault a policeman? Why had Law put the word out for Morgan? Why had Law been killed? Why were these three men linked?* He knew he was missing something, and even had a copy of the file in his briefcase to take home for further perusal. If he could find the missing link he wouldn't have to have Alexander Law's death verdict recorded as 'murder by person or persons unknown', which would ultimately leave the file open and the crime classed as 'unsolved'.

He spent as much time as necessary at the house that had been broken into. He had in fact completed all that was required of him in a very short time, as there was little information available without Forensics getting involved, but after providing the usual instructions about nothing being touched until the fingerprint man arrived, he remained to listen to the Robertsons' complaints regarding the state of the country. He was really just doing a public relations job, and even though he was personally blamed for every fault in the police force and government, he realised it was just the elderly couple's way of letting off steam and coping with the shock of having all their prized sentimental valuables stolen.

He finally left the house and stood by the front garden gate, looking across the road, to a car he recognised and immediately remembered why the road name Symonds Avenue was so familiar to him. That was Bob's car and this was the road in which his mother-in-law lived. *Which house was it?* He racked his brains to remember. *I bet he's working on something in that shed of his,* he thought, knowing of his friend's passion for woodwork and thinking of the lovely occasional table he had made for Rita and him on their wedding anniversary last year. *If I knew which one it was, I might even drop in to surprise him – I might even get a morning cuppa,* he mused as he slowly crossed the road to his car, looking around for a house that he could identify. But he couldn't. As he put his key in the car door lock, though, he noticed a face looking at him through a window. The features he recognised instantly – it was Mary's mother; although he had only met her once, at the police ball, he would have known her anywhere. He removed the key and, smiling, walked round the car and up the pathway to the front door, waving a greeting at Mrs Sharpe.

Barry had risen that morning in excellent spirits, the high of the previous day still coursing through his veins as he planned his day. He had a lot of work to do, a lot to catch up on, but he had all day to concentrate on getting his money hidden properly. As he drove, he mused over the very pleasant evening he and Mary had spent together; especially their spontaneous lovemaking, during which both were very enthusiastic participants. *Just like the old days.*

His broadening smile, a result of the memory of the previous night's events, briefly faltered as he pulled into Symonds Avenue due to the fact that he couldn't get his car up the drive as someone had parked over the entrance. Normally he didn't like to leave his car in the street where it could be seen, but preferred to conceal it by leaving it in the driveway. Still, it probably wouldn't matter, he told himself – after today, the money would be well and truly hidden. He pulled up behind the car outside his mother-in-law's and while locking the door, noticed the marked police car parked fifty yards down the street. He immediately dismissed its presence as he walked up the path and round the side of the house. *Maybe old Mrs Sotcliffe has finally killed that waste of a*

173

space of a husband of hers, he mused before proceeding into the kitchen to share a cup of tea with Mary's mother; who, although initially surprised to see him, quickly became a willing accomplice to his subterfuge as he furtively explained that he was working on a secret project for Mary.

Barry was back in excellent spirits as he entered the shed and, seeing his previous attempts untouched, he didn't bother to replace the wedge under the door. Without donning his gloves, he started to remove some of the wood he had used to conceal the bag, even though this left its contents in full view. He wasn't unduly concerned as he knew that the old woman wouldn't be calling with a cuppa anytime soon, and besides, the wood he had removed would soon be attached to what he had previously accomplished and his ill-gotten gains would then be well and truly hidden until he was ready. That was when he saw the spider …

No one, not even Mary, knew that since childhood Barry had suffered from an acute form of arachnophobia. He had endured years of recurring horrific nightmares where spiders of all shapes and sizes would crawl over his body and lay eggs under his skin. Even the sight of the smallest specimen would send him into abject panic, but this one was a *monster*; and it had positioned itself in the exact place that Barry's head would need to be to complete his task.

Without turning away from the huge beast he started to feel about the workbench for a hammer, a screwdriver … anything! There was no way he was going to take his eyes away from the beast for a second and leave himself open to attack, and he started to sweat profusely as he continued to grope around for a weapon with which to defend himself. For reasons best known to itself, it was at that moment that the spider flicked its two front legs before scurrying out of sight into an area in the top corner of the shed where the roof met the wall.

Barry knew that for him to carry out any more work on

hiding the money would be impossible until he had dispatched the spider, as he'd never be able to concentrate on anything else knowing that his greatest enemy lay hidden in the corner ready to strike at any opportunity. He moved over to search his toolbox and selected a sharp-pointed wooden-handled chisel – part of an engraving set given to Mary's dad by his wife on their last wedding anniversary together before he left; the ten carving tools were each honed to a fine edge to enable the user to carve intricate effects into the wood.

This'll make sure the bastard gets the point, he thought dryly and pulled the stool towards him. He would stand on it as best as he could for greater advantage – he had absolutely no intention of reaching upwards and having that thing run down his arm towards his face; he shuddered uncontrollably at the thought and all the hairs on his body went stiff, his eyes constantly flicking back to the area he had last seen the spider.

He looked again at the stool and held it tightly with one hand as he kicked the loose leg back into place. With only three legs, one of which was only just hanging on, it should have been on the scrapheap long ago, but Mary had insisted it would serve Barry nicely in the shed; along with the workbench, which was in reality an old kitchen table that had had the leaves removed and required a small block of wood wedged beneath it to stop it wobbling dangerously.

Barry had forgotten the number of occasions on which the rickety stool had almost collapsed when he put weight on it, and he had almost thrown it out several times. However, a sharp kick in the right place generally did the trick and the stool had loyally remained in service. This time he placed it as close as he could to the target area and gingerly stood up on it, feeling the loose leg slightly wobble as he placed his left hand on the beam that ran down the centre of the roof, and gripping the pointed chisel in his right.

He was so engrossed in what he was doing that he never heard the shed door open.

Mrs Sharpe stood curiously watching the man on the pavement opposite her house as he looked up and down the avenue. He was obviously searching for something or somewhere and seemed completely lost, but she thought there seemed something vaguely familiar about his kind face. She had seen him come out of Mr and Mrs Robertson's house, in front of which he was now standing, and she was curious as to what was going on – after all, she had seen a uniformed policeman come out of the same house moments earlier. Thinking that she could go over later, perhaps under the pretext of asking after their daughter Betty, who was expecting her fifth child – *each of whom had different fathers* – Mrs Sharpe noticed the man was now looking directly at her and was surprised when he smiled and started to walk up the path to her front door. She moved towards the door to see what he wanted and opened it before he had a chance to knock.

'Mrs Sharpe? I bet you don't remember me. We met at the police ball. I'm Martyn Crowe, I work with Bob – sorry, Barry.'

She smiled as she recognised the nice man who had been so polite and had even danced a waltz with her. 'Yes, I remember now – I'm sorry, I just couldn't place you. Won't you come in?'

'If it's not too much bother. I only came over on the off chance of seeing Barry. I saw his car parked outside.'

Mrs Sharpe smiled and opened the door wide for him to enter. 'He's in the shed. I'll make us all a nice cup of tea and you go straight through and see him.'

Grinning, Martyn walked down the hall and through the kitchen, and strolled up the short path to the shed, softly pushing open the door in the hope of surprising his friend.

He looked up as Barry, who was about three feet away, started to sway as the stool on which he was perched finally collapsed.

Martyn saw Barry turn and launch himself in his direction with both arms outstretched before he fell across him. The excruciating pain in his head was the last thing Martyn would ever experience.

Barry automatically spun round as the light from the open door suddenly flooded the shed, his engrossed concentration on defeating the hairy eight-legged foe unexpectedly broken in a moment of absolute surprise. Because of his sudden movement, his left hand slipped off the roof beam as one of the legs of the stool totally collapsed, and he started to awkwardly fall across the shed in the direction of his turn. *Oh shit!* Having completely lost his balance, he flailed desperately at the air as he briefly saw a quizzical Martyn standing in the doorway, before landing heavily and squarely on his friend. Both men flattened with the force of the impact.

Dazed for a second or two, Barry slowly pushed himself up. 'Jesus! You OK, Martyn? Shit, you startled me!' Having raised himself into a kneeling position, he shook his head and looked down at Martyn, whose knees appeared to be nudging him to get off and allow him to rise. Then he saw the chisel handle.

It was as though time had stopped as he knelt in the doorway, his knees either side of his friend's legs, his upper half lying outside the shed. Totally confused, he distantly heard high-pitched, frantic screaming, as he stared at the vision before him. Martyn's whole body twitched as a deep crimson tide poured from around the chisel handle, which was the only part of the tool left protruding from his right eye, and started to pool around his mouth, where tiny sprays of blood and foam were flicked into the air with each tortured breath. Trying to comprehend what was going on,

177

Barry dimly realised that the screaming which had been emanating from his mother-in-law had finally stopped, only to be replaced by the single high-pitched note of a police whistle.

Mrs Sharpe was filling the kettle when Martyn had opened the door of the shed; through the open back door she had heard the anguished, strangled cry and, dropping the kettle in the sink, rushed into the garden in time to witness her son-in-law talking as he knelt over his friend.

As she walked down the path to enquire if everything was all right, her eyes were drawn to the bright fluid seeping from the prone man's face. When she saw the handle of something sticking out of Martyn Crowe's eye and all the muscles on his face twitching, stepping past the two men, she grabbed hold of the door frame for support, suddenly feeling very sick as she realised that the incessant screaming she could hear was coming from her own throat.

Traumatised by the scene, she collapsed against the inside of the shed door, and as she did so her eyes caught sight of something at the back of the shed, causing her screeching to instantly stop. She was looking at a bundle of Bank of England notes sticking out of a canvas bag.

PC Rodgers, having just said cheerio to Mr and Mrs Robertson, was standing by the police car looking for the DS when he heard the female ear-splitting shriek of utter horror. Thinking immediately that the burglar had chanced his arm again and, in repeating the crime, had subsequently been disturbed in the act, he drew his whistle and signalled for assistance as he followed the audible trail of terror emanating from across the road. Running up the side of the house, his boots crunching on the gravel strip that divided the centre of the paved driveway, he had just drawn his truncheon when he rounded the corner and was halted instantly by the screaming suddenly stopping and by the gruesome scene before him.

Detective Sergeant Crowe, with one final flutter of his arms and legs, simultaneously coughed a final spurt of blood before remaining motionless on the ground. The dark pool of blood that covered his face was penetrated by a six-inch wooden cylinder pointing skywards. Bob Bourne was staring open-mouthed at the DS lying directly beneath him, then collapsed sideways and landed heavily on his backside as he started to weep silently, his eyes never leaving the body. The elderly female, who had obviously been the one screaming, was leaning in the frame of the door gawping incredulously, with her arm pointing at something inside. Suspecting an intruder to be within, PC Rodgers carefully approached until he saw what had affected her so dreadfully. His truncheon arm fell to the side of his body as he too looked on in disbelief at the bag stuffed full of money stored in the back of this suburban shed.

The eerie silence which engulfed the occupants of the garden was finally shattered by the sounds of distant sirens, approaching ever closer.

Part Two

Chapter 25

Barry Bourne sat shivering in the interview room.

The last hour had been an unbelievable blur, like something out of an Alfred Hitchcock film. Mr Robertson, hearing the scream and seeing the police officer sprint across the road blowing his whistle, had dialled 999 immediately. The police car had arrived in less than four minutes and the ambulance only five minutes later, but Barry had instinctively known his friend was already dead. The young PC, finally spurred into action by the cacophony of sirens, had moved Barry and Mrs Sharpe back into the house, both to avoid any contamination of evidence and to remove them from the gory scene. Barry had occupied his normal chair in silent disbelief until he was finally transported to the police station where he worked. If anything had been said to him since the start of the incident, he had no recollection of it.

He sat there trying to collect his thoughts. It had simply been a terrible accident – he was only looking to kill that spider, and surely they would understand that. *They must. Where were they, anyway?* He had been sitting alone for what seemed like forever. Oh! He knew – they would be telling Mary and Rita. The thought of Martyn's sons caused him to shut his eyes tightly as if to try and block out the notion. *It was a bloody accident!*

The door of the interview room opened and Detective Chief Inspector Kelly stepped inside, his face like stone as he slowly closed the door and occupied the chair opposite Barry. Before the DCI could say anything, Barry spluttered, 'It was an accident, sir. I was trying to get the spider and the sodding stool broke.'

The DCI spoke quietly, his manner not friendly as usual, but extremely cold and detached. 'Save it son, I shouldn't be here. I've come to say one thing – get yourself a solicitor, a good one – you're going to need it.' With that, he rose and walked briskly out of the room.

Barry sat forward in the chair and lowered his head into his hands until they were almost touching his knees, muttering, 'It was a bloody accident – what do I need a brief for? They've got to believe me!' His thoughts spiralled from his friend to the spider, from the spider to the shed, and from the shed to the money. *Oh no! Holy shit!* His temples started to pound and his throat suddenly dried up. With everything that had happened he had completely forgotten about the money! The DCI was right – he did need a solicitor, and he finally began to understand just how much trouble he was in.

Maurice Flowers, a small, balding, weedy man, was sitting behind his desk, having completed his paperwork for the day. The senior partner and the only criminal solicitor in a medium-sized law practice within the city; he had just packed away the last two dossiers in his drawer when the telephone rang. *Damn!* He had just been about to leave. As he reached across his desk for the receiver, he silently reaffirmed that he was going to go home early tonight whoever it was; besides, he was the only one in the firm who dealt with criminal matters, and any client that needed him would just have to stay as a guest of the judicial system until tomorrow.

He lifted the receiver to his ear and listened intently to the caller. Mesmerised by what he was hearing, he knew that despite his previous intention to leave early, this was going to be too good an opportunity to miss. The only note he made on the notepaper in front of him was a continually overwritten figure 9, before finally crossing it out and scoring the figure 10 into the page. Maurice Flowers judged all his clients on a scale of one to ten, not to reflect their innocence or guilt nor even to indicate whether the cause was just or not, but simply to indicate whether the client would earn him a sizeable profit. The richer the client or more high profile the case, the higher the number. *This client was a potential gold mine.*

The voice at the other end having fallen silent, Maurice Flowers stated categorically, 'Tell him not to say anything at all until I get there!' before replacing the receiver and grabbing his topcoat and briefcase from the nearby chair. As he exited his private office through the connecting door into the general office, he declared to all present, 'If you want me I shall be at the police station.' Almost as an afterthought he added, 'Phone my wife, tell her I shall be late,' and without waiting for a reply he shut the door as he briskly walked to his destination.

Mary Bourne was in the kitchen cleaning the oven, when she heard the knock on the front door. *I wonder who that could be?* she wondered as she swore mildly to herself at the inconvenience. She had seen the police car arrive at Rita's thirty minutes earlier and watched as she was ushered into the car before being driven away. *Why didn't she asked me to look after the boys?* She removed the rubber gloves and brushed down her apron before opening the door and was surprised to find Barry's uniformed inspector and several other police officers on the doorstep.

Inspector McFarlane, who she knew quite well, addressed her formally. 'May we come in, Mrs Bourne?' Without waiting for a reply, the strange procession filed into her house, before separating to proceed to different destinations within her home until the hallway was empty. Mary closed the door and followed the inspector into her sitting room where the discussion of the next few minutes left her in complete bewilderment and turmoil. *Martyn Crowe was dead. Barry had been arrested. Thousands of pounds had been discovered in her mother's shed. A warrant had been issued to search the house.*

No matter how hard she tried, she just couldn't comprehend what the inspector was talking about. At first she attempted to laugh at what must surely be a joke, but soon realised that there was nothing friendly about his tone, and even though she tried to argue and object, they were obviously here in an official capacity and whatever she said was not about to stop them. The facts duly explained, the inspector remained with her silently as the other officers went about their business, until she finally said, 'Can I please see my husband? I would like to speak to him.' Coldly he replied, 'He is being held in custody at the police station. I will see what I can do.'

When they finally left, she noticed that one of the uniformed officers had been stationed outside her front door. Judging by the movement of curtains in adjacent houses, the neighbours had noticed also.

Barry had remained in the interview room for nearly four hours, now just wrapped in a rough woollen cell blanket, his clothes and shoes having been taken away for forensic examination. *What on earth's going on?* He tried to imagine the form of the investigation and how it would be progressing; he knew they would search his house and he wondered how Mary would react and what she would have to say about it. *How the hell am I going to explain all this to her?*

He couldn't get rid of the bitter taste in his mouth; even his request for food and a drink of water had been curtly refused – obviously the rumours had begun to circulate and he had apparently already been found guilty by his colleagues. Where he had expected sympathy and their continued comradeship, he had discovered only contempt and hate. His lips were so dry. He kept trying to moisten them with his tongue, but when he was finally told that his solicitor had arrived, he was not sure he would be able to speak even when he got the chance.

Despite all his mental rambling beforehand, upon hearing his solicitor was present Barry instantly came to a decision. *He was going to tell the truth.* It had crossed his mind earlier to try and bullshit about the money and say he had experienced a magical winning betting streak on the horses. However, his police logic discarded such lies for he couldn't back up the false answers and they would immediately catch him out. Plus, if he started lying about the money, then they would immediately assume he was lying about the death of Martyn.

With his decision to come clean made, he felt a great sense of relief, as though a large weight had been removed from his shoulders. Even though he now wished he had never seen the money, he knew that wish had come too late.

Maurice Flowers sat across the table, palms flat on the surface as he watched the blanketed figure in front of him eagerly telling his tale of woe. He knew from experience that, from the straightforward way the story was unfolding, along with the unhesitating answers to his questions, he was being told the truth. However, knowing the police as he did, he had an uneasy feeling that a dead DS on one hand and a constable in custody for the death on the other was not conducive to a verdict of 'Accidental Death'. The colleagues of the dead policeman would undoubtedly demand their pound of flesh.

'Is there anything else, Mr Bourne?' asked Maurice as soon as Barry had completed his explanation.

'I would appreciate some clothes to wear; I have nothing on under this.'

Maurice merely nodded and, without another word, left the interview room.

* * *

Detective Chief Inspector Kelly walked into the police station and immediately sought out those involved in the search of PC Bourne's house. *Had they found anything?* He wasn't at all surprised or disappointed at the negative responses his questions received: apart from the money in the shed, they had found nothing else at the home of the mother-in-law.

So all he had was one copper in the morgue, another in a cell, and a bag full of money; along with in-house speculation that the money was the missing piece of the puzzle in Martyn's recent murder enquiry. *At least now, wherever you are Martyn, you finally solved the case.*

DCI Kelly walked towards his office and recalled the conversation he had just had with the Chief Constable, who he regarded as a yes-man without bottle who insisted his force appear whiter than white to the public regardless of the actual morals of his men. The DCI was well aware that to the public an arrest was sufficient proof of guilt; the trial, when it happened, was almost a side event. How many times he had heard 'They wouldn't arrest unless they were sure' or 'There's no smoke without fire'. He had originally asked his superior if he could conduct the interview with Bourne his way, deal with the money side first and then wait until the experts had unearthed some incriminating evidence before proceeding on to the death of DS Crowe. The terse answer was, 'Formally arrest and charge with murder! That, Chief Inspector, is an order!'

Barry was well aware that he would have to remain in police custody until he made his appearance before the Magistrate's Court the following morning. He had endured the formal interview in the presence of his solicitor, and on Mr Flower's advice he had told the truth; the statement had been taken down in writing by the DCI and had been

188

witnessed by a DI brought in from another division to assist. On completion, Barry was formally arrested and charged with the murder of Detective Sergeant Crowe.

After the inspector and other police officers had left, Mary Bourne walked around her house in a daze, her thoughts in chaos. Every drawer and cupboard had been ransacked; even her underwear had been searched for evidence of her husband's guilt. She started to automatically refold her intimates when she received a call from the station requesting her to take a change of clothing for Barry when she visited him; she did not understand why and still had absolutely no idea what was going on, apart from the absurd 'facts' told to her by the inspector.

She ignored the state of the house and systematically gathered underwear, socks, casual trousers and a shirt for Barry; the last item she hugged to her face as she whispered softly to herself, 'Oh God, oh God, oh God!' as if to gain strength and inspiration from her husband's scent. Placing the items into a small case, she went into the bathroom and splashed cold water on her face as she collected herself together. Looking in the mirror, she saw a woman with dull, expressionless eyes and didn't recognise her. She went downstairs, slipped on her coat, and, case in hand, locked the front door and stepped past the constable stationed on her doorstep before heading towards the bus stop. Throughout the journey to the police station, even though no one actually paid her attention or even looked in her direction, she felt as though disapproving eyes were watching her. At the station, although she was treated with basic civility, the friends of her husband with whom she had in the past socialised lowered their gaze as they passed her without acknowledgement.

She handed over the small case to the desk sergeant upon her arrival, and after waiting for what felt like an age, she was finally escorted through to the interview room, where she was left alone with her husband. She held him in her arms and then they sat down together for the first time in a long time and talked. Barry carefully explained what had happened; her eyes widened in surprise but she listened to the whole story without interruption. When he'd finally finished she felt physically sick about what had happened to Martyn, but more by instinct than planning she held him in her arms once more as he cried. They stayed together like that for what felt like a lifetime.

Rita Crowe couldn't come to terms with the death of her beloved Martyn.

She'd been happily ironing in the kitchen, singing along to the latest ballads on the radio and looking forward to picking up her sons before preparing tea. She'd gaily answered the knock at the door, the fact of unexpectedly being interrupted not denting her good mood – until she set eyes on Detective Chief Inspector Kelly and saw the look on his face.

For Rita, the next hour had gone by in complete and utter confusion. It was as though she was under hypnosis. The whole conversation was one-sided as DCI Kelly, accompanied by a policewoman, verbally walked her through the sketchy details. In the end though, all she could take in was that Martyn was dead and Bob Bourne was under arrest. *Martyn was dead! Bob Bourne was under arrest!* A car was outside, its engine running, waiting to take her to the station before she was escorted to the hospital, where she would have to formally identify his body. Did she have someone who could pick up the kids? Rita blankly replied, 'Old Mrs Steele at number 131 said she would take the boys at any time,' before allowing herself to have her coat put on and be led to the patrol car, in which she sat next to the DCI.

'Get hold of the woman at number 131 but don't tell her

what's happened,' Kelly instructed the policewoman. 'Then stay in the house until we get back.' Then they drove off.

If Barry thought being charged with the murder of his friend was unbelievable, worse was yet to come, happening quite by chance following his thirty-minute respite with Mary. He was in the process of being moved from the interview room to the cells when he turned a corner and came face to face with Rita Crowe. Both walking along with their heads bowed, they almost blundered into each other and for a brief instant looked directly into each other's faces. He tried to say how sorry he was. He tried to tell her it was an accident. He wanted to wrap his arms around her and comfort her; but the look of pure, unadulterated hatred in her eyes stopped him dead in his tracks. He was struck with an anguish he had never before experienced; no one had ever displayed such absolute contempt towards him before. As the escorting officer yanked his arm to move him out of the path of the late DS's wife, he realised that she, like all the others, had made up her mind already. *Guilty!*

The initial confusion had turned not to sorrow or grief with the words of sympathy and condolence she received from all the police officers at the station, but to uncontrollable rage. Never feeling less like crying in her life, she seethed, wanting Barry Bourne to fry and then to rot in hell for destroying her life and that of her boys. She had barely contained her anger when she inadvertently walked into him in the corridor; all she had wanted to do was smash her fist into his face and keep hitting him, but she had restrained herself, willing her hands to remain at her sides as the escorting officer pulled him around her while he looked at her with that stupid expression. *What had he expected her to do, take him in her arms and pat him on the back saying, 'There, there, it's OK really'?* She turned and watched as he was taken towards the cells, inwardly screaming, 'Murderer, murderer!'

Accompanied by Detective Chief Inspector Kelly into the anteroom of the hospital mortuary, she had looked down at Martyn lying there, appearing so handsome. Wondering why she could only see half his face, she removed the sheet as she bent to kiss him, gasping in horror at the gaping black hole where his eye once was, before collapsing into the arms of DCI Kelly and letting the first of a flood of tears stream down her cheeks. An attending doctor, seeing her distress, had decided she should stay in hospital and admitted her overnight after prescribing sedatives.

Her elderly neighbour Mrs Steele, along with the WPC, brought the boys in to see her a while later, and she hugged and cried over them, not knowing what to say. Through her tears she explained that Daddy had gone to be with Jesus, but it was clear that they didn't understand – their daddy had been away before, and they would just wait until he came home.

Chapter 26

Barry spent the night in the cell totally unable to sleep. Each time he closed his eyes he had seen Martyn's stone-white death mask and heard Rita's screams of hatred. Even when he had lain awake staring in the blackness towards the ceiling, the eyes that constantly peered through the permanently open grille in the cell door bore into him. He was definitely their prize exhibit. It wasn't every day that a DS was killed and a fellow police officer and close friend was charged with his murder, and he realised that the daily papers and television news would have a field day with this story.

He had been informed by his legal representative that he would stay in the cell until the morning. Raking up his knowledge of the basics of law, he had asked about the possibility of bail, even though he knew in his heart that his chances were less than zero, and when Mr Flowers had told him there was no chance on this earth, at least he knew his solicitor was being honest with him.

Just after eight o'clock, when the morning shifts had changed over, Barry was handcuffed and moved to the cells located under the courts. He had often followed this procedure as a police officer but never dreamed in his worst nightmare that he would end up on the other side of the system, let alone totally disowned and ignored by his former colleagues. Unless it was to ask an official question or give him formal directions no one at all spoke to him. Men he had worked with for over five years, men he had helped to arrest suspects, men to whose assistance he had unquestioningly gone, all averted their eyes from him. *Innocent until proven guilty, what a bloody joke!* He had already been convicted by his peers.

Mrs Margaret Handle had been a lay magistrate for a very long time and had often heard herself described as one of the 'good old school'. She was greatly respected by the police for her no-nonsense approach to removing hardened criminals off the streets, while showing restraint and leniency if the case required, and she in turn respected every decent and hard-working police officer for taking on a near-impossible task.

Upon her arrival at court that morning she had been informed of the unhappy circumstances and told that the constable charged with the crime would be appearing before her. When she read the outline of the case, her immediate sympathy went out to the family of the deceased officer, a private prayer extending to the widow; but she had also felt a great sadness as the accused officer was brought up before her. She did not know at this time the full facts of the case and wondered what terrible circumstances had brought this tragedy about. As she looked directly at the accused man, Barry did not avert his eyes, and for that she gave him a modicum of respect.

Her eyes lowered to the defence table and she inwardly groaned as she saw Mr Flowers. He had so often in the past tried to get acquittals for his clients by discrediting the police officer involved in the case in question; she did not like Maurice Flowers one little bit, for his attitude or his manners. A consummate professional, her dislike of the man was immediately dismissed as she listened intently to his impassioned plea for bail. However, she knew that had it not been a policeman charged with murder, the question of bail would never have arisen. She was determined not to let these circumstances influence her decision, knowing that a defendant charged with murder was automatically refused bail on his or her first appearance, irrespective of the circumstances; but she allowed a discreet passage of time to elapse before stating, 'Defendant to be remanded in custody.' As Barry was taken down the court steps to the cells below, the courtroom emptied, and the press contingent fought its way out to the nearest telephone.

Mary Bourne had decided, after consultation with Barry and Mr Flowers, that she would not attend court. It had been explained to her that as it was a first appearance, Barry would only be there for a few moments, while she, if she were there, would undoubtedly be left to face the wrath of the press contingent if they discovered who she was. They had decided that if she felt up to it, she would visit Barry in prison later as neither expected him to get bail. Mary had also made her mind up that, for the time being, she was going to stay with her mother. She had gone straight there after leaving the station and her mother had seemed genuinely pleased to see her. Mary also pondered over whether to try and see Rita.

Chapter 27

During the following months Barry Bourne gradually became institutionalised – he did what he was told, when he was told; even his thoughts weren't free from routine as he gave his answers to the same questions. *Why did he think he could get away with taking the money? Why did the stool break at that exact moment in time? Why did his friend have to die?* The only time he experienced respite was during Mary's visits and his excursions to court. The large black police van, known colloquially as a Black Maria, would arrive at the prison, and the prisoners on remand would be locked inside the small individually caged cubicles contained within. For Barry, the only downside to these monthly outings was the fact that the grille in the van's side only enabled him to catch glimpses of the pavement when in transit; in his current state of mind, he had totally forgotten that the idea behind the design was actually to prevent anyone from the outside seeing in.

They were always driven to the back of the court through a large set of iron gates; the first time he had made this journey and he had seen the iron railings, he remembered how he had walked past these same gates on his last visit to the mortuary what now seemed like a lifetime ago. Once through the gates, the prisoners were individually released from their cubicles and, still shackled, ushered in line through a door in the far wall and down a well-lit, white-tiled tunnel to central reception. Here they remained until it was decided in which courtroom they were going to appear; once

196

the lists had been prepared the prisoners were separated and taken to the appropriate cell directly under their allocated court. The route from cell to court was via a short wooden flight of steps, and once at the top, they stepped directly into the area set aside for prisoners, the dock. Barry still wondered why it was called the dock. Once the court appearance, however brief, was over, for those going back to prison the whole procedure was repeated in reverse.

Mr Flowers always took the trouble to visit him each time he appeared in court. The fact that he was being paid very well for his services meant he always had a sunny disposition, which in turn made it easier for him to conceal the fact that he really couldn't give a damn about his client's innocence or otherwise.

Maurice was delighted when he had been able to convince Barry to make the committal proceedings a formality by explaining that this was just a simple legal procedure which officially transferred the case from the lower Magistrate's Court to the higher Assize Court. Barry was already aware that the Assize Court was the only one capable of hearing a murder trial, but was not aware, because Mr Flowers had neglected to tell him, that they could have contested the transfer on a 'no case to answer' basis, and might have been able to get the whole murder conviction thrown out. Mr Flowers was devious enough to know that although his client was a serving police officer and totally innocent of murder, he was still sufficiently ignorant of the law to allow himself to be manipulated. By transferring his case to the Assize Court, Mr Flowers' earnings had immediately increased ten-fold.

Maurice Flowers had also been very successful in his choice of counsel to represent Barry at his trial; he had managed with a little know-how and a lot of luck to secure the services of Mr Jerome Peregrine-Richards QC. The man might have a preposterously pompous name but he was a brilliant barrister and Flowers was well aware that if

Peregrine-Richards were successful in his defence then his own reputation would prosper as well.

Mary Bourne had come to enjoy the routine she was experiencing very much indeed. She easily fitted the twice-weekly visits to her husband in with her normal daily life. She particularly liked the fact that she knew where he was at all times. Although she wasn't happy that he was in prison awaiting trial for murder, secretly she was delighted that the turn of events had caused their love for each other to be rekindled with a passion. Like so many others in her position, she fantasised about what her life would be like upon his release; her greatest desire that he would be found innocent of everything, with his release, they could start their life together anew.

Rita Crowe hated the routine that she now had to deal with, especially the monotonous boredom of doing the same things at the same time every day. One of the things she had always loved about being with Martyn was the uncertainty; meals had never been at the same time two days running – in fact, every aspect of her husband's job had been unpredictable and she had loved it – it had kept her feeling alive and stimulated. It didn't help that both boys regularly cried themselves to sleep as the truth finally sank in that their dear father was never coming back. She was as dead inside as her husband, a walking, talking corpse whose broken heart missed her dear sweet Martyn so very very much.

Chapter 28

As late summer rolled along Jerome Peregrine-Richards sat at his large leather-bound desk and stared at the file in front of him. He had allowed himself all afternoon to go through the papers of the policeman accused of murdering a colleague and, in doing so, affirmed the British judicial system to be the best in the world. He had been sent all the papers collected by the prosecution counsel, containing every detail of their case against his client, and yet he had not been required to supply them with one detail of his defence; with what little he already knew about the case he was extremely glad, because at the moment he wished he had one.

He leaned back in his chair and sipped tea from his china cup as he glanced around his office. Afternoon tea in his chambers was a ritual – possibly, he surmised, a greater institution than the Crown itself. Everything without exception stopped for afternoon tea. The world might be coming to an end, multiple disasters and calamities imminent, but afternoon tea continued. He was thankful now that he had followed the family tradition and practised law, even though at one time he found its study to be a tedious blight on his university social life. But going into law ran in the family and as the eldest son it had been expected if not demanded of him. He was well aware that in time he would be appointed as a judge, his future already mapped out for him because of his family ties and traditions. The fact he might become a judge because he was an excellent barrister had, in fact, never entered his head.

His tea finished, he pushed the cup to one side and again pulled the papers detailing '*Rex v Bourne, B.O.*' towards him. He opened the file and began to read. When he stared at the end of the last page, having given the dossier his full attention, he allowed a grudging smile of admiration to slowly appear on his face. 'The crafty old so and so,' he mused aloud as he turned the pages over to the beginning. *I wonder who Prosecuting Counsel is?* He slowly flicked the pages until he found the name he was seeking. *Bartholomew Compton, QC.* The name stared back at him and he let his normal upper-crust decorum slip as he muttered, 'You are a bastard, Barney Compton, an out-and-out bastard!'

He started to reread each page, this time taking notes. The prosecution had deliberately intermingled the details of the deaths of Detective Sergeant Crowe and Mr Charles Morgan with the opportunistic theft of the money by his client. He stopped again, bringing his silver fountain pen up to tap against his temple. *That is crafty. Take out the theft of the cash and all the witnesses relating to it and what's left? Nothing. Nothing at all!* It was immediately apparent that Prosecution intended to have Barry tried by inference and had deliberately mixed up the details of the death and theft so much so that it now appeared to be one continuous set of circumstances. *Because Barry had stolen the money, then he had also committed the murder of Detective Sergeant Crowe, and so he was also responsible for the death of a Mr Charles Morgan.* There was nothing, however, in the file about Charles Morgan having originally stolen the money and ultimately being responsible for his own death, and certainly no mention that Barry was actually in bed asleep at the time Morgan was run over.

Peregrine-Richards turned to the album of photographs enclosed with the papers containing pictures of the money laid out, together with photographs of the dead policeman, which would be presented as an exhibit so the jury could study them. He knew that no death was pleasant, but the sight of a body with a screwdriver – he paused and checked – 'Damn it, Jerry get it right,' he chastised himself – a *chisel* sticking out of a sightless eye was more than the average person could stomach. His client openly admitted he'd caused the death of his friend but was adamant that it was an accident.

He looked again at the separated pile of photographs of Martyn Crowe. *How hard would it be to deliberately aim to stick a chisel into someone's eye, even if they weren't expecting it?* he wondered. *Surely the natural reaction would've been to turn the eye away, if only a fraction, and the chisel would certainly have missed. OK, it might have caused a severe injury to the cheek, but it wouldn't have been fatal.* Mr Peregrine-Richards was absolutely sure of this and reached down for the long-handled paperknife on the front of his desk, picked it up and walked over to the mirror on the wall, where he always checked his appearance before leaving the office. He gripped the paper knife in the same way as the chisel was described as having been held, raised it above his head and brought it quickly down at the reflected image. He knew that he was about to stab a mirror and yet he still flinched – he had instinctively moved his head so that his image should not be struck by the tool. He remained staring into the mirror, thinking just how many other parts of the body would be easier to aim at than the eye in order to cause death. *His client was innocent of murder.*

His mind retraced all the facts of the case as he returned to his desk. Discarding the paperknife on the adjacent leather chair, he bent over the papers and reviewed the statements made by his client during questioning, the details not altering one iota since they had initially been told to Mr Flowers. What exactly was he up against? He knew he certainly had an opportunistic thief for a client, a corrupt policeman who had taken money purely through greed, yet he definitely wasn't the cold-blooded murderer that Prosecution was claiming. If he could read between the lines and understand their tactics then everyone could. Without the theft details being craftily intermingled there was absolutely no case for murder; in fact, had there been no theft at all then Prosecution would have been hard pressed to even present a case to the coroner, let alone to the Assizes. *Why, then, had Police Constable Barry Oliver Bourne been charged with murder?*

He sat and contemplated the problem for a quite considerable time before straightening up in his seat and remarking out loud, 'That's got to be it!' He picked up his notebook and flicked to a fresh page to jot down his thoughts: *'A highly venerated, senior police officer has been killed in unusual circumstances and someone must be charged in connection. Had they not charged my client, then in the next genuine murder case of a police officer, a clever solicitor might use these circumstances to get their client acquitted. The police are determined this will not happen, and Police Constable Bourne has become their sacrificial lamb whom they are determined to try and slaughter.'*

He sat back and imagined the numerous telephone calls that had occurred late into the night; each caller in turn making sure they didn't personally have to make the decision, the onus and burden having to be passed squarely onto the shoulders of the court. His client would, of course, come before the judge and plead guilty to the theft and when he was subsequently found not guilty of the murder, then all those sitting in their ivory towers who secretly hoped that he would be found culpable could simply shrug their shoulders and point out that it wasn't their fault, they had sent him for trial by his peers. They had done their best and complied with the law. *But what if he doesn't get off? What if my client is found guilty of all charges?*

Peregrine-Richards knew one thing for certain: he had got to prepare and present a submission to the judge at the start of the trial, and it was imperative that he convince whoever was presiding that to have the facts of two individual events presented and judged together would be a travesty of justice. He had, he knew, a lot of hard work to complete between now and when the case came to court. If he lost this initial submission then he would be hard pressed to convince a jury of his client's innocence. And if the judge did decide that the facts were to be heard simultaneously, then he could not comment to the jury on the decision. He pushed these negative thoughts to the back of his mind; what he had read in the file had riled him since it went against his sense of justice, and he was infuriated that he had become a mere puppet in this matter. He pressed a small button on the side of his telephone and waited until his secretary appeared at the door. Not taking his eyes from the paperwork strewn over his desk, he simply said, 'Sit down, Miss Shaw, we have a lot of work to do.'

Mary Bourne had received word, via a letter from Mr Flowers, that Barry's trial had been programmed into the autumn Assize list. She felt mildly confused; on one hand she was disappointed because she didn't want the routine that she had become so used to to be disrupted; on the other, she was glad that the end was in sight, as she wanted nothing more than her husband to be by her side again.

Rita Crowe had also been informed the approximate date of the trial was the first Monday of October, remembering how Martyn had once told her, when it once seemed like their holiday plans were ruined, that an exact trial date was never confirmed until the last moment. She had decided, however, that if possible she would be present at the trial every day and all day so that Martyn would see what was happening through her. In a bid to combat her grief she had attended her local church and tried with all her might to turn to God for help. However, her prayers remained unanswered, for Rita wanted nothing more than her husband to be by her side again.

Maurice Flowers made a point of attending the prison during the single meeting between Barry Bourne and Jerome Peregrine-Richards, not for the benefit of Barry, but to be seen in the same company as the barrister by the other inmates, thereby further boosting his reputation as a big-time solicitor.

He had quickly understood the importance that counsel was placing on the pre-trial submission and knew from the amount of time it had taken to prepare that a great deal of hard work had been done. He didn't really care about that as long as he got paid, but realised that his choice of barrister might yet pay further dividends. His wife would give everything to mix in the upper echelons in which the Peregrine-Richardses moved. Though he had repeatedly told her that as a solicitor he could only work and appear at the Magistrate's Court, while a barrister was the one who wore a wig and gown and appeared before the higher courts, he knew that she didn't really understand, but if there was the slightest glimmer of hope that he could introduce her to these higher social circles, it would give his home life and, more importantly, his sex life, a much-needed boost.

Mr Peregrine-Richards had actually enjoyed his meeting with his client, if one can ever enjoy a visit to prison, though he was certainly glad he only had to do it rarely. *How could anyone get accustomed to that abominable smell?* he thought as he entered the inner sanctum of the penal complex. It had hit him straight in the face – stale bodies, stale urine, stale faeces – he was sure he could almost taste it as it assaulted his senses. How on earth anyone could sign up to be a prison officer and then voluntarily spend thirty years in a place like this was incomprehensible, he pondered as he entered the interview room where Barry Bourne was already sitting.

He was satisfied, almost immediately, that his client was telling the truth, having reviewed each detail of the case with him. He had deliberately got facts wrong or put things out of context, but each time Barry had patiently corrected him. However, he'd had an extremely difficult time trying to convince his client of the importance of the pre-trial submission. Police Constable Bourne appeared to him to be simple; no, 'simple' was the wrong word … naïve … That was it, his client was naïve! Mr Peregrine-Richards was convinced beyond a shadow of a doubt that his client was innocent of murder, but unless he did an excellent job, he knew that to satisfy the hunger of the penal system, his client could well hang for a crime he didn't commit.

Barry Bourne returned to his cell a little easier in his mind; he had liked the counsel appointed to represent him and felt that apart from the fact that they were from completely opposite ends of the social spectrum, they had got on well with each other. He was fairly certain that he had convinced his barrister that he hadn't deliberately murdered Martyn; he knew that Mr Peregrine-Richards was concerned how the case might be presented by Prosecution, but Barry felt that his life, literally, was in safe hands. He had discovered from Maurice Flowers that the trial was listed in the autumn Assize catalogue and was relieved that it hadn't been deferred until the following January. At least now he had some sort of date to aim for. All that anyone involved in the trial could now do was wait.

Chapter 29

The last Friday afternoon before autumn Assizes saw the judge's quarters, situated in a quiet, secluded, well-to-do area of the city, completely bathed in sunshine, and the policemen who constantly patrolled the exterior of these premises felt relaxed and content. This building was solely used for housing the top judges of the land during their stay in the city, when they had control of the courts of quarter session and assize. The quarter sessions had concluded their business and there were now only two Assize Court judges in residence. The judges dealt with either civil or criminal matters, depending on what they had been allocated or how the case lists progressed. Each was aware of the entire case programme but didn't know until the last minute which particular trial they were to preside over.

Mr Justice Summerfield leaned back in his very comfortable leather armchair, his glass of port never far from his right hand and the decanter equally well within reach. He always enjoyed his visits to the city, being escorted by the police wherever he went, chauffeur-driven limousines at his beck and call, guarded day and night whilst in residence. Yes, he thoroughly enjoyed being completely and utterly spoilt by the legal system. He was, however, not looking forward at all to Monday morning. He had hoped the trial he was about to supervise would be allocated to his fellow judge, but the malicious wounding and attempted murder case he had been presiding over had suddenly ended when, during cross-examination, the accused's alibi had collapsed so much so that he changed his plea to 'Guilty'. The judge had in fact passed sentence about a week earlier than he had previously anticipated, and the guilt of the accused, on the evidence presented in trial papers, had never been in doubt in his mind.

He paused for another sip of port before glancing down at the forthcoming trial papers he had been reading. Never a fan of murder trials generally, and certainly not of those involving the murder of a serving police officer with a colleague accused, he recognised the negative publicity this one would generate and the public indignation that would inevitably follow. From his reading of the national and local newspapers he was blatantly aware that the press were already clamouring for blood in this case, and, knowing he was going to be in for a hard time, he sighed heavily as he reviewed the outline of the case once more. Justice Summerfield had in fact studied the papers several times already since they were delivered by his clerk and was not convinced in his own mind of the guilt of the accused. *What was his name?* He lifted his half-moon spectacles back into place on the end of his nose as he searched for the answer. *Ah yes, Police Constable Barry Oliver Bourne.* It was obvious from the way Prosecution had prepared the papers that the two unrelated circumstances had been cleverly entwined; he realised that since there was only very scant circumstantial evidence, insignificant forensic evidence and not a great deal else for the murder charge, the whole case probably would depend upon his decision.

To enable him to consult the appropriate legal textbooks in preparation, he had already been advised that Defence was initially going to present a strong submission to have the theft and murder cases dealt with separately. He knew that if he agreed and removed the theft charge, then there would be little, if anything, on which a jury could convict for murder. *But was that the right decision?* If the jury didn't convict in the murder case of a police officer, how much media and public outcry would rain down on him? Would that be the crucial criticism that would destroy his chances of ever being raised to an Appeal Court judge, the ultimate position as far as he was concerned, and one he had strived for continuously for several years? If he left both charges to run simultaneously then the media couldn't condemn him, and if for some reason the accused was found guilty, then the case would automatically be sent to the Appeal Court, where the decision could be reversed.

He wouldn't give his official decision until after all the submissions had been made and he'd theatrically appeared to give the matter a great deal of thought. But he already knew what he intended to do and turned back to the front page where the two individual charges were typed.

An assize judge, under normal circumstances, would not have dealt with such a minor offence as a theft of money, but as it had been passed on to him with the murder, he pencilled in the figure '5' alongside the charge in relation to the theft of the money and circled it. He knew that under the Larceny Act the maximum sentence for 'theft by finding' was five years, and that was the sentence he was going to deliver; provided, of course, he was acquitted of the murder.

He leant back in his chair, looked out at the bright autumn sunshine and smiled, raising the glass of port to his lips. *It really is a lovely afternoon, after all.*

Jerome Peregrine-Richards was leaning back, his office chair tilted on two legs, with his hands clasped behind his head, trying to rest his eyes, which were aching beyond belief from reading. He had reread the case papers for the murder trial for what he supposed must have been the hundredth time, but his thoughts started wandering and he opened his eyes to look at the unopened newspaper left on his desk that morning. The impending trial was getting a lot of coverage, much of it on the front pages, and he was aware that it wouldn't do him or his career any harm at all. Like so many others in his profession, he reflected, he made his living from the misfortune of others and the reputation gained through television coverage and what got into the newspapers. *Ah well – that's life, or, in this case, if we don't win – that's death!*

He picked up the slip of paper that had been placed on his desk by his clerk and read the name aloud: 'Mr Justice Summerfield'. Well, it could have been worse, as he wasn't usually a cut-and-dried 'hanging' judge. He reasoned that the judge couldn't possibly form a decision on the case before he had heard any submissions, and so at least his client would get a fair hearing. *Had he done enough though?* The thought niggled him; he knew that if his submission on Monday went against him, then it might be a considerable factor in bringing the rope a little closer around his client's neck. *Too late to worry now, I've done my best – now it's up to Summerfield*, he thought, and let the two front legs of the chair drop back onto the floor. He decided to have one final check through his plea just as the telephone rang, and there followed a short conversation with his instructing solicitor regarding the final details of the case. 'Thank you, Mr Flowers. I will see you in court on Monday,' he finished, nodding at the response he got before replacing the receiver. He turned once more to the papers, his mind wandering to the social event he was looking forward to attending that evening.

Maurice Flowers replaced the receiver and glanced down at his own desk, which seemed to overflow with papers requiring his attention. He smiled as he recalled his first day in office, many years ago, when there had only been one piece of paper and he had wondered if business would ever improve. The fact that every one of the hundreds of pieces of paper that now littered his desk represented money in his pocket made his smile grow even larger.

He picked up the papers on Barry Oliver Bourne and looked at the list of witnesses to be called by Defence; no need to contact or worry them just yet, he decided, Prosecution would take up most of the first week and if Mr. Peregrine-Richards' submission went as planned then he may not need any witnesses at all. He anticipated the press to be in full attendance and made a mental note to have enough business cards available to ensure they spelled his name correctly this time; the expected publicity would do his reputation and bank balance nothing but good.

He knew that the majority of his clients were habitual criminals, but the money he received for representing them kept his family in a style to which they all had become very accustomed. He enjoyed his lifestyle, which was of an exceptionally high quality considering that most of his work resulted from word of mouth by previous satisfied clients. He smiled again. *Whoever said that crime doesn't pay couldn't have been a solicitor.*

He picked up the phone and started to dial his home number. He didn't want to be late home this evening because he intended to make the most of his last weekend off for a while. As he waited for the phone at home to be answered, he muttered, 'I wonder what the jury will be like.'

As he stood at his bench on Friday afternoon, George Wright was both happy and nervous that his week at work was almost over. He was in high spirits knowing that another week of assembly-line drudgery was complete, and he was especially looking forward to the prospect of a weekend that he could spend tending his hydrangeas, providing, of course, that the weather forecasters had actually got it right. He was, however, very apprehensive about Monday morning, and raised the question for only the second time in his life: *Why me, God?* The first instance occurred in 1914 after the Army refused his entry due to chronic asthma and flat feet, while all his friends enlisted; he had finally understood the reason four years later when most failed to return.

His first reaction upon receiving the letter was to immediately try to obtain a note from his doctor, and when that failed he had unsuccessfully attempted to obtain a letter from his employer stating that his presence at work was too vital for him to have time off. Both were efforts to be excused jury service. He had never been on a jury before and had fretted about the whole scenario since being summoned. *What will I have to do? Will I do it right?* Too late to worry now, he started to pack away his tools; he would just have to go, and try to make the best of it.

Why on earth his wife should be so pleased that he had to attend he had no idea. Ever since he had handed her the letter she had clucked around him like a mother hen. 'My George, specially chosen,' she had claimed to all her friends with a look of pride, as if he had been awarded a knighthood rather than simply chosen from the electoral register. 'They don't just pick anyone, oh no!' Thoughts of his wife led to the moment that she had commented about how he had put on weight as he had tried on the suit she had pressed for him and was insisting he should wear. Her subsequent lecture about how he should be more careful to resist the in-between-meal snacks from the canteen now he was in his early fifties became blurred, as he battled valiantly to pull in his stomach in order to fasten the trousers. He hoped he didn't have to sit for too long with the buttons straining against the material. It suddenly crossed his mind to wonder whether you were allowed to go to the toilet and what would happen if you were caught short. Whatever happened, the quicker jury service was over and life in the Wright household returned to normal the better. As he reached for

211

his clock-card his thoughts had already switched to one of the most important questions in his world: *what's for tea?*

Barry Bourne sat on his bunk, the tin plate resting in his lap as he studied the contents, wondering what it was supposed to represent. The prisoner who had served the meal had described it as 'sausage and mash', but he wasn't quite sure as every item on the plate seemed to be the same colour and consistency.

Although he was classed as a remand prisoner and, like the others on this wing, was able to wear his own clothes rather than prison garb, he was alone in having to spend all day, apart from one hour in the exercise yard, locked up with his own company. Under normal circumstances he would have probably shared a cell and been allowed to spend his days in the recreation hall, but in view of his profession and the offence he was charged with, he was kept on his own and closely guarded, more for his own protection than anything else. He was fully aware, from the caustic shouts and graphic threats emanating from the other prisoners, that he couldn't remain safe forever though, and understood exactly what would happen to him once he had been sentenced for the theft of the money. He was dreading the prospect and shuddered at the thought of a prison sentence; maybe he could ask to be kept in solitary confinement? Even then, he didn't think he could stand another few years of this, so his only hope was leniency and probation.

Barry had just had the pre-trial conference with his solicitor and it had finally sunk in just how important the submission to be made by his counsel was. Never in his wildest dreams had he visualised the ensuing events when he had first found the bag. He had spent his many solitary hours mentally reviewing all the events of the past six months, and really couldn't understand why no one, other than his wife and defence team, believed his insistence that the death of his closest friend had been a pure accident. Surely the blokes at work, who really knew him, would know it couldn't have been anything else?

He'd been advised that Mr Flowers intended to call Rita Crowe as a character witness, to give evidence on his behalf, and he hoped that she would speak the truth about his friendship with her husband. He desperately needed her to, but Barry was still haunted by the vision of hatred in her eyes when they had briefly met. Rita couldn't possibly think that he had deliberately murdered Martyn, could she?

He used the plastic fork to gently explore the grey mass congealing on his plate and after moving the majority of goo from one side to the other, he located a single black finger-like object; he had found a sausage. *How much longer can I stand eating this shit?* He shook his head in disbelief and carried the plate over to the corner and emptied the contents into his slop bucket, calculating that he still had enough room left in it for his dinner, before he got chance to empty it in the morning.

He sat back on his bed and his thoughts automatically wandered to Mary, as they had done a lot lately. What a pity it had taken this for them to regain their old feelings. *If only …*

I wish I could see him tomorrow! Mary Bourne dismissed the thought as quickly as it had come into her head, remembering the agreement she had made, albeit in a somewhat disgruntled way: no more visits before the commencement of the court case. Not wanting to complicate their newly refreshed relationship, she hadn't told him of her visit to the doctor and his optimistic view that they would certainly be able to have children. She would wait until she was one hundred per cent sure, by which time – and more importantly – she would also know exactly what fate awaited her husband.

I will wait for him, whatever he gets, she had promised to herself. Knowing from their conversations together how much Barry had come to rely on her again, she had no doubt now that their marriage was going to work. Although she had often wondered just what sentence he would receive for stealing the money, not once had she ever given the slightest consideration to him being convicted of murdering Martyn. They had, after all, been the best of friends and it had simply been a tragic accident – that was what Barry had told her, and that was good enough for her. She silently whistled a tune as she made her way into the kitchen to prepare tea. Her mother would be home soon with their dinner – kippers – a real treat! She smiled as she suddenly realised just how hungry she was.

Rita Crowe forced herself to get out of the chair and prepare tea for her sons; after all, all this wasn't their fault. She tried to remember the last time she had been happy. It seemed such a long time ago that the world had seemed such a grand and perfect place. Now it was just an empty wilderness of despair, her life ruined by that evil, selfish, bastard Bourne. *Jealous,* she reasoned as she placed the loaf on the board and picked up the bread knife, *he was jealous of everything Martyn and I had together!*

She slowly plodded to the cupboard to collect jam. She didn't mind that she would have to be up bright and early on Monday morning; it would make a change from her monotonous routine. Mrs Steele had said she would look after the boys, before and after school, for as long as the trial took. She had been very kind and the boys liked her – in fact, the only time Rita saw smiles on their faces lately was when she collected them from Mrs Steele.

Thankfully I don't have to worry when I walk past her *house,* she mused, feeling physically sick at the thought of seeing Mary, who wasn't living at home these days.. *It was* her *husband who killed Martyn. It was her bloody husband who's destroyed our lives.* She seethed. It was Mary's husband who was still alive, and for that she hated her. Her rage flaring, she stopped buttering the bread she had sliced and looked at the photograph of Martyn she always carried with her. She intended to be at the trial each day to ensure he got justice. The tears started to flow and between the sobs, she spluttered her promise: 'Darling, I will make sure you're not cheated.'

Chapter 30

Monday morning started cold and damp. The wind that blew around the court building seemed to match the cold chill of apprehension that was being felt by the whole cast about to play their parts in the performance about to unfold in Assize Court Six, the main court.

In his chambers, well away from the morning draughtiness, Mr Justice Summerfield allowed the attendant allocated to look after him throughout the trial to assist him on with his robes. He enjoyed wearing the scarlet and ermine that denoted him as a criminal judge; however, he was not yet ready to put on his wig. Sometimes, particularly on days like this, it seemed to weigh very heavily and today he felt every one of his sixty-nine years of age.

After a large and relaxing lunch the previous day he had again started to read the file, but must have unknowingly dozed off, for when he awoke the papers had been placed back in their folder on the small table beside him. Since he had not changed his mind on the decision he would make, there they had remained until this morning. He looked at the clock on the wall: just after ten o'clock. He still had time for a small cigar before he made his entrance. One thing he was absolutely certain of: the trial couldn't start without him, whatever the time, and he didn't want to see either barrister in a pre-trial conference before they met in court. Although he knew both men and had respect for them, this morning he simply wanted his own company.

Maurice Flowers positioned himself in Courtroom Six, directly behind and to the right of where Mr Peregrine-Richards would sit. He knew that the counsel did not like being interrupted whilst he was on his feet speaking, but he felt he needed to be in a position where he could lean over and pass anything on to Peregrine-Richards's assistant that he wanted drawn to the barrister's attention, without actually disturbing him. As he sat in the second row from the front of the court, he looked around the impressive courtroom, where everything, with the exception of the metal dock rail and the rich leather seats, was carved or crafted from wood. Whoever had been responsible for designing the building had certainly known their business: it oozed tradition and instinctively felt like a place where justice could and would be served.

He glanced back at the dock where Barry Bourne would soon sit; it consisted of a hard bench surrounded by a cylindrical brass rail and he knew that was where the term 'prisoner at the bar' had originated; it was, appropriately, a very dismal-looking place. He turned round to review the front of the court; the barristers for the prosecution and defence would occupy the front row of benches, their position facing but slightly lower than the clerk of court, who sat immediately below the judge. Accordingly, the whole court was designed so that the judge sat higher than anyone – except those in the public gallery – so that he could look down on the entire proceeding and of course everyone in the courtroom had to look up to him. On his first visit to a courtroom he had wondered why the accused sat so much higher than the legal profession, the prisoner and judge being almost at the same height, until he realised that from this position, the judge could watch the prisoner with an uninterrupted view, whilst the prisoner sitting in the dock was left in no doubt as to who was in charge.

Jerome Peregrine-Richards stood in the bar dressing room

silently rehearsing his pre-planned forthcoming lines. He glanced over and standing at the far end of the room, saw Bartholomew 'Barney' Compton, a fellow Kings Counsel, and the chief prosecutor for the trial. He knew Barney was a fair but hard adversary and they signalled their mutual respect for each other in the form of a nod; he knew, however, that he was in for a difficult ride.

George Wright had decided to take the bus into town, not being sure where to park or how long they let you stay; besides, he and his wife always took the bus because he didn't like driving into the city. He walked through the doors to the main court to stand in the large public reception area, feeling very self-conscious in his less-than-comfortable suit. Wondering if the other people milling around would assume that he was some sort of criminal, he felt a sense of relief when he saw the 'Jury in Waiting' sign and moved over as quickly as possible to stand directly below it, signifying to all in sundry, 'This is why I am here.'

As he waited his eyes wandered over the magnificently ornate architecture of the building. *They don't build them like this any more. There are no craftsmen left with the skill to construct a building as beautiful as this nowadays.* He was so engrossed with the finer details of the design that he nearly missed his name being called and, spinning round, caught sight of a small lady with a clipboard in her hand and wearing an official-looking black cloak that seemed to be losing its battle to remain on her shoulders.

He walked over and stood in front of her as she asked, 'Mr Wright? Mr George Wright?' All he managed to do was meekly nod his head as he watched her tick off his name and indicate with her pencil where she expected him to stand. Feeling very nervous, as if at his first day in school, he moved gingerly over to a small group of people standing by an imposing double door. No one seemed keen to be friendly and he remained equally silent, trying to hold in his stomach as he looked above the door at 'Court No. 6' carved in the stonework. He again wondered what the case was going to be about. *If I've got to be here, then I hope it's half interesting.* He smiled briefly. *At least then I might have some tales to tell down the local when it's all over.*

Barry Bourne sat nervously on the only chair in the cell below Court Six, which, he remembered from his police days, was the main criminal court, while a tight-lipped, stern faced prison officer he had never seen before stood with his back against the wall silently watching him. He could hear nothing from the court above, but knew it would by now be a hive of activity; his solicitor and barrister had already been to see him and then had gone up the steps into the courtroom. *It'll be my turn soon,* he thought, just as a door at the top of the stairs opened and a face appeared. 'Bourne?' He nodded as the voice continued sharply, 'Come on up, then!' and he began to climb the short number of steps, aware that the prison officer was on the stairs right behind him.

Blinking at the sharp lights of the courtroom, he heard the murmurings of those present in the courtroom abruptly stop as he stepped directly into the dock. Told to sit down on the hard wooden bench, as he did so the steady drone of chatter returned. Barry tried to get his bearings: in front of him but slightly higher would sit the judge; directly below the judge, the clerk of court was already busily shuffling papers in preparation for the trial's commencement. He could see the backs of his solicitor and barrister below and in front and, turning round, noted the seats immediately behind him were empty; he couldn't remember which group was supposed to sit there. His gaze lifted up to what he knew was the public gallery, where rows of curious faces looked down at him.

He turned back to face the front and looked sideways at

the two prison officers who would flank him for the duration of the proceedings, their faces seemingly saying, 'Don't even think of trying anything, pal. We've seen every trick in the book.' He had just decided to treat them as if they weren't there when his solicitor, Mr Flowers, turned round to speak. 'Are you all right, Mr Bourne? Any last-minute problems?' Not sure whether he was allowed to speak or not, he simply shook his head and then saw Mr Peregrine-Richards turn round and nod confidently at him. Barry focused his attention on the back of his barrister, who seemed very relaxed and in control; he had started to wonder just how good he really was when his thoughts were interrupted by a loud shout of, 'Court rise!'

Automatically standing to attention, Barry found himself looking directly at Mr Justice Summerfield as he moved impressively into the Court. Counsel bowed sombrely to the judge, who gave a short, curt bow in return. Barry swallowed hard. This was it; his trial was about to begin, and he felt very alone indeed.

George Wright, now on his own outside the courtroom thinking perhaps they didn't need him after all, literally jumped when his name was called and meekly followed the female court usher through the double doors and into the court. Aware that all eyes were now on him, he felt his cheeks grow warm and begin to glow red. He followed his guide as she led him to an enclosed area that contained two rows of seats, then sat on the only vacant chair left.

'Will you please stand!'

George Wright knew that the hissing voice was addressing him, and was just as aware that his cheeks were now burning crimson. *Why had he sat down?*

The man to whom the voice belonged, sitting directly below the judge, stood up and turned to face him. 'Are you George William Wright?'

George Wright gulped and nodded affirmatively.

'You must answer yes or no,' said the voice in exasperation.

'Yes, sir,' said George submissively, sensing everyone watching him and wondering if he was going to get anything right. He heard the judge say to someone, he didn't know who, 'Any objections?' and watched as two men, dressed identically in wigs and gowns, stood up in turn and proclaimed, 'No objections, My Lord.' The clerk of court then addressed George Wright, asking him to pick up the Bible from the ledge in front of him and helping him through the solemn oath that had to be taken by all jurors. He managed to complete this task without further mishap, even waiting to be told to sit down before doing so again. *I'm beginning to get the hang of this,* he thought. *It's just like home; don't do anything until you are told to.* As he took his seat, he attempted a wry smile at the thin man sitting next to him but got no response. When he realised the judge had turned to face them and was about to speak, he took a deep breath and tried to concentrate on what was being said.

'Members of the jury, you have been chosen to sit and hear a very difficult case. However, there are a number of points of law that have to be raised before the trial can begin. Now, the law is solely my province and I intend to deal with it in your absence. It is not a matter that you need concern yourselves with. You might feel, however, that this would be an ideal opportunity for you to elect a foreman of your jury. I apologise for the inconvenience right at the start, but will you now please follow the court usher and leave the courtroom.'

No sooner had the final words left the judge's lips than a previously unnoticed door, carved in the same wood as the rest, opened at the back of the jury box and George Wright got up and shuffled along the row of seats towards it. He found himself in a bit of a bottleneck of bodies, and while waiting for the other jurors to get into the side room, he found himself looking into the face of a young man sitting between two prison warders, whose eyes returned his gaze before he began to move towards the side room again. *I wonder what you've done.*

The rising of Mr Peregrine-Richards immediately silenced the hushed conversations that had started as soon as the jury started to file out, and he formally requested to be allowed to present a submission to the court. The submission had been agreed beforehand and this was a legal formality to be recorded in the court records so that justice was seen to be done.

Having received Mr Justice Summerfield's formal consent, for the next forty-five minutes he reasoned, pleaded and practically begged that the two matters in this case should be dealt with separately. When he finally sat down he knew that he had done the best he could. Almost immediately, Mr Bartholomew Compton stood up for the prosecution to contest the submission, and proceeded with far less compassion to indicate his belief that the matters should be dealt with together.

Barry Bourne listened intently to both speeches, and although he knew his opinion was biased, it seemed to him a mere formality that the cases would be split; based on Defence's arguments, there was clearly no other decision.

Mr Justice Summerfield sat motionless as he listened to the respective counsels' arguments. He had discovered long ago that it was easier to sit with his elbow on the top of the desk in front of him with his head resting on his open hand. Through years of practice he had found he could comfortably spend all day like this in court and not miss a word being said. To many in the court it gave the mistaken impression that he was asleep, and on a number of occasions he had added a couple more years to the sentence of a prisoner who thought it clever to mock him while he supposedly slumbered.

He was very pleased he hadn't allowed a pre-trial conference with counsel, for out of courtesy and protocol, he would have been required to inform them that he had already made his decision on the submission. Both cases would be dealt with together and he would leave any criticism of his decision to the Appeal Court judges. Mr Peregrine-Richards and his client, he knew already, were going to be very disappointed men.

George Wright had found an empty chair in the jury room and sat down. He turned to the man sitting beside him and tried to break the icy silence. 'Hello. Any idea what this case is about?'

The man looked at him with surprise written all over his face. 'Don't you know? It's been in the papers for weeks. It's about those two coppers, they say the one in there murdered the other.'

George Wright winced. *A murder case!* He instinctively knew he wasn't going to like this one little bit. He had of course read all about it in the papers and heard it on the news, but hadn't expected to be involved in it.

The court usher addressed the jury. 'It might be a good time now, as His Lordship suggested, to select a foreman. I use the word *man*,' – he looked apologetically at the four women present – 'because His Lordship prefers just that, a man to be chosen.'

Not exactly sure why or how it had happened, fifteen minutes later when the jury were recalled back into the court, they had selected as their foreman of the jury a bemused George Wright.

A bitterly disappointed Barry Bourne watched the jury of eight men and four women as they filed back into the court, and who would never know of the decision that had been reached in their absence. He felt very tired, his dejected thoughts rudely interrupted by the clerk of court, who stood up and spoke directly to him.

'Prisoner at the bar, please stand.'

Barry stood less ramrod stiff than before and held on to the rail in an effort to stop his knees shaking, as the clerk continued, 'Are you Barry Oliver Bourne?'

Barry, having earlier decided it would be unwise to seem flippant by using the title 'My Lord', simply replied, 'Yes, sir.'

Reading from an official-looking piece of paper he was holding in front of him, the clerk stated, 'There are two charges on the indictment against you. Firstly that against the peace of our Sovereign Queen, on the seventeenth of February 1952 you did wilfully murder Martyn Christopher Crowe. How do plead – guilty or not guilty?'

There was a momentary pause, during which the courtroom was in complete silence, before Barry lifted up his head and replied in a clear voice, 'Not guilty, sir!'

The clerk of court bent down and recorded the official response on the Court document before continuing, 'The second charge states that on the fourth of February 1952 you did steal property, namely cash to the value of twenty-five thousand pounds, the property of some person or persons unknown. How do you plead – guilty or not guilty?'

Barry was aware of the collective gasp that had reverberated around the court as the amount of money had been read out; he knew that in most cases these people were working all hours to take home a mere three pounds a week, and for some reason he became very irritated when he saw, out of the corner of his eye, his barrister nodding. He heard himself answer in a clear voice, 'Guilty, sir!'

The clerk bent down once more to annotate the court document and Barry felt a pressure on his right shoulder as the prison warder ushered him to sit back down. He did so with immense relief, for only he knew just how shaky his legs were, as the strangest thought crossed his mind. *I never knew Martyn's middle name had been Christopher.*

George Wright's eyebrows had automatically risen when he heard the amount of money followed by a guilty plea; he had thought it only to be a murder case. He was wondering what the cash had to do with it, when he overheard a female member of the jury sitting behind him whisper softly, 'You can tell he's guilty. Just look at his eyebrows. Never trust anyone with eyebrows like that.' *What the bloody hell had the shape of his eyebrows got to do with anything?* George Wright immediately made up his mind. *There might be others here who already think he's guilty but I am going to listen to all the evidence and then come to a decision.*

Mr Justice Summerfield listened to the crescendo of disbelief in the court as the sum of money was read out and the plea made, realising that his earlier decision was now having the negative effect he had feared. He could almost hear their minds whirring, '*Charged with theft and murder. Guilty of theft, so therefore must be guilty of murder. They wouldn't have charged him with both if he wasn't guilty of both.*' He glanced to his left at the jury and in particular at the plump middle-aged man they had chosen as their foreman; at least he seemed alert and fairly intelligent. Looking at the clock, he made up his mind to give everyone involved some breathing space and announced his decision to break early for lunch, hoping the extended interval would give them an opportunity to calm down. To the call of 'Court rise,' he pushed back his chair, got up and slowly exited the courtroom.

Barry Bourne returned to sit in the cell below the court and lit a cigarette, watching the smoke slowly curling through his yellow, nicotine-stained fingers. Since his arrest he had started smoking heavily, often feeling too nauseous to eat. He flicked ash on the sandwich he had been provided for lunch, which steadfastly remained on the plate. He was not looking forward at all to what was about to follow.

Chapter 31

During the successive days, as one court session followed another, Prosecution resolutely presented the facts of its case. However, as each witness was called and gave evidence, it became painfully obvious to anyone possessing a modicum of legal knowledge that the decision made by the judge at the commencement of the proceedings was the only thing making this murder trial continue. Mr Justice Summerfield, having adopted his favourite position, listened as the case unfolded and realised without a shadow of a doubt that his pre-planned decision had been the wrong one. Prosecution so carefully and skilfully blended the theft with the death that it was almost impossible to separate one from the other, resulting in the accused being incorrectly tried for murder simply because he was a thief.

The album of photographs had images graphically showing the bloodied dead body followed immediately by pictures of the money stacked in piles, with the bloodstained notes highlighted to the greatest effect. The bloodstains on the cash had in fact nothing to do with the murder of Detective Sergeant Crowe; however, the way the evidence had been displayed was certainly having the desired effect where it mattered most – on the jury.

Mr Bartholomew Compton went to great lengths to prove that the blood on the money belonged to David Smith; he had gone to the same lengths to prove that the blood on the handkerchief found secreted in the canvas bag belonged to

David Smith and had skilfully proved that the handkerchief belonged to the accused. The evidence that David Smith was killed by Charles Morgan, who was himself dead, was presented in scant detail; however, the fact that Charles Morgan had been killed in an area normally patrolled by the accused was given great prominence.

Mrs Sharpe, the accused's mother-in-law, gave rather sensational evidence of what she had seen inside the shed, after the incident with Martyn had happened; the fact that she had in fact witnessed nothing of the death itself was not mentioned.

The Forensic Science Officer dramatically showed to great effect the position of the fingerprints of the accused as they appeared on the handle of the chisel, thinking it of no importance to explain that it would probably have been held that way during the course of its normal use.

The confession statement of the accused was read out by the prosecutor, who kept referring, with laughter in his voice, to the 'very convenient spider' that happened to be in 'the right place at the right time', using every trick in the book to ridicule the series of events as told by the accused. He even described how a detailed search for the offending creature by police officers had proved fruitless.

By intermingling murder and theft witnesses, Mr Bartholomew Compton continued to ply his crafty trade. That this method was starting to cause confusion to the legal minds present left little doubt as to the effect it was having on the unlegal minds of the jurors.

Mr Justice Summerfield was also painfully aware that his decision had meant that the defence counsel were unable to cause any upset of evidence during cross-examination, as there were very few points to question. He leaned forward to make a note on his pad to remind him when the time came, thinking perhaps he could assist during his summing up. As he finished writing he discovered he was looking straight into the eyes of Mr Peregrine-Richards and, unable to hold the gaze, he looked away quickly.

Yes, you've made an utter mess of this, haven't you? Mr Peregrine-Richards looked accusingly and saw the judge look away, embarrassed. It had been a ridiculous decision; they might just have well charged his client with being an accessory to the murder of David Smith. Prosecution, by using every sneaky ploy, was ultimately controlling the evidence and he wasn't able to retaliate. He started to tap his pencil on the table out of sheer and utter frustration, well aware that to the onlookers in the courtroom, who didn't understand what was occurring, he would appear to be failing in his duty to defend his client by not cross-examining the witnesses with any vigour. *How the hell could he?* He was only legally able to cross-examine on particular questions asked by Prosecution, and that cunning bastard was avoiding asking any of those.

As he tapped the table, like an uneven metronome, he was conscious of the fact that the judge had expected him to vigorously attack the fingerprint expert, and he had dutifully obliged. 'Could the chisel have been used that way in the normal course of woodwork?'

'Yes, possibly,' was the begrudged response.

Mr Peregrine-Richards he knew couldn't labour the point – after all, there were only so many different ways to ask the same question before the hackles of the jury started to rise and they became bored. He tried to be firm when questioning his client's mother-in-law, and although he got her to freely admit that she hadn't actually seen anything of the death of Martyn Crowe, he had been unable to prevent her becoming hysterical when she'd described seeing the body, and before he could stop her, she blundered into the details of the cash. *That money will be the death of you, Mr Bourne,* he mused while returning to the bench as Prosecution called its next witness. He turned his head slightly so that he could see his client out of the corner of his eye. *You had better be bloody good in that witness box, my lad.*

He was still deep in thought when he heard the judge speak his name. 'Your witness, Mr Peregrine-Richards!'

He forced his mind back to the present and instinctively replied, 'Thank you my Lord,' as he slowly climbed to his feet trying to think what he was going to say.

Maurice Flowers, sitting directly behind, could almost feel the frustration radiating from his barrister; he knew that try as he might, Mr Peregrine-Richards was getting absolutely nowhere at all with any of the witnesses. He realised that the case could well hinge on what he had discussed with counsel during their pre-trial meetings, when they had both questioned how effective PC Bourne was going to be when put on the stand and, the biggest question of all, whether the jury would believe him.

Maurice Flowers looked over to the eight men and four women who held the fate of his client in their hands. One of the women was indifferently filing her nails, two of the gentlemen in the back row looked almost asleep, and one fellow had spent the last few minutes smiling at an attractive young lady in the public gallery; at least the foreman seemed to be paying attention. Maurice Flowers had never been a strong believer in the jury system; how could you have the best legal brains arguing and discussing the intricate facts of a life-or-death case and then leave the final decision to butchers, bakers and candlestick makers, whose choice often depended on which opposing counsel they liked best or what the media suggested should happen.

George Wright ached from the effort of trying to sit still and concentrate on every word while his waistband dug into his stomach. He sneaked a glance at the others in the jury box. Was he the only one paying attention? Was he the only one who realised the awesome responsibility that had been placed on their shoulders? He had long ago given up trying to take notes; finding that while he was writing down the point he wanted to remember he was missing what was being said afterwards, and so he decided to concentrate and hope he could remember all that was being said.

From conversations in the jury room during the regular breaks afforded by the judge, he discovered that all four women had found the photograph album upsetting; two had even been reduced to tears there in the courtroom. George had never seen a photograph of a dead body before – come to that, he had never seen a dead body, even though there had been two world wars in his lifetime. He was surprised by how unmoved he was – in fact, he found them rather interesting and studied them in great detail.

However, he was aware that on the evidence of the photographs alone, some of his peers had already made up their minds as to the guilt of the accused and so weren't paying any attention to the words being spoken. He had even picked up a piece of paper dropped accidentally by a female juror and found it to be a shopping list. He'd become slightly depressed at the conversations taking place during the lunch break: 'Waste of time, he's as guilty as sin'; 'it's obvious that even his own Defence thinks he's guilty, because he's not trying very hard.' *Am I the only one who's hearing the evidence that it was an accident?* George realised that his fellow jury members were being influenced, albeit subconsciously, by the actions of the defence team. He tried to push the impending headache away as he leaned forward and renewed his concentration.

Barry Bourne had long given up his act of confidence and sat shell-shocked and frightened as he remembered the words of Maurice Flowers: 'Mr Bourne, when it comes down to it, your life could depend on how you appear when giving evidence. Martyn Crowe was the only other person who could have told the jury it was an accident, but he's dead.'

How the hell do I convince these people that I'm not a killer, when I've already admitted to being a thief? He was also seriously starting to doubt his counsel's wisdom in calling Rita Crowe to give evidence for the defence. Sure, she knew that he and Martyn had been good friends and that he had no reason to kill him, but did she believe he was innocent? He had considered asking Mary to have a word with her, but if it came out in court that any collusion had taken place, the jury might get the wrong impression and presume he was trying to interfere with a witness, and that would just be another nail in his coffin. He inwardly squirmed as the thought entered his head. There had been times during the trial when he had wanted to stand up and scream at the top of his voice that it had been an accident, an unfortunate and tragic accident, but who would believe him? Only Mary! Would this nightmare never end?

Mary Bourne sat in the same place every day, at one end of the public bench in main reception, frustrated that she couldn't hear any of the evidence that the media were reporting proved her husband was a murderer, which she knew he was not. *Perhaps, when it's my turn, I can convince the jury he is innocent.* She wasn't confident in the task even though she would certainly try and do her very best. She turned slightly to look at the former friend at the other end of the reception area where Rita sat face forward, her knees and feet together with her hands in her lap, alongside the policewoman that permanently accompanied her. Mary had been told Rita was going to be called as a defence witness and wondered how she felt and what her reaction would be in Court.

Rita sat motionless, as she had done during each day of the trial; she was there to keep the promise made to the photograph of her dead husband to ensure justice was done. Or was it revenge? Throughout the days she had silently chanted her own personal mantra: *An eye for an eye! An eye for an eye!*

Rita still missed Martyn with all her heart. The hollow feeling that filled her stomach every day would not go away, but the nights were the worst. When she did eventually manage to cry herself to sleep her mind played tricks on her and she often woke thinking Martyn was still alive. She had forgotten how many times she had mistaken a shadow on the pillow next to hers for her husband's hair and how she had stretched out her arm to draw him closer, only to find the space empty. She felt totally alone and didn't know if she could cope for much longer. With a loud sigh, her eyes seemingly sinking further into their black-edged sockets, she forced herself to promise to carry on for the sake of the boys.

Mr Justice Summerfield looked at his watch again. There was only two hours left until the end of the Friday afternoon session and therefore the week's sitting. As Prosecution's case was almost at an end he decided not to let Defence begin its evidence today. He would give all the parties concerned the weekend to mull over what they had heard, and that way the jury should come in on Monday morning and listen to Defence with a fresh and open mind. *Yes,* he thought, *it'll do the jury good to have a couple of days' rest.* He then looked up and saw the desolate expression on the face of the accused, as he stared into space. The judge's thought then mirrored that of the defence team: *I hope you are good, young man, when it comes to giving evidence. Your life is surely going to depend on it.*

His attention returned to the proceedings as he heard Mr Bartholomew Compton declare, 'That is the case for the prosecution, my Lord.'

'Thank you,' Mr Justice Summerfield replied, simultaneously raising his hand in a motion to stop Mr Peregrine-Richards from rising. He turned to the jury. 'Members of the jury, this has been a long week and I feel that we can all benefit from a break.' He paused to let his words sink in. 'You are of course reminded not to discuss the case with anyone other than fellow jurors or follow the media, so as not to be influenced by the views of others; rather you must decide the case on the evidence alone, when and only when you have heard all the facts of the case. The Court will now adjourn until ten thirty on Monday morning.'

As he saw the judge begin to move from his leather chair, the clerk of court ordered, 'Court rise!'

Mr Peregrine-Richards leaned uncomfortably back on the bench seat, which seemed to catch him on the same spot so that his back ached, and spoke quietly to Maurice Flowers. 'The old man's probably right for once. We've all had enough – I know I have. Perhaps it will go better on Monday.' Without waiting for a response, he turned back and gathered up his papers as he started moving along the bench, relieved to be getting out of the courtroom.

Some cases left him with a nasty taste in the mouth, and this was certainly one of them. He wasn't winning, he wasn't even drawing – no, he knew he was lagging far behind on points and had no knockout blow to counteract it. His client was innocent and it was down to him to convince the jury. *But how?*

George Wright was glad that the week was over and he couldn't get away from the jury room fast enough – even now he dreaded the thought that he would have to return on Monday. The past five days had been nothing at all like he had expected and he certainly didn't want the responsibility for another man's life on his conscience. As he made his way towards the bus stop he hoped that it would be fine weather tomorrow so he could lose himself in his garden, where he knew what he was doing. *Time to plant the potatoes. At least with my flowers and veggies I know exactly where I am.*

*   *   *

Sitting down without thinking as he arrived back in his cell beneath the courtroom, Barry suddenly shot to his feet and caused his escorts to leap back defensively.

'Sorry about that,' he apologised. 'I've had enough sitting down; I just wanted to stretch my legs.' He saw the warders relax as he walked around the perimeter of the confined space using his hands to rub some life back in the cheeks of his backside, wondering whether to be happy or sad at the adjournment. He had half hoped that he would give evidence today to explain his side of the story; he had worked himself up and was ready. He only hoped that he would be as ready on Monday. Barry was relieved Mary would not be allowed to visit him in prison while the trial continued, but hopefully it would soon be over and then they would both know what the future held in store for them.

Mrs Sharpe had decided to take her daughter away for the weekend, arguing that the break would do her good. Mary was at first reluctant, knowing how difficult it would be for him to keep his spirits up in that dingy place, but she would actually see him again on Monday, when she was due to give evidence. As she finally left to go to the police house they had shared for so many years, to pack the few extra things she would need, she remembered their parting kiss as she left Barry in the cell. It was wonderful, and no matter how long she had to wait for him, that kiss held the promise of far better things to come.

Mary stood unhappily in their old house which held nothing but bad memories for her. She had packed the few additional items she needed and, opening the front door, went to leave. As she did so, she became frozen to the spot. A police car slid silently to a halt at the kerb three doors away and Rita Crowe stepped out; an officer from the station had dropped her home. Mary knew that all the sympathies of their husband's ex-colleagues and families were with her old friend, but funnily enough she didn't care. She heard the officer shout through the open car window, 'See you Monday morning, Mrs Crowe, same time as usual,' before he drove off.

Mary was glad she would be away for the weekend and, glancing at her watch, she locked the door and began to hurry down the road, hoping to be in time to catch an earlier bus.

Rita Crowe stood with her back against the closed front door. She dreaded spending time in her house on her own, as it felt like her tomb; at least the boys would be there in about a quarter of an hour, and although they always came running in and hugged her, they were sad now where they used to be happy. Her head bent down dejectedly and she noticed the two buff-coloured envelopes lying on the mat. After bending to retrieve them she slipped off her coat and took the letters into the sitting room.

Both letters open on her lap, she sat absolutely confused and dumbfounded on the settee, the ripped open envelopes lying where they had dropped on the floor. Her mind struggled to comprehend the two pieces of earth-shattering news she had just received. She picked up the top letter and read it again. *A summons!* It was a witness summons for her to give evidence on Monday morning for the defence, in the murder trial of her husband. *Surely they've made a mistake?* She reread every line, but soon realised they hadn't. 'How dare they!' she exclaimed as she screwed the letter into a ball and flung it across the room. She had been informed several weeks ago that she was on the Defence Witness List but had dismissed the idea as a ridiculous formality, however, the letter on her lap stated the contrary, it was confirmed that on Monday she was to give evidence on behalf of the man who had killed her beloved Martyn. Her initial outrage subsided into a mood of sheer and utter despair as she turned to the second letter. *An eviction notice!* She forced herself to read past the heading in red ink at the top of the paper which seemed to scream at her – 'Notice of Eviction'. She had known that sooner or later she would have to leave the police house where Martyn and she had made their home, but had never expected it to happen so rapidly, even though the letter explained that it was being done in her own best interests, for she would be immediately re-housed by the city council. As she repeated the word 'eviction' to herself, she felt a deep stigma of shame, one that she knew she had no cause to feel as she had done absolutely nothing wrong. But when it came down to it, this was really the final straw: she'd been made a widow by a rotten bastard of a murderer, her children had no father, and now none of them had a home.

She laid her head back and sobbed. *Martyn would've known what to do.* He had always made her feel so secure, like she was cocooned in a shell of safety. *Why aren't you here when I need you most?* she inwardly pleaded, as she picked up the crumpled letter, which she then flattened as best she could before placing it with the other on her lap underneath a notepad she retrieved from the bureau drawer. Calmly, Rita Crowe began to write.

Mindlessly, she rose and walked over to the mantel shelf, where she picked up the small bottle, hidden behind the clock, full of the yellow sleeping tablets she had been prescribed. She hadn't wanted them but was now thankful for the doctor's insistence. In a daze she moved into the kitchen and, lighting one of the gas rings, poured some milk into a saucepan, before including the contents of the small bottle, watching the tablets float until they dissolved in the warming liquid. She threw the empty bottle towards the bin in the corner, neither noticing nor caring that it missed its intended target and landed on its side upon the kitchen floor. The words 'Warning: Do not exceed the stated dose' flashed their advice to the world. She pulled out a tray before pouring the hot milk equally into three cups and adding a plate of biscuits. Carrying the tray and its contents into the sitting room, she placed it on the small table in front of the settee, just as the front door burst open and her two sons came running in. 'Hello, Mummy,' was their joint shout as they hugged and kissed her, before seeing the milk and biscuits on the tray.

'Thanks Mummy,' said James as both boys started to devour their biscuits.

'Come and sit down beside me and let's have our warm drinks together,' she said, and both her sons jumped onto the settee, one either side of her as they drank the warm milk.

Rita smiled, finished her milk in two gulps and settled back with her arms around each of her sons, who nuzzled into her.

Chapter 32

Mr Justice Summerfield was glad when Monday morning arrived. He had left the judges' quarters for his own home on Friday evening but it had been a very disappointing and uneventful weekend. He was looking forward to getting the trial out of the way. This was the last one of the present assizes and all being well, on Wednesday or Thursday at the latest, he should be safely back in his own house with this mess well and truly behind him. He could then enjoy a welcome break until January, when the next session began. Regrettably, he was beginning to enjoy the breaks more than the work and considered that perhaps he was getting too old. Seeing the chauffeur who had been sent to pick him up standing discreetly by the door, he smiled.

'I won't be a moment,' he said, rising from his chair and receiving a slight bow of the head in acknowledgement.

Mr Peregrine-Richards and Mr Flowers stood in their respective offices looking at the paperwork that had amassed on the desks during their enforced absences. Both knew that they would be pleased when this matter was over and done with, so they could return to the normality of their particular lives.

George Wright was in very low spirits as he travelled to the court by bus. Although the weekend weather had been good and he had spent the time he wanted tending his crops and flowers, he had not been able to rid himself of the depression that hung over him like a dark cloud. His wife had wanted to know every detail of the trial and seemed indignantly surprised and shocked when he would not tell her anything. Even when he tried to explain what the judge had said and told her that he had taken an oath on the Bible, she had simply muttered, 'Whatever happened to the trust between a man and his wife?' Subsequently they had hardly spoken to each other and he didn't like the atmosphere at all. They had never behaved like that in their thirty years of marriage, and the sooner the trial was over the better.

Barry Bourne was grateful that Monday had arrived, wanting to get it over with. He had surprised himself by missing the routine of prison life while he had been in court. In prison he didn't have to think for himself; every minute of every day and night was mapped out for him, when to eat, when to sleep, when to walk and when to wash. Feeling protected and secure there, all he wanted to do today was to give his evidence and get back to the safety of the prison.

Mary Bourne had enjoyed her weekend away at the cottage of her mother's cousin. They had shopped together on Saturday and her mother had treated her to a blouse she had seen and liked. It would have been extra special had Barry been with her, but she was quite content knowing where he was and that she didn't have to worry what he was up to. Like her husband, she too wanted to get the ordeal of giving evidence over and sent a mental prayer hoping she would not let him down.

Police Constable Trevor Arnott knocked at the door of what he still thought of as Detective Sergeant Crowe's house and was surprised when he got no reply. Every day last week he had received an immediate answer, almost as if Mrs Crowe was glad to see him and get out of the house. He knocked harder this time and felt a sudden chill travel up his spine as the door swung silently open. He stepped inside, shouting, 'Mrs Crowe? Are you there, Mrs Crowe? It's me, Trevor Arnott, I've come to take you to court.' With no reply forthcoming, he felt the hairs on the back of his neck stand up and a terribly uneasy feeling come over him. He shouted again as he moved towards the open sitting-room door.

PC Arnott reached into his pocket and pulled out his handkerchief to cover his mouth, trying desperately not to vomit, although his stomach was performing cartwheels and threatening to immediately expel his breakfast. He picked up the telephone on the hall table and began to dial the station. He did not know or care who would answer, for all he could say when the connection was made was, 'PC Arnott, I need assistance. Please get some help. They are all dead, even the kids.' He let the receiver fall to the floor and leant back against the door frame with his head on the wall, as the tears began to flow down his face. He was unable to move or to say anything; all he could see in his mind's eye was those two tiny lifeless bodies curled up in their mother's arms and a note lying on top of two crumpled letters. The words of the note etched forever in his brain.

'*Gone to find Martyn. He will know what to do.*'

Chapter 33

Maurice Flowers remained completely unfazed as he was informed about the death of his witness and her two children, never once giving the slightest thought to the fact that it might have been his summons which had caused her to commit suicide. His biggest concern was that his client didn't find out before he'd had the chance to give evidence, and his only regret was that he couldn't stop word circulating around the courtroom. He could only wonder what effect the information would have on the members of the jury, when they heard.

Mr Peregrine-Richards stood with his eyes raised to the heavens as Mr Flowers informed him of the sombre news. *Why did I take the blasted case in the first place?* He had arrived at court that morning with a fresh optimism, believing that everything that could go wrong with this trial had already gone wrong. *Just shows you how mistaken you can be*, he reflected before agreeing with his solicitor, who said, 'We've got to get Police Constable Bourne into that witness box before he gets a chance to hear the gossip!'

Barry Bourne plodded up the stairs and into the dock, where he sat down on the now familiar bench, quickly sensing an atmosphere of apprehension and disbelief as he peered over the rail to look around the courtroom. Where were the barristers? They were normally present in plenty of time to await the arrival of the Judge. *What the hell's happened?* he wondered as he watched small groups of people whispering animatedly. A cluster of media people listening intently to the words of a woman with a press pass suddenly lowered their heads in a display of mourning before she scurried off to the next huddle. No one looked in his direction, and Barry tried to shake off the feeling of concern, believing it was his own nervousness at the prospect of giving evidence that was causing him to have the jitters. *I'm as ready as I'll ever be*, he thought as he looked up at the courtroom clock and wondered what the delay in starting was all about.

Mary Bourne had arrived at court early, and as she had been instructed by Mr Flowers, had not spoken to anyone, but had headed directly for the witness room, for she could not go into court until after she had given evidence. She had also been informed by Mr Flowers that Rita had been called as a character witness but hadn't considered, until now, what would happen if Rita entered the room. *What on earth will I say?* She mulled over the thought, before hoping that perhaps they would save her the embarrassment and have her waiting in a different room. She hadn't noticed the time and the delayed start.

It was the court usher in charge of the jury who whispered the reason for the delay, and the words went round the jury room like wildfire. George Wright, the depression of the previous week still in his system, nodded eagerly when he, one of the male jurors commented, 'The bastard should hang for them as well,' as they heard that the dead police officer's widow had take her own life and that of her two young children. He immediately felt extremely guilty at having allowed himself to agree without thought and he chastised himself, knowing he had to keep a clear mind so he could do the job properly, but his head had already started to ache and he knew it was going to be a bad day.

Mr Justice Summerfield could not believe the news when it was relayed to him by his allocated attendant, 'Unbelievable!' his only reply. *Well,* he thought to himself as he straightened the collar of his robes, *I know one thing for sure; I'm not going to delay the trial. Mr Peregrine-Richards will just have to carry on.* He had never been certain in his own mind that calling the deceased officer's widow as a witness for the Defence had been such a good idea, although he'd understood the logic of the Defence barrister, who'd wanted to use her to destroy any motive that Prosecution may have tried to establish. *Well, they can't call her now, so let's see what else they've got in their bag of magic tricks.* He rose from his chair and, with a slightly despondent sigh, dismissed all further cynical thoughts and settled his wig on his head, before moving wearily towards the door to the court.

Barry Bourne returned to the dock after giving his evidence and sank gratefully onto the bench. He was suddenly surprised just how different the court looked from the witness box. *Nowhere near as foreboding as from here, but I guess that's how it's supposed to be.* His position in the witness box had placed him slightly above but next to the fattest man in the jury box, and because he had a jolly, rounded face, Barry had tried to look at him constantly as he spoke. Thereby he had discovered the whole experience not to have been as terrible as he had previously imagined. He had concentrated on simply telling the truth, no matter how firm or unpleasant Prosecution had tried to be; he had definitely coped better than he'd previously thought he would. Throughout his evidence, Barry had tried very hard to convince everyone present that despite stealing the money, which he now honestly bitterly regretted, the death of his friend, through a horribly tragic accident, was the worst fact of the whole scenario.

He had not been sitting back in the dock long when Mr Flowers reached back and handed one of the prison warders a folded piece of paper. Quickly scanning the words, he passed the note to Barry. Thinking it a note to say how well he had done and how pleased his counsel was with his performance in the witness box, Barry smiled as he opened the paper before his jaw literally dropped as he read. He immediately glanced in the direction of his solicitor, hoping to see a huge grin and hand pointed in his direction to conclude the sick joke. But instead, Mr Flowers gravely nodded his head and turned his back. *Rita and the boys, dead – suicide!* He sat looking at the floor of the dock as he asked himself incredulously over and over, *Why?* Then his thoughts started to darken. *I was godfather to James – oh no! Oh no! Don't tell me she did it because of me? Please God, don't let that be it!* Barry had not noticed that his wife had been called and was starting to give evidence. He could hear nothing except the loud pounding of blood in his head. He began to feel faint and grabbed hold of the edge of the bench to stop himself from falling.

Mary Bourne was concerned and confused as she sat in a seat at the back of the Court. She couldn't understand why Barry hadn't looked at her at all during her time in the witness box, even though she had smiled broadly in his direction when she had entered. He had seemed to be looking at his feet the whole time and she thought he looked ill. Had her evidence gone that badly? Had she said the right things? As instructed, she had stood up straight and spoken in a clear voice in answer to all the questions presented by Mr Peregrine-Richards and had calmly waited for Prosecution to quiz her. She had been uneasily puzzled when she heard him say, 'I have no questions of this witness,' but was now totally confused as she had heard Barry's Defence counsel say their case was over, just as she was taking her seat. *Where was Rita?*

Chapter 34

Maurice Flowers sat and listened to the closing speeches from opposing counsels, paying close attention to their words, taking in their whole manner of presentation. He always found these to be an invaluable source of material from which he would unashamedly copy select statements for his future attempts to confuse and bamboozle the ordinary lay magistrates presiding in his cases. As he made relevant notes, he recalled his client, PC Bourne, who he considered had performed excellently in the witness box, with no dramatics or stupidity as had often happened with others in the past. PC Bourne had been calm and straightforward. *But,* wondered Maurice – and it was an enormous 'but' – *had he been able to convince the jury?*

Mr Peregrine-Richards sat down knowing that the text of his closing speech had not flowed as he had intended it to, because of the last-minute alterations following the death of Mrs Crowe. He looked down at his crib sheet and noted all the deletions and amendments that ultimately had watered down the argument proving his client's innocence, and as a result his professional pride had been dented with the knowledge of having not done his client justice. He settled down to pay attention, as he knew everyone else was, to the closing speech from the judge.

* * *

Mr Justice Summerfield knew that the twelve persons of the jury had sole control over what the verdict was to be. However, first they all had to agree on one verdict or else the trial had to be held all over again. He shuddered for a moment at an idea mentioned in a recent legal conference, which had alluded to the idea that in order to speed up trials in the future they might only have to rely on a majority of the jurors agreeing. Imagine having to sentence a man to death if only just over half of the jury thought he should hang! He didn't know what to dread the most, verdict by majority or all-women juries; both seemed equally obnoxious.

Without a doubt he knew that the accused, Barry Oliver Bourne, was not guilty of the murder of Martyn Christopher Crowe, and now he had to convince the jury during his summing up to agree with him. He always prepared his text by following a tried-and-tested method passed on to him by a senior judge, basing it on what he thought the verdict should be. If he believed the accused was guilty then he began by giving all the reasons why he should be found 'not guilty', before concentrating on the other side, which would drive those reasons out of the minds of the jury and thereby convince them of the guilt of the accused. In this case he used exactly the same strategy, but with a 'not-guilty' verdict in mind – he briefly listed the reasons why they should convict PC Bourne of murder; and then, for the considerable remaining period, he discussed in great detail each piece of evidence as to why they should acquit him of murder. He endeavoured, without actually ordering or shouting at them, to drum into the heads of each jury member the phrase 'beyond reasonable doubt'. *Surely one of them, perhaps the foreman, must have formed a reasonable doubt? After all, I only need one!*

Not by accident, Mr Justice Summerfield completed his

summing up first thing on Tuesday morning. He could have finished his speech late on Monday evening and then sent the jury out to deliberate their verdict, but that might have meant they would have been stuck in court all evening or even worse overnight, and putting them up in hotels plus the additional expense of extra security was heavily frowned upon for budgetary reasons. He had originally planned to finish about twenty minutes after the session had started that morning and was only three minutes out in his timing. That, he surmised, would give the jury the rest of the day which he hoped would be long enough, to consider their verdict. He felt that his summing up had been more than fair; Prosecution might complain it had been biased against them, but Mr Justice Summerfield doubted it, and Defence would have been more than pleased. Of course, there would be criticism from the Court of Appeal should the case have to go there, which he earnestly hoped wouldn't happen. All in all he was extremely pleased with himself as he prepared to send the jury out; he intended now to relax in his chambers with a well-earned large cigar and an even larger measure of port.

Mr Peregrine-Richards and Maurice Flowers both agreed, as the members of the jury disappeared through the door, that the judge's summing up had gone in their favour and it was obvious to them both that he had thought their client innocent, which made a welcome change from most of their cases. *Surely no juror who had been paying the slightest attention could have failed to realise what the Judge was almost telling them to do?* Both men noted with satisfaction the grimace pulled by the prosecutor at the end of the summing up; he was clearly in no doubt either.

Barry Bourne slumped down on the chair in the cell below the court and refused any offer of food, knowing that it would have simply stuck in his throat. He dejectedly lit a cigarette in place of nourishment and mulled over the events of the morning. Had he not heard about Rita and the boys he would have been elated – even as a legal layman, he knew that the judge's summing up had been extremely biased in his favour, but none of it held any pleasure for him, with Martyn's wife and sons dead.

Mary Bourne heard as she stepped out of the courtroom. The news hit her like a gigantic body blow so that she had to sit down quickly because she knew if she hadn't she would have fallen. It was too unbelievable. She had only seen Rita going into her house late on Friday afternoon. *Oh my God, surely they couldn't blame Barry for this as well?* As the realisation set in she sat with her head in her hands, grateful she was staying at her mother's, for she knew she couldn't face going back to the police house ever again.

George Wright was the last to enter the jury room, and stood behind the vacant chair at the head of the table while the court usher closed the door behind him and sat down directly outside the door, preventing anyone from entering or leaving until the twelve were ready to deliver their verdict. He viewed his fellow jurors as he pulled at the collar so freshly starched by his wife and that was beginning to rub at his neck. Two of the ladies had gone to the toilet, and most of the men had undone their ties and removed their jackets. One was counting seats before scraping three more chairs along the floor so that they could all sit around the table that was in the centre of the room. He stood and waited the agonising minutes until all the other jurors had settled into their seats before he sat down. He saw eleven faces looking expectantly at him: he was the foreman of the jury, he should take charge. Self-consciously he cleared his throat and said a little nervously, 'I'm not sure what we should do, but perhaps if we each wrote down what we each think the verdict should be then things may become a little clearer.' He was pleasantly surprised when they all agreed, each turning to their pads and writing.

Unknown to the others, George Wright had already made up his mind that the best chance to avoid any confrontation between the jurors and thereby keep some resemblance of order was to utilise a method where verdicts were anonymously written. He smiled as the pieces of paper, each one folded in half to conceal what had been written on it, were passed to him. When he had twelve folded verdicts on the table, he opened each in turn, placing it on the appropriate pile while making a mental note of the result, until he looked up at the expectant faces and said, 'There are seven for guilty, one for not guilty and four don't knows.'

Any previous expectation turned to annoyance on several of the faces with the realisation that it was going to be a very long day. *Thank God they don't know that their foreman is the Not Guilty*, thought George Wright.

The Defence team individually pondered on whether to attempt some work or simply relax and enjoy the break. If either of them commenced on a new brief which turned out to be problematic then the interruption to return to court may spoil their labour; however, time was precious and any missed opportunity to work might be regretted later.

Mr Flowers wanted nothing more than to stay and indulge in polite conversation, enjoying the experience of being in such illustrious company, while Mr Peregrine-Richards wanted a respite from the incessant chatter of his instructing solicitor. Both men separated for their respective offices, knowing they could be back in the courtroom within a few minutes of their office juniors conveying the message that a verdict had been reached. During his short journey, Mr Peregrine-Richards recalled a previously quoted adage: 'solicitors and barristers do not mix'. He had never truly believed it until now.

*　*　*

With nothing else to do – he had no trial papers to prepare, as this was the last one of the session – Mr Justice Summerfield had decided that sleep was the best course of action. He dismissed his attendant, slipped the small bolt on the door, and with his feet on another chair, settled down to a relaxing afternoon snooze.

Barry Bourne sat on his bunk and reluctantly began to play patience. He didn't want to, but he needed something to occupy his mind, and the other option was even less desirable – conduct small talk with the prison warders who were sitting quietly with their backs to the bars. As he laid the cards on the woollen blanket he tried to recall what he had heard about juries and the time they took to reach a verdict. *The longer they were out the better – or was it the other way around?* He couldn't remember, and he closed his eyes to pray. *Please God, let it come down on my side. Please! Just this once be with me!*

The atmosphere in the jury room was heating up, not so much from the steady temperature provided by the radiators, but from the tempers that were beginning to fray. Since the initial recording of their verdicts, each person had in turn voiced their point of view. When it had come to his turn, George Wright had endeavoured to remind them that it was a man's life at stake and that the judge had practically instructed them to find him not guilty. In return, several tried to convince him that all talk about acquittal was simply British fair play and it really meant he was guilty. After another once round the table for further opinions and sentiments, during which all twelve people in the room agreed that if the facts of the theft weren't important they wouldn't have been presented in such detail, George Wright called for another vote, this time on a show of hands. He felt all in the room turn against him at the result: eleven for guilty and one for not guilty. He started to speak about their duty, but immediately stopped as he saw several pairs of eyes raised towards the heavens, while two jurors actually turned their backs on him. He felt despondent knowing he was fighting a losing battle to convince his peers to acquit.

After one last valiant attempt, which quickly failed by ultimately falling on deaf ears as the other eleven people individually or in couples rose from the table and mingled in various groups throughout the room, George Wright was left quietly sitting at the table alone with his head bowed. No one spoke for some time until suddenly one of the male jurors, fists clenched and eyes bulging, rushed at George Wright, making him jump from his seat, the chair clattering on the floor behind him. As he ranted, spittle flew from his mouth. 'Look at the bloody clock, nearly half past sodding seven! We've been stuck in here for over seven bloody hours!' He paused to draw breath as he tried to control himself. 'Seven bloody hours in this stupid room! What the hell are you playing at?'

Indeed, during the time they had been in the room the only interruptions had been the silent delivery of sandwiches and a message from the judge asking if they were close to arriving at a verdict. They weren't, and the tension was now unbearable.

The angry juror, with sleeves rolled up past his elbows and large dark stains clearly visible under his armpits, stopped in front of the shocked foreman so their faces were only six inches apart. His fists were still clenched and his eyes seemed to bulge out further as, having difficulty getting the words out because of the anger in his voice, he continued, 'Just what is the matter with you?'

George Wright could only mutter 'I'm not sure.'

With his forearm, the man wiped away the spittle that had again formed on the edges of his mouth. 'Look – all of us' – and he indicated with a sweep of his arm the other ten people in the room – 'think he is guilty, and you are not sure? What is it going to take to get you to see sense? I don't intend to be here all night; I've got things to do!' With his closing remark the other jurors voiced their agreement, in a cacophony of blame that had nothing to do with the trial but everything to do with the fact that they were holding him solely responsible for lost meetings, missed appointments and spoilt plans.

The verbal bombardment made George Wright feel so nauseous that he thought his head was going to explode, until he finally capitulated with the thought, *Ultimately, I suppose, the Appeals Court can always sort it out.* He shut his eyes and raised his hand, causing an uneasy silence to fall in the room. Then he heard his own voice, sounding a million miles away, utter in defeat, 'All right, you win – Guilty!'

He picked up his fallen chair and slumped into it, not noticing the smirks of satisfaction on the eleven other faces in the room as he berated himself for letting down the man in the dock. For having done that, he felt utterly ashamed.

Mr Justice Summerfield glanced at the clock: coming up to a quarter to eight. *What on earth is taking them so long? Another fifteen minutes and I'll have to send them to a hotel for the night.* He had already sent yet another message asking if they were close to a verdict, to which he had to be satisfied with the single-word reply – 'No'. It told him nothing. *Didn't they listen to a word I said?* The subsequent knock at the door, informing him that the jury had finally reached a verdict, came as a blessed relief. He called for his attendant to assist him with the now heavy robes and wig before collecting the ornamental white gloves and square of black cloth – he was certain he wouldn't need it, but he was legally required to carry it – and then moved to the door leading into the courtroom.

Chapter 35

Barry Bourne was the only prisoner left in the court cells, the verdict having been so long in coming. Sitting on his bunk, he closed his eyes and replayed in slow motion the events that had occurred after the verdict had been given: the court usher moving towards the judge, picking up the black cloth and unfolding it to place it on top of the judge's wig, so that one corner lay on his forehead pointing towards his chin. A single thought crossed his mind as he stood silently to attention while the judge addressed him: *It was an accident! Oh God, I don't believe I'm going to hang because of a spider!* Afterwards, his counsel saying to him, 'Not to worry, everything will get sorted out at the appeal' had not helped either. In fact he was becoming very annoyed with people telling him not to worry – that was easy for them to say, *he* was the one who was going to hang and he was *very* bloody worried. *I don't want to die!* he sobbed as his head bent forward and his shoulders began to shake uncontrollably.

Mr Peregrine-Richards had turned to look at his client during the passing of the sentence of death and had seen a very white and frail man with no hope looking back at him from the dock. He immediately indicated to the judge his intention to appeal, which was approved without delay, and the instant the trial was ended he marched straight back to his office and slammed the door shut behind him as he headed for the drinks cabinet. 'Guilty!' he shouted in

254

exasperation. 'How the bloody hell did even those twelve idiots reach a stupid verdict like that? Didn't they bother listening to the summing up of the judge? Complete and utter nonsense!' he shouted to no one as he slammed a glass on the counter and poured himself a larger-than-usual drink.

Mr Maurice Flowers stormed dramatically into the general office still occupied by some of his staff. 'Bloody guilty,' he shouted to anyone who looked at him, and threw his papers over the first convenient desk. He then proceeded to loudly chastise Mr Peregrine-Bloody-Richards, declaring that the youngest clerk in his practice could have done a better job. He slammed down in his chair behind his desk. 'Shit!' he uttered as he realised the verdict would do his reputation no favours at all for the following few weeks, which ultimately meant losing money as potential clients would look elsewhere for a solicitor to get them off. *Perhaps a short holiday, give everyone time to forget this case,* he mused, but then noticed the piles of paperwork that cluttered his desk. They all represented work and therefore money, and he immediately felt better. With a single thought, *Ah well, tomorrow's another day,* he reached over and picked up a file from the top of the mound in front of him.

Chapter 36

The appeal was heard three months later, a day Barry Bourne had waited for what seemed like an eternity, feeling frustrated on every count: he'd been refused permission to attend the funerals of Martyn and his entire family, which had taken place ten days after the trial had finished; they had all been buried together in a family plot. And on top of that, he wouldn't know what sentence he was to receive for the theft of the money until after the results of the appeal.

Barry knew that another reason for his frustration was that he was now yesterday's news. For so long he'd been on the front page of every newspaper, until their headlines had declared, 'Policeman to hang', whereupon he'd been filed into some dusty archive and forgotten. More important news had since filled the papers; the war in Korea had escalated; tea rationing had ended and so everyone would soon be able to enjoy unlimited cuppas for the first time in twelve years; Agatha Christie's murder-mystery play *The Mousetrap* had opened at the Ambassadors Theatre in London; and there was a lot of talk about a future British expedition trying to climb Mount Everest, at 29,028 feet, the highest place on earth.

Barry Bourne had come to realise that he was now just a small part of history and he didn't like it. He wanted people to know he was still around, he wanted them to care that he was waiting to hang for something he didn't do. The last straw had been when he was refused permission to attend his own appeal, the official letter stating, 'You will be notified in due course of the outcome.' Mr Peregrine-Richards and Mr Flowers would be pleading his case to three new judges who knew nothing about him; they would be pleading for his life, for his right to live. He could only hope that they would do their best ... But would they still care enough?

His wife's continued visits were the only thing outside prison life that was constant. Throughout this ordeal she hadn't let him down, and the more he reviewed their past life together, the more he knew it was in fact him who had let her down: he had stolen the money, he had wanted to leave her. Barry shuddered as he realised that in less than twelve months the things he subconsciously feared the most had dramatically and suddenly come to fruition: dread that his marriage would dissolve into a loveless one like Mary's parents, or that they would grow old without children; fear that he would let down his best friend Martyn, who had helped him so much over the years, or that his colleagues would lose all respect for him. These he knew now, were his true fears, not a dislike of spiders, and if he were allowed another chance then it would all be so different.

Mary was pleasantly relieved she had made the decision to move in with her mother. She had never really enjoyed the atmosphere of the 'Police Colony', as it was known locally, and certainly didn't deserve the treatment she would undoubtedly have got from the other wives if she had stayed; after all, she had done nothing wrong – she hadn't stolen any money, and she hadn't caused the accident that resulted in so many lives being lost. She also had no intention of waiting for the eviction notice she would receive when Barry was officially dismissed in disgrace from the police force. They had decided to sell everything, and it was pure relief for her the day the furniture van took their possessions away and she knew she didn't ever have to return. That place held nothing but sad and hateful memories, and when Barry did come out of prison they could start afresh with everything new.

Mr Peregrine-Richards sat down at the end of his impassioned address to the three Appeal Court judges, who had listened in silence and with apparent interest. It was a difficult atmosphere and he felt almost detached as he attempted to express his feelings in such a small room and before three such important senior law lords. *Well, I've done my best, but is it good enough this time?* He had already decided that if the appeal did go against him, he would get in touch with Mr Justice Summerfield and plead with him to write to the Home Secretary to get the death sentence commuted to one of life imprisonment. Barry Bourne may have to serve a sentence for a murder he didn't commit, but at least he wouldn't hang for it.

Mr Justice Summerfield sat reflecting in one of the wicker chairs in the conservatory of his home, his thoughts still full of that guilty verdict. He had known as he passed the death sentence that, even though it was required by law and was the only sentence he could give on the guilty verdict, it was wrong. Whether it was simply because the case was so fresh in his mind or whether it was his conscience talking, it had bothered him every day since. *The Appeals Court was bound to put it right ...* His thoughts were suddenly interrupted by a sharp pain shooting down his left arm, to be replaced by a considerable ache in his chest. *Must be the cold weather making the arthritis play up.* He pulled the blanket that lay across his knees further up his body and closed his eyes for a rest.

George Wright sat at home having his third alcoholic drink of the day, and it wasn't yet lunchtime. He had been thoroughly sickened by the congratulations and back-slapping he'd received from his friends and by the bragging of his wife; him having been elected foreman was the icing on her cake. Every one of his colleagues expressed the happy opinion that he was a 'grand lad', but none were the slightest bit interested in his thoughts or feelings, in the fact that there was going to be a hanging for which he was responsible. The only 'friend' he could truly confide in was Johnny Walker, and he found the amber liquid to be extremely comforting, and so regularly sought solace in the bottle. He was off work yet again, claiming he was suffering from a bad back to avoid facing both his work colleagues and, more importantly, the reality that what he was actually suffering from was a terrible case of guilt. He was finding it harder and harder each day to live with his decision. 'Why, oh why was I picked to be on that cursed jury?' he muttered to himself for the hundredth time before he raised his glass to his lips once again.

Chapter 37

Barry Bourne walked to the visitors' area, where his solicitor was waiting to see him. He looked eagerly into the faces of his guards to see if he could gauge from their expressions the decision of his appeal; but each remained unreadable as he was escorted along the corridors. He became more and more nervous with each step even though he tried his hardest to be hopeful. *Hope is all I have left ...* As he entered the room, Maurice Flowers failed to look him straight in the eye. Barry instantly knew all was lost. *The appeal had been denied.* He stood absolutely rigid; his fists clenched by his sides, and then started shaking uncontrollably as months of pent-up frustration and anger rose within him like a volcano. In his state of upset he didn't see his solicitor slowly back away or sense the prison officers bracing themselves for the impending explosion of an enraged prisoner. But the anger left him as quickly as it had come as he realised the futility of his actions. Feeling himself visibly calm down, he moved over to a chair and sat down to listen calmly and rationally to his solicitor. *Mary will help!* his mind reasoned. He knew she was in the process of preparing a petition to present to the Home Secretary that was sure to get him off where his appeal had failed. *Mary promised me she would sort it and she will!*

His meeting with Mr Flowers over, he left the visitors' area and automatically turned right towards his cell. He was therefore surprised when the prison officer stopped him and guided him in the other direction, with the command, 'This way!' He was accompanied down a corridor that was previously unknown to him, until he reached an open doorway and was guided into to a bigger and more spacious cell, with a second door at the back. His throat went dry and he held on to the steel bar door as he suddenly realised his destination. He was in the condemned man's cell.

Mary Bourne was beginning to despair, her petition nowhere as near as successful as she had hoped, for the people she approached were just not interested. She had also been genuinely surprised at the nasty reaction she had received at the police station from her husband's former colleagues; she had gone there against her mother's advice. Even though she felt frustrated, her promise to Barry fuelled her determination to succeed, if only to give her husband renewed hope; with time ticking against her, she was rapidly losing hers and there was still one other piece of news she had neglected to tell him. She had finally received the results of her hospital tests: one very minor surgical procedure would correct her problem and then there would be nothing to stand in the way of them having a family. *But that was something to celebrate on a happier day.*

Mr Peregrine-Richards sat at his desk, the file on Barry Oliver Bourne under his right hand as he reviewed his concern. After considerable thought, he had finally been able to reach an honest conclusion. 'With what I had to work with, I did the best I could. You win some, you lose some. Buck your ideas up and get on with helping your next client!'

He picked up the papers, and after staring at them for a few further seconds, tossed them unceremoniously into the out tray before noting the time. 'Roll on afternoon tea!' he said, deleting the name Bourne from his memory.

*   *   *

Mr Maurice Flowers held a similar bundle in his hand. He was sure there was probably more he could have milked from the case, not certain by any means that he had covered all angles. But finally satisfied in his own mind that he had not missed anything worthwhile and that he had claimed all the expenses he was entitled to, he dropped the file into the tray marked 'Requiring Final Payment'.

Mr Justice Summerfield heard about the appeal dismissal with amazement, knowing that his summing up, which had been rejected by the jury, must surely have been noted by the law lords, whom he knew well and who usually took a great deal of notice of his opinion. He recognised that, as the trial judge, he was entitled by law to communicate directly with the Home Secretary, and he was determined to write him a letter, in which he could detail his beliefs and suggest a pardon for Police Constable Bourne. He knew he was more than capable of convincing the Home Secretary of the man's innocence.

'No time like the present,' he decided aloud. Looking through the conservatory door to his wife, who was busily writing her shopping list, he realised that he could continue uninterrupted for the moment. *I'll write it now, while the facts are still fresh,* he decided. He stood up to retrieve the headed notepaper from the drawer and was totally unprepared for the violent pain that gripped his chest and spurted up and down his left arm. He momentarily wondered what was happening before crashing lifelessly to the floor.

Chapter 38

Barry Bourne had not celebrated New Year, for it was certainly not going to be either a happy or a prosperous one for him. He had, however, thought a lot about God as his mind became obsessed with the 28th of January and eight o'clock in the morning. A few days before Christmas, during one of his many bouts of depression, he had picked up the Bible, which had previously lain untouched on the table, and let it fall open on his lap. *The First Book of Timothy*. He recalled his surprise when he had discovered that there was even a book in the Bible by someone called Timothy. His eyes had been drawn to Chapter 6, verses 9 and 10, which he had read so often since, he could now recite them by heart:

> But they that will be rich fall into temptation and a snare, and into many foolish and hurtful lusts, which drown men in destruction and perdition.
> For the love of money is the root of all evil: which while some coveted after, they have erred from the faith, and pierced themselves through with many sorrows.

He had often sat and thought about what had happened as a result of his actions, continually reeling off the names of the people who had died since that fateful morning he had found the money and wondering if they were all waiting somewhere beyond to condemn him to purgatory when he soon joined them in eternity. What Barry was not aware of in his victim count was that he was missing two names: Mr Justice Summerfield and Mr George Wright. All the deaths really saddened him, and none, with the exception of that of David Smith, would have happened at all if he hadn't stolen the money he found in the canvas bag at the top of the alleyway. He had come to realise that those deaths were ultimately his responsibility and that soon he was going to have to make the ultimate payment for them. Rather than question why fate had shaped his life the way it had, he became more reflective and considered what his actions would have been had he understood the consequences. He knew hindsight to be a wonderful thing, but what, he wondered, would he have done differently then if he had known what he knew now?

Having long ago demolished the shed, Mary Bourne and her mother had decided to put up for sale the house in which they were living and move to another part of the country where they were unknown and where Mary could revert to her maiden name of Sharpe.

'We'll move and then you can go ahead and have that operation,' said Mrs Sharpe matter-of-factly. 'You never know when you'll meet another man, and you might as well be ready!'

Mary and Barry met for the last time the afternoon before his execution. The first few moments amid the mutual tears and sobbing had been very difficult as both attempted to splutter out their innermost feelings of adoration and requests for forgiveness simultaneously. They had cried a lot in each other's arms, pledging one another their undying love.

But all too quickly their last moments together had passed and they were finally parted, never to see each other again in this world. Barry had stood in silence after his wife's departure before moving into a corner to face the wall, desperately wanting to be on his own but knowing he wasn't, for those standing on the other side of the barred tomb in which he stood were watching his every move.

He wanted so badly to be brave and face his punishment with as much dignity as he could muster, but to do so he had to make his peace with God, and so he sank to his knees, head against the wall, and prayed.

Chapter 39

Barry Bourne's frame jerked upright as the pain seared through his body and screamed into his brain, a pain so intense that he thought his head was going to explode …

He sat bolt upright in the inky black darkness, the movement causing his helmet to fall off his head and onto the floor. *Where am I? What the hell's happening?* Slowly his eyes focused and he saw the huge white blisters starting to form on the pads of his right forefinger and thumb, the glowing red end of his cigarette on the ground beside his helmet. His mind raced to place his thoughts in some resemblance of order, as he instinctively placed his finger and thumb in his mouth in an effort to suck out the pain. 'Shit!' he loudly exclaimed as he realised he had fallen asleep while having a crafty smoke break during his night shift. *What time is it?* He pulled his watch close to his face to make out the luminous hands and noted with relief that it was only fifteen minutes past four.

Nursing his injured hand, he climbed off the oil drum and picked up his helmet, trying to explain to himself why he had fallen asleep – it had never happened before. He had been tired when he started his shift, and even though the overtime he had drawn had been during the peak period traffic, which had been busier than usual, he had done the same stint of overtime before and not fallen asleep.

Barry had the niggling feeling that he had been dreaming,

a dream that seemed to have turned dramatically into a nightmare, but couldn't be certain. Even though the details had gone he couldn't understand the inexplicable feeling of extreme relief he was experiencing, and yet suddenly, as he placed the helmet on the oil drum, his thoughts went to Martyn and his family and he felt a great sadness. *They were all right when I last saw them*, he recalled, remembering kicking a ball about with James and John, while trying to separate the confusing thoughts from the facts.

'Pull yourself together!' he ordered himself as he shook his head, trying to remove the strange feelings that continued to creep around the edges of his mind, until finally his thoughts settled on his recent success at the promotion exam. *It was a bloody good job I met the Sarge before I took my nap*, he thought. He smiled as he looked at the state of his fingers, which were still sore, but at least the agonising pain had ceased to a dull roar.

He suddenly shuddered and muttered, 'Who just walked over my grave I wonder?' as his fingers pulled his collar, which seemed awfully tight all of a sudden, away from his throat. *Doesn't normally feel this snug*, he mused as he looked up towards the heavens and saw a glimmer of light breaking through. It was the start of another day and he realised he hadn't felt this rejuvenated in a long time. *I must have needed that kip!* Still unable to shake off the feeling that he was missing something important, he retrieved his helmet and placed it back on his head, calculating that he had time for one full set of rounds and then could be off home to bed and a real sleep as he brushed off his tunic and trousers before he resumed his patrol.

As he moved up the adjacent alleyway he kicked a discarded tin can out of his path, which clattered and crashed as it rebounded off both walls before coming to rest in a tumultuous crescendo on several half-empty dustbins. He felt a happy tuneful whistle about to break from his lips when he saw a canvas bag lying on the ground at the end of the alley.

PC Barry Oliver Bourne frowned as he moved stealthily towards the bag …